"Listen. Turn off the motor. Take a deep breath. And don't say anything for a minute."

Her immediate impulse was to hit him, but she obeyed, not quite in the order he had commanded, taking the deep breath first.

"Don't say anything," he cautioned again. "I've got a message to give you. I'm going to give it to you, all of it, and I don't know anything except the message. Don't boil over with questions, because I don't have any answers."

She stared at him. "All right, J.Q."

"A man called. He did not give his name. He asked for you. I said you would be back in a little while. He said to give you a message. He's coming here, this afternoon, about two, to talk with you. He believes he may know where your son is."

The world went into a tiny cone of awareness, a buzzing quiet. . . . The sound of her own blood in her ears.

"Marty?" she said wonderingly. "Marty's dead. . . ."

By B. J. Oliphant
Published by Fawcett Books:

DEAD IN THE SCRUB
THE UNEXPECTED CORPSE
DESERVEDLY DEAD
DEATH AND THE DELINQUENT
DEATH SERVED UP COLD
A CEREMONIAL DEATH
HERE'S TO THE NEWLY DEAD

HERE'S TO THE NEWLY DEAD

B. J. Oliphant

FAWCETT GOLD MEDAL • NEW YORK

A Fawcett Gold Medal Book
Published by Ballantine Books
Copyright © 1997 by B. J. Oliphant

All rights reserved under International and Pan-American Copyright Conventions. Published in the United States by Ballantine Books, a division of Random House, Inc., New York, and simultaneously in Canada by Random House of Canada Limited, Toronto.

http://www.randomhouse.com

Library of Congress Catalog Card Number: 97-90321

ISBN 0-449-14992-7

Manufactured in the United States of America

First Edition: September 1997

10 9 8 7 6 5 4 3 2 1

1

J.Q. WAS STANDING at the kitchen sink, looking out across the parking lot while he sipped meditatively at his third cup of morning coffee. By the time this cup was finished, he would be able to consider this particular Sunday, the last day of August, as a proper, functional day in which he no doubt had a proper and functional part. Until then, he would be an unwilling participant in whatever went on.

"What's got you so grouchy this morning?" Shirley McClintock asked, penciling in a word on the morning crossword. On Sundays, the local paper indulged itself by printing the *New York Times* puzzle, full of puns and weird definitions. She dropped the pencil, then rose to her feet and stretched to her full six-foot-three. "Six-foot-one-and-a-half in socks," she told people who asked. "Six-two in flat shoes, six-three in my boots." Though lately she'd felt slightly shrunken, as though her horizons had drawn in.

"I'm still sore from moving all the hay on Friday." He grimaced, rubbing his shoulder. "Next time instead of one helper, I'm going to hire several younger persons. Young. Like those two."

She came to stand behind J.Q. and peer over his shoulder, their heads exactly level. There was nothing at all in the parking lot of Rancho del Valle except box-on-wheels-type cars; one cat-type creature sitting; one dog-type creature bone chewing; and a pair of lovebirds, presumably human.

"You mean the newlyweds?" she asked, puzzled. "They don't look muscular enough to lift a bale, much less stack it."

"She—what's her name, Buscovitch—looks about fourteen," he said grumpily. "And him, Jones, he's maybe sixteen. Give or take a year or so. He's told me five or ten times they got married last Tuesday, as though he either needed to convince himself or he felt that fact was of world-shaking importance. I give it two years, tops."

"The only words I've exchanged with them were when he came to tell me there was no light in the closet. I agreed with his observation that indeed there wasn't."

"They're in the Garden House, aren't they? The closet is two feet deep! What do they need a separate closet light for?"

Shirley shrugged. "I thought maybe she was planning to undress in there. Or he was. But they can always undress in the bathroom, or the kitchen. So, I thought maybe they had something kinky planned that needs a tightly closed but lighted space."

2

"They're not old enough for anything kinky. Though maybe they *are* old enough to have robbed a bank."

"A bank!"

"He asked me yesterday if I could change a thousand for him."

"He must have been joking!"

"He wasn't. He had the bill in his hot little hand. He told me he'd be glad to give me a hundred as a fee, looking at me like a puppy. Eerie. I told him to change it at the bank in town."

"Somebody probably gave it to them as a wedding present." She patted his bony shoulder and went back to the kitchen table to gather up the morning paper. "It's our week for adolescents. There are two infantile sisters in the Frog House. They talk baby talk to the rabbits; they're afraid of the goats; they won't drive up to Bandelier because the road makes too many turns; they won't take the high road to Taos because they might get into trouble between towns, and if they had to stop, there might be wild animals. They went walking yesterday. A pickup truck came by with a radio playing loud Spanish music and the men in the truck had mustaches. They considered this a sign of incipient rapine and ran all the way home."

"Where are they from?"

"Downtown Philadelphia. Where, as I recall, there are some very bad critters that walk on two legs. Speaking of critters, how are all ours this morning?"

He grunted, mock annoyance. "Flourishing, as usual! I estimate we have a two-hundred-pound rabbit out there, the rate it's going through rabbit food."

"The children like them." She unbuckled the belt of her jeans, tucked her shirt more neatly into the waistband, rebuckled, and ran her fingers through her short

3

gray hair, making it stand untidily on end. "Did you see the Wilson cousins out in the warren the other day, five or six of them, all under the age of ten, hunkered down feeding carrots to the bunnies. It made me feel all warm and grandmotherly."

"Human or rabbit?"

"Both." She grinned at him. If J.Q. had his way, they would keep Dog and the horses, possibly the cats, but every other critter on the place would be banished to make room for two cows, which is all there would be room for. J.Q. missed cows. Come to think of it, she herself missed cows. However, she had to admit that having a smaller place that catered to paying guests made up in amusement what a thousand Colorado acres full of cows had once provided in the way of tranquillity.

Her thoughts were interrupted by the arrival of her sixteen-year-old foster daughter, Allison. With her hair pulled back and a shiny, just-washed face, she looked as young as the lovebirds out in the drive.

"Who's grandmotherly?" she asked, opening the refrigerator door and rummaging. "Not you, Shirley."

"Why not me?" Shirley asked in astonishment. "God knows I'm old enough. Why, at my age, I could have a twenty-year-old grandchild, at least."

"The Big House people," J.Q. muttered, "are loading themselves into four trucks for a day's sightseeing. This is the first time I can remember our having a single family of guests who arrived two by two in a fleet of pickup trucks."

"They're from Texas," she said, as though this explained it. "Maybe they planned on buying enough Indian art to make a large load."

"Planned on winning it, maybe. They spent yesterday

4

at the Camel Rock Casino. I asked them how they did and they said they lost. I told them everybody did, and got a dirty look back. I'll bet they still believe in Santa Claus."

"You mean there isn't any Santa Claus?" said Allison, eyes very wide. "Oh, oh, I'm going to cry."

J.Q. took no notice. "And if they buy stuff, it won't be Indian art. Yesterday they drove fifty miles south to see the new factory stores between Santa Fe and Albuquerque. Don't they have any factory stores in Texas?"

"Shopping in a foreign country is always more fun," said Allison.

"Set a rock on it," said J.Q. "Speaking of which, your proliferating rabbits are digging out of the warren again. Shall we let a dozen escape before we put a rock on the tunnel? Or shall we just open the gate for a few hours to thin out the population?"

Allison moved her load onto the counter: bread, butter, milk, eggs, orange juice. "I don't know why they're *our* rabbits when all the little children are feeding them carrots and apples and their mommies and daddies are taking snapshots and everybody's going ooh and aah and isn't that cute, but they're *my* rabbits whenever they dig out. Or whenever some horrible woman like that Osinsky person lets her brats chase them and corner them and kick them, and then when I tell her to stop them, she says they'll get tired pretty soon and besides, she has no control over her own children."

"Dr. Osinsky," said Shirley. "And she was quite correct. She had no control over her brats at all. I stopped them beating on a baby goat. I stopped them teasing Dog. Both times she stood there, showing no signs of wanting any control over them. In all the time we've been here,

5

I've never seen such little monsters. They're not even in school yet and they're already on their way to sociopathy."

Allison snorted. "Well, don't let her come again."

"We won't," Shirley soothed. "She's on the never-again-never list. As a matter of fact, she called just last week asking about early September, and I said we didn't have a thing."

"Which doesn't answer my question about how many," said J.Q.

Allison shrugged. "Personally, I'd like to keep them all."

Shirley leaned on the counter, still staring at the newly-weds. They couldn't be as young as fourteen. Eighteen maybe. Or they could be in their early twenties, though she doubted he shaved more than once every week or ten days.

"One two-hundred-pound rabbit is enough," said J.Q. turning away from the window.

"How many is that in actual bunny units?" Allison asked, busy buttering bread.

"Oh, thirty, more or less. All the way from owl-bait size up to about twenty-pound great-great-grandmas, black ones, white ones, others various shades of brown and gray. All indolently lying about, waggling their ears and eating their heads off."

The two lovebirds unwound their arms from one another and started for the kitchen door.

Shirley said, "We are about to receive a visitation."

She opened the door just as they were about to knock, and she fumbled mentally for what they would be calling themselves. Well, Jones and Buscovitch, of course. Their children would undoubtedly be Jones hyphen Busco-vitch. Or Buscovitch-Jones.

"Good morning," Shirley offered. "What can we do for you?"

"This is my wife," Jones murmured from cherubic lips as he ran a hand across his silky black hair and cast an upward glance from melting hazel-green eyes. "We were married on Tuesday."

"She knows," said blond Buscovitch from an Alice-down-the-rabbit-hole face, all flyaway hair and a bemused expression. "You already told her."

"Of course," Shirley said cheerfully. "Are you having a pleasant trip?"

Jones nodded, blushing. Buscovitch merely stared through Shirley as though she were a roadside monument of not even passing interest.

Jones put his hand on his wife's shoulder. "My wife and I are going on a trail ride this morning. At the Silver Saddle Stables." He fell silent, struggling to find words.

"That's nice," encouraged J.Q. "A lot of our guests go riding down there, and they all seem to enjoy it."

"We want to plant a tree," he said. "To . . . to sort of, memorialize our . . . honeymoon."

Shirley cocked her head, waiting.

"Where would we go, to buy a little tree?"

"To take home with you?"

"No, no," he said. "To plant. On the trail ride."

Shirley looked at J.Q., her eyebrows rising. Allison choked and suddenly remembered something she had to do elsewhere. J.Q. came to Shirley's rescue.

"You've ridden a lot?"

They shook their heads, two marionettes with but a single string. "No. Not ever."

J.Q. smiled his patient smile. "Well, to plant a tree, you'd have to carry the tree, a shovel—"

7

"I wanted to ask if you'd lend us one."

"And some water," suggested Shirley.

"Right," Jones said eagerly.

"Why here in New Mexico?" Shirley blurted. "Why not back where you live? California, isn't it?"

Momentary silence. He took a deep breath. "We want to come back every year and visit our tree." He looked adoringly at Buscovitch, who returned his gaze with a placid one of her own. "We want to make an annual pilgrimage. Someone suggested a Chinese elm. Where can we get one?"

"You can't," said Shirley. "Or, I should say, you wouldn't want to. They're a weed tree. There are fifty or a hundred of them out along the driveway. We chop them out every year. If someone suggested you plant one, it's because they grow like weeds, but you'll be riding up into the Pecos Forest on your trail ride. Wouldn't a pine be more . . . appropriate?" Though why one would plant one more teensy tree among a forest of millions, God only knew.

"Whatever," said Buscovitch, with the tiniest yawn. "Where can we buy one?"

"Look up nurseries in the Yellow Pages," Shirley suggested. "Call them first. Tell them it'll have to be a tiny one. Quart-pot size. You won't be able to carry anything bigger on a horse." If that, she thought. Though a quart-size pot would fit into a saddlebag.

"Can we borrow a shovel?" asked Jones.

She nodded grudgingly, not really willing to be a part of this. "There's an old trenching tool you can borrow, out in the garage. You should be able to tie it on the saddle. And take at least a gallon-size plastic jug of water."

Jones turned liquid eyes on Buscovitch, silently worshiping, and she took his hand as they strolled away. Ten minutes later Shirley saw them leaving in their shiny little coppery-red car with the wire wheels and the sunroof. The discussion about trees was making her feel guilty. She had promised their housemate, Xanthippe Minging, that she, Shirley, would plant some shrubs along the ditch where old growths of lilac and juniper had died out. The various viburnums and spruces had been sitting in their pots for weeks, being faithfully watered, but otherwise ignored. It would take only an hour or two to plant them, but she'd been putting it off ever since Xanthy left. Gardening was not one of Shirley's interests.

She resolved to do it today. When she'd finished her own second cup, she went out to the garage, full of resolution, only to stomp back ten minutes later cursing audibly.

"What?" called J.Q. from the kitchen door.

"Those . . . those *brats* took my poacher's spade! The one you gave me for my birthday." The object referred to had been made in England, had a stainless-steel blade, a straight-grained ash stirrup handle, and it was just the right size to fit nicely among tree roots or shrubs or garden plants. It was still new and shiny and had cost, so Shirley suspected, more than any six ordinary spades. The gift had convinced her J.Q. was in on the conspiracy to get her interested in horticulture, but nonetheless, it was a gift, and treasured for that if no other reason.

"Well, they'll bring it back," J.Q. offered, sounding insincere even to himself. His experience was that things lent to others either didn't come back or came back bent. The posthole auger they had lent to their neighbor last month had come back unusable and had cost seventy-five dollars to straighten. It had evidently been used to bore holes in rock.

"My own damned fault," muttered Shirley. "I didn't realize they were leaving right away. I didn't realize they wouldn't know the difference between an almost new stainless-steel spade and what I called an old trenching tool. Damn."

Allison came out onto the patio, munching on a fried-egg sandwich. "I have an announcement. This being Labor Day weekend, it's the last family time before school starts, and we have not yet decided on our familial thing for the weekend."

"Ultimo out of town, is he?" asked J.Q., referring to her current best young male friend, which is what Allison called him.

"Not boyfriend," she asserted whenever someone used the word. "He's not a boy. He's very mature."

Now she retorted, "J.Q., that's not nice. I don't neglect you for Ultimo. Family stuff on weekends is important to me, and Ultimo doesn't have that much time to spend with me, even if I wanted to."

"But he's out of town," J.Q. persisted, with a grin.

"He's down in Albuquerque because one of his sisters has a new baby and the whole family is going to the christening. And that isn't what I'm talking about. I'm talking about the fact that it rained Friday, and Ultimo told me there are always lots of mushrooms up Santa Clara Canyon, and I thought, maybe . . ."

The idea was appealing. J.Q. nodded, pleased. Shirley relaxed. They hadn't been myco-gallivanting in a long time. Late August, early September was a good time.

They could pack a picnic lunch. Even if they didn't find anything, it would be nice to wander around in the trees.

"All the houses are full, so nobody's coming today," Allison went on, wheedling. "You said hardly anyone would be calling for reservations, because it's dead time. . . ."

Early September was usually dead time, too late for summer and too soon for fall and winter reservations, which were more often spur-of-the-moment trips, not planned far in advance as summer and holiday ones usually were.

"And we haven't been anywhere for a long time," Allison went on.

"No sales talk needed," Shirley agreed. "What have we got for a picnic lunch?"

"Cold fried chicken, and ham for sandwiches, and there's potato salad left over from the other night."

"Done," said J.Q. "You put the lunch together, and I'll clean out the Jeep." Each morning, when he went out to pick up the daily paper, J.Q. drove up and down the quarter mile of frontage road to police the area that hordes of trolls had littered during the night. The trolls pitched empty beer cans from their cars to prevent their being caught driving with an open container. Along with the beer cans the trolls also donated a lesser scattering of McDonald's, Burger King, and Taco Bell wrappers. Since J.Q.'s cleaning out the Jeep always involved several other tasks that occurred to him as he went along, it was past eleven before they were ready to leave.

They drove west to 285, the main Santa Fe–Taos highway, then farther west on 502, toward the Jemez Mountains, the canyons before them shifting in and out of visibility as clouds moved eastward to mass overhead.

As they approached the Rio Grande they turned north, toward the Santa Clara pueblo, where they paid the fee the pueblo charged to enter the canyon. By noon they were contentedly moving across grassy clearings and through ponderosa forest, finding enough bulgy-stemmed boletes and pink-gilled field mushrooms to make the trip worthwhile, plus a number of oddball fungi to amuse themselves trying to identify.

At one point the three of them became separated, and Shirley, off by herself, found a large, pristine agaricus, which she was admiring when a voice asked from behind her:

"Is it to eat?"

She turned to confront a round-faced and twinkly Asian gentleman clad in denims and sandals, a sack in one hand and a trowel in the other. She handed him the specimen she'd been admiring. "This one is. It's very good."

"How do you know?"

She took the mushroom back and turned it over. "It grows out in the open, in the grass. Pale pink gills on the new ones, rapidly turning dark brown from the spores. White or whitish stem and cap . . ." She twisted the stem, which came away easily. "Stem separates easily." She poked the cap hard, then displayed it. "It doesn't stain yellow when bruised. *Agaricus campestris*."

"All that?"

"All that." She grinned. "Are you mushrooming?"

He shook his head. "No. My older brother goes for mushrooms. Matsutake, mostly, in the fall. Me, I dig tiny trees to do bonsai. You know bonsai?"

"I do. I've seen exhibits in San Francisco and Washington, and one time when I was in England, as part of the big Westminster flower show. They are beautiful."

"Some," he admitted. "Some are not beautiful but have . . . character. Very old ones, sometimes. My brother and I believe that is more important even than beauty. Character." He rummaged in a deep pocket and brought forth a lacquered card case from which he produced a card, rather with the air of a magician plucking one from thin air. "My card."

Nosura Akagami, it read. *Gardens, landscapes, bonsai.* She bowed in his direction. "Thank you."

He smiled himself away among the trees, and from the other direction J.Q. approached with a single specimen of something that looked suspiciously like a chanterelle.

"Who was that?" he wondered.

"A nice Japanese man who's collecting seedlings to make bonsai."

Allison joined them soon after, and when they'd wandered long enough to make them doubt the existence of any mycological mother lode just beyond the next tree, they turned back to the clearing where they'd parked and spread out the picnic.

"I wish Mingy would come home," Allison mumbled around a mouthful of cold chicken. Xanthippe Minging, Shirley's longtime friend and Allison's teacher, was Xanthy to Shirley and J.Q., Mingy to Allison. Xanthippe had "retired" and moved to New Mexico with Shirley, J.Q., and Allison, but she had recently been spending a lot of her time visiting kinfolk on both coasts. To pay her keep in Santa Fe, so she said, she had taken on the gardens at Rancho del Valle as her responsibility while she tried to teach Shirley the difference between spurge and spirea.

Shirley nodded. "Xanthy's coming back next month. I just hope I get those shrubs planted before she gets back. I promised her I would."

"She's been gone most of the year!" Allison complained.

J.Q. offered, "She's almost eighty, Alli. She says she wants to see all her family and get to know them again while she's still in good shape to travel."

Allison snorted. "She'll be in good shape when she's a hundred."

"Very probably." Shirley rolled up her sandwich wrapper and put it in the garbage sack, meantime casting a wary look at the sky, which had darkened considerably while they'd been eating and was now muttering ominously. "In about five minutes it's going to pour."

Her words were lost in a growl of thunder. They folded up the blanket and stowed everything back in the Jeep, managing to get under cover before the first big drops splatted on the hood. By the time they were back at the canyon entrance, the rain was in full spate, a mini-cloudburst, coming down in curtains so unbroken it was difficult to see the road. During the next thirty minutes they went into and out of half a dozen downpours, and by the time they reached the ranch, the skies had settled into a sullen, grumbling seep, a slow leak of sky accompanied by disgruntled sheet-metal noises and far-off brightenings behind the clouds, like celestial flashbulbs.

"So much for planting," Shirley commented. "The newlyweds aren't back yet. I don't see their car."

"They probably stopped somewhere," said J.Q. "It's their next-to-the-last day here."

The day disintegrated as rainy days often seemed to do, good intentions and lifelong work habits dissolving in the higher humidity. The animals were fed and brought

14

in for the night, half-grown baby goats and lambs safe from coyotes. The peafowl began their nightly flight into the tall cottonwoods along the acequia. The sky darkened even more, with no hint of sunset except a baleful red bar above the mountains. J.Q. suggested they go into Espanola and have supper at Jo Ann's Ranch-O-Casados, a former fast-food kiosk on the main road through town now owned by a family who grew most of their own vegetables. Jo Ann's was a well-kept secret among local residents, who hoped the tourists would never discover she served the best Southwestern food in at least five counties. Surfeited variously on burritos and chimichangas and the world's best beans, they returned home at eight.

"They're still not back," Shirley observed, a frown forming between her eyebrows. "They should be back by now."

"They're not kids, Shirley."

"They are too, J.Q. You said so yourself, just this morning."

"They could be having dinner in Santa Fe. Or they could have driven over to Chimayo. Or they could have taken the high road through Truchas to have supper in Taos."

"Could have," she growled. "Could have anything. Doesn't mean they did."

The little coppery-red car had not returned by nine. The two sisters from Philadelphia chose that hour to check out, explaining that they had to drive to the Santa Fe airport at six in the morning to catch a flight to Albuquerque, twenty minutes away by air, less than an hour by car from the Santa Fe airport.

"Santa Fe," commented J.Q. "Not too many of our guests fly out of Santa Fe. It's pretty expensive."

15

"Oh," sighed one. "We know. But we were afraid to drive to Albuquerque. What if something happened out there on the desert!"

"It's about an hour's drive on a busy four-lane highway patrolled by state police," J.Q. said. "I doubt much could happen."

"Oh, that's what we mean," said the other. "That it's busy. Anybody could come by."

They departed, seemingly quite happy to have been too timid to have seen anything of what most people came to New Mexico to see.

"Do you believe that?" Shirley asked. "They're mice, both of them."

"City mice," said J.Q.

Allison added, "I talked to them yesterday. They're not as young as they act, but they've never been in the country. Open space scares them because there's no place to take shelter if it rains. Thunderstorms scare them because they might be hit by lightning. Trees scare them because if you were under one, it might be hit by lightning. Roads without lights scare them because you can't see where you're going. Roads that climb hills scare them, because there might be something in the road just over the top. Horses scare them. I tried to get them to go riding with me, but they were too scared. The thing that got me, they seemed kind of proud of how scared they were."

"I remember that as a feminine thing," said J.Q. "Shrinking violets, covering their mouths with one dainty hand while shrieking like banshees at a mouse. Though cowering in corners is rather out of fashion at present."

"Since the time of Fay Wray, and praise God for that," said Shirley, yawning. "I don't know why I'm so sleepy.

We haven't done diddly all day." She peered out the rain-streaked window. "Those kids still aren't back."

"Those kids aren't your kids," said J.Q. "Go on to bed. Sleep an extra hour. Wallow in sloth."

Surprising herself, Shirley fell asleep almost at once, lulled by the splash of rain falling from the roof canals outside her windows. No gutters in Santa Fe. Just wooden troughs protruding some distance from the side of the house and emitting a splashy downpour whenever it rained. Smart people made sure the water ran away onto something that needed it, like trees or bushes or flower gardens. Or vegetable gardens. Lots of people seemed to have them.

Midnight came and went. Along about three, a bombardment of thunder roused her. It was followed by six or eight similar crashes as the upper-atmospheric percussionist whaled away at his sky drums. By the time the tattoo subsided, she was thoroughly awake, so she got up, bathed her face in cool water, and decided she'd like a drink of something. Juice maybe. Or Scotch. Or maybe a beer, if there was any in the refrigerator. Beer was always soothing.

Once in the kitchen, however, instead of stopping at the refrigerator, she went out the patio door into the windy night. The lights around the parking area were subdued by the rain, now dwindled to a drifting mist. Nothing moved except the wildly waving trees, leafy arms summoning. Come on, wind. Come on.

The little red car still wasn't there.

She went in, got her master key, and walked to the house the young people were staying in, the mist curling her hair and running down the back of her neck. Perhaps they had come back late, packed up, and left.

They hadn't packed up and left. The house looked like a cyclone had hit it. If nothing else had convinced Shirley of their ages, the condition of the house did. They were teenagers. They had to be. Clothes on the floor. Without thinking about it, she picked up a blouse. The label caught her eye. One of the most expensive boutiques on Rodeo Drive. Good Lord. Pure silk, handmade, and that label. The blouse couldn't have cost less than three hundred dollars, and probably twice that. She dropped it where she had found it and looked at others. A few more California labels, some Santa Fe labels, the most expensive shops in town. Hand-beaded and embroidered vests. Handwoven fabrics in jackets and coats. Cashmere and silk and hand tailoring, for both him and her. There were shoes everywhere, and handmade boots, hideously expensive, everything thrown about and nothing put away in the closet. Not a stitch.

She left the house, locking it behind her, and came back to the kitchen to stand by the phone for a long, indecisive moment. Joe Cisneros at Silver Saddle Stables would not appreciate being called at three in the morning. Joe Cisneros usually got up at six. She could wait until then.

She did wait until then, sitting up in the library with a throw wrapped around her and a much-read book in her lap, listening to the recurring snaredrum rattle of rain on the window, staring at the page without reading a word of it until she dozed off.

At six she was wakened by a hand on her shoulder: J.Q., in stocking feet, carrying his boots. "What are you doing in here? You'll have a crick in your neck all day!"

"Thunder," she said, trying not to yawn in his face. "Oh Lord, you're right. I do have a crick. Get the coffee on, J.Q. I'll be in as soon as I'm dressed." Drawing the throw around her shoulders, she padded off to her bedroom. From her disordered bed, two cats looked up lazily from the warm spot she had left last night. Great. Now there'd be cat hair on her sheets. Normally the creatures slept on her feet, not around her neck, but they'd been here before she had. She was the interloper.

Brushing teeth and hair, washing face, dressing in clean jeans and a newly pressed shirt made her feel only slightly more alert and functioning. Getting really awake would take several cups of coffee, or maybe just the sight of the little red car in the parking area.

It wasn't there. She took the mug proffered by J.Q. and sipped at the hot brew while she looked up Joe Cisneros's number.

"Who?" asked J.Q.

"Silver Saddle Stables."

He made a face, but didn't remonstrate with her.

"Hello? Joe, I can hardly hear you? . . . That's better, yes. Joe, did two young kids in a little red car show up for a trail ride yesterday morning?"

Long silence while Shirley listened, made faces, scratched her head, her ear, her wrist, where she'd evidently been bitten by a mosquito during her sojourn last night.

"All right, Joe, I get the picture. I'd have been mad, too. But what happened?"

More buzzing on the phone. J.Q. brought the pot over and topped up her mug as she made a helpless gesture. Joe was going to tell it his way, at length.

"Okay, so they weren't there. What about the horses?"

More, much more.

"And the car, Joe? What about the car?"

19

Another spate.

"All right. J.Q. and I will be out in an hour or so. Can you give us two of your horses?" Pause. "Of course I'll pay for them, don't be silly."

A final buzzing shout, then silence. She hung up the phone.

"What?" demanded J.Q.

"He's fit to be tied. The kids got there. She was wearing shorts and sandals. Joe made her put on some jeans and shoes. He keeps a few pair, different sizes, for the purpose. Jones had my spade and a gallon jug of water and a sack with what Jones described to Joe as a really nice little tree in it. They told Joe what they planned. Joe told them to forget it, he had fifteen people on the trail ride, and they weren't going to stop along the way so two of them could plant a damned tree in the middle of a forest, for God's sake, or words to that effect."

"Lovely. Destroying love's young dream."

"Well, he didn't, actually. She, Buscovitch, batted her eyes at him, and he told them he'd leave them halfway along the trail and they could fool around with their damn tree while the others went on, then they could rejoin the ride on the way back. Then he tied all their stuff on their saddles and they started out."

"How long a ride?"

"Three to four hours, with a twenty-minute dismount and pee-behind-a-tree stop in the middle. Starting at ten, ending at one or two. He takes two rides a day that way, one starting at ten, one starting at two or two-thirty, and sometimes dawn and sunset rides, too. So, anyhow, they start out, and halfway up the canyon he drops the two of them off, ties their horses to a nearby tree so they won't wander off, and tells the kids not to get out of sight of the horses."

"And?"

"And as he rides off he hears Jones ask Buscovitch where she wants to put it, and he hears Buscovitch say every place has rocks on it. Well, about an hour and a half later, down the trail he comes with his other riders, and the horses are gone. He says the canyon is fairly steep along there, and the trail is pretty much the only place to ride, so he figures the kids got tired of waiting and rode back to the stables. Sure enough, when he gets back, here's the two horses outside the corral, scratching themselves on the gateposts and wrecking the saddles in the process. Which makes him mad, of course, because they should have at least had the sense God gave a nit to put the horses in the corral."

"And?"

"And their car was still there, so he figured they wandered down to the river maybe to have a little picnic. Or, as he put it, a newlywed nooner.

"Anyhow, when he got back from the afternoon ride, late, in pouring rain, he didn't think about the car, didn't even look. This morning, though, he walks through the parking area on his way to the stable, and it's still there, but there's no sign of Jones or Buscovitch or the stuff they were carrying like the water jug or their tree or my spade."

"You want your spade back."

"Damn right."

"We'll leave a note for Allison."

"Fine by me. And we'll take the rest of the coffee in a thermos."

The skies had cleared, and the morning sun dazzled the

surfaces of a newly washed world as they drove south, through town, beating any early-morning holiday traffic and turning onto the road that would take them toward the Pecos Wilderness. The Silver Saddle Stables was located down a side road, and as they drove in, Joe came out of the tack room. He looked grumpy and sounded irritated as he told them they could ride whatever they could catch, he wasn't going to saddle the string until he'd had breakfast and his helper had arrived.

Most of the geldings in the corral were feeling a bit feisty. While Joe stood by with a sour face J.Q. caught a sorrel with a white face, and Shirley managed to get a bridle onto a sensible-looking black. Ten minutes after arrival they were ready to depart.

"Okay," said Joe as he opened the gate. "You head up this trail here until it hits the canyon up there about a quarter mile where it splits. Take the right fork. You go up maybe two miles, two canyons come together, and the trail forks again. You take the left one. Just a little way along there, you'll find the place I let those kids off. There's a big red stone pillar with a white capstone off to the left, down the slope. It's the only one like it along there. There's other standing stones, but that white hat, that's the only one."

"What is it, ponderosa forest?"

"Solid ponderosa's a little higher up, so it's kind of mixed for about a quarter mile through there. Scattered ponderosa, some young piñon and juniper, even. The canyon burned out about fifteen years ago, but it didn't kill the big trees. It's pretty open except right down in the canyon bottom."

Shirley nodded and urged the black out the gate and onto the trail. He laid his ears back and she spoke to him

22

sharply. "I know it's not your routine, you lazy critter, but you settle down." The horse turned to look at her out of one dark eye. Recognizing a kindred orneriness, he settled. The sorrel followed, nose to tail.

The trail was well worn, leading up a gentle slope toward the canyon, where it grew abruptly steeper but still well kept, without intrusive growths or protruding stones to offer any excuse for a horse to forget what he was doing. The horses had been up and down this stretch so many times they didn't even bother to look around them. They came to the first fork and automatically turned right, ambling along. Shirley was out of patience with the pace, but she had no intention of urging a horse she didn't know to run on a trail she didn't know, with her aboard, no matter how good either trail or horse might be. She checked her watch, thirty minutes out.

Ten minutes later they came to the second fork. Higher on the hill she could see ponderosa pines looming, their fluffy boughs deceptively feathery in this morning light. The horses stopped. Evidently the left fork wasn't a constant, though they turned into it without protest. The trail now scalloped itself around half pillars, rounded protrusions from the main body of the mountain, cut and smoothed on either side by V-shaped vertical erosion channels, both pillars and channels dwindling in size as they rose to the mesa rim, far above. The trail had been built, well built, a long time ago. Many of the filled areas were sprouting trees that looked thirty or forty years old, and even the shallow fill dirt was grown up with wild geranium, strawberry, and native grasses.

They came around a corner to confront a staggered file of pink rock pillars extending up the canyon on their left. The second one in the row had a stark white capstone.

The others were lower, pink to salmon to red, streaked with brown, rounded by rain and wind into gigantic chessmen. When they had ridden to the point on the trail nearest the white-capped stone, Shirley dismounted and tied the black to the branch of a tree that rose from below. The trail wound on, up the canyon and out of sight. To her right the wall of the mountain went straight up. Downhill to her left were a few dozen ponderosas, big ones, well spaced, with occasional piñons and low junipers scattered among them. Below this open forest the standing stone was rooted in a large outcropping of red rock, and below that a thicker growth of trees furred the canyon bottom. Something down the hill shifted and glittered at her. They had seen no stream in the canyon, and Shirley mentally tagged the sparkle as a pool, left over from yesterday's rain.

"There's a place back a way where I can climb down," said J.Q. "Down looks like the only way they could have gone."

"Not really," Shirley opined. "They could have gone either direction on the trail, up or down. They could have remounted and done that. If there are turns up above, they could have gone off on a different fork. . . ."

He tugged at his hat brim and said in a surly voice, "May I suggest we consider one alternative at a time?"

She scratched her ear. He had a point. "Right. I'll come with you."

They went back down the trail to a point at which the slope below was shallower and easier to climb, then cut diagonally across the slope toward the white-capped pillar. Around it was only the ruggedly eroded base rock, and below that the hill dropped steeply into the more

24

thickly wooded canyon bottom. Shirley looked at the pocked and rounded stone with a troubled frown.

"What?" demanded J.Q.

"I saw something shining from up there. I assumed it was a rain puddle, from yesterday, but there's none here in these hollows. The stone is porous."

"A spring?"

"Look down there, J.Q. If there were a spring we'd see a lighter green; aspen or cottonwood, maybe. Or some willow. Something water dependent."

"Tell you what, you go back up there, see if you can see it again, and yell down to me which way."

She clambered back up the slope, pulling herself onto the trail by a conveniently located branch. Standing beside the black horse, she looked downward once more, seeing nothing. She shifted right, then left to catch that glimmer of reflected sun.

"To your left downhill," she called. "It looks like it's just this side of those pines."

He eased himself down the slope, quite steep at that point.

"Farther left," she called as he disappeared among the trees. After several minutes he reemerged and beckoned. Even with the distance, Shirley thought he looked unlike himself, enough so to make her apprehensive. She went back down the trail, let herself down onto the slope, and climbed slowly down.

"Well?"

"Through here," he said, leading the way. Inside the arc of pines was a wide stone shelf, a complicated, mostly flat, king-bed-sized protrusion of the same stone that appeared above. Lying on the stone beneath a sheltering overhang was Shirley's spade, the blade glinting where it wasn't smeared with a dark stickiness that crawled with flies. A few minutes later and it would have been completely in shade.

"Oh, God," she said. "Oh, J.Q."

"Don't leap to conclusions. Do we look, or do we go back for help?"

"We look, first. They could be down here somewhere, needing help. . . ."

Wordlessly, they split up, he going west off the stony floor, she east, searching the trees at either side, then dropping down toward the canyon bottom, right so many steps, then left so many steps, covering the area, guided by the stone pillar above them, meeting in the middle, dropping farther down, and doing it again.

It was J.Q. who found them. Shirley went in the direction of his shout, farther down, quite a bit farther west. Jones and Buscovitch lay side by side beneath a huge tree, cradled between a lichened boulder and a buttress-like root. A gaping cut on Jones's neck and skull had been rinsed clean by the same rain that had washed their hair back from their faces. Their clothes were saturated. At their feet lay a capped plastic gallon jug, and beneath it, an empty shopping bag with fiber handles, soaked flat, neatly folded. Buscovitch's face was unmarred. Jones's eyes were open, staring blindly through pale lashes at the sun glints sifting through the needles above them. The freckles on his face stood out like rust stains on skin as white as the clouds, cold as the stone itself.

"Babes in the woods," Shirley said softly. Poor, poor children. They looked like infants, skins as smooth as silk, Buscovitch's blond hair darkened by the rain, Jones's black hair baby fine, slightly curling in wisps around his face. She didn't know whether to cry or be angry. Such a waste. She turned, examining the clearing. J.Q. was doing the same thing.

"Looks like armillaria," he said, pointing at the ground beneath the nearby pines. Creamy domes of fruiting fungus shone against the forest litter, some of the caps eight or ten inches across. Once she had noticed them, she saw them everywhere, all around the clearing. "The weekend rain must have brought them up. Early for them." His voice was expressionless. He had retreated inside himself somewhere.

"Early for these children, too," she said, feeling a hard lump in her throat. She turned and slogged away, J.Q. close behind her. Her watch read eight-twenty. They had time to get back to Joe Cisneros and have him call the sheriff, or the state police. Whoever one called, it should be before there were riders on the trail, messing up the scene. That's what one had to do, no matter one felt like howling. One had to be sensible. One had to react with poise and decorum.

"Why would the person leave them there, or put them there, but leave the spade out in the open?" Shirley asked as they mounted up and turned the horses toward home.

J.Q. had pulled his pipe from his pocket and was trying to light it. He shook his head, meaning he didn't know, didn't want to think about it.

She did think about it. The location of the spade was a discordant note. And so was the death of the newlyweds. Why them? If ever there were two inept, inexperienced, naive, unthreatening creatures on earth, surely they had been Jones and Buscovitch. Silly, yes. But not the sort of people who got killed!

She was still puzzling over it when they arrived back at the stables and told a shocked Joe Cisneros the news.

27

"Then they didn't bring the horses back?" he cried, unable to believe it.

"They didn't," Shirley affirmed. "Someone else untied the horses, Joe. Someone who didn't want you to find them still there on the trail when you came back down."

The local sheriff never turned up. Instead, once Joe said the word *murder* over the phone, the sheriff said he would refer the call to the state police, and it was they who arrived in two dusty state cars shortly before Joe was due to take his morning riders out onto the trail. After a few words with the lieutenant, a bulky, indomitable-looking man with an angry mouth and stern, almost ferocious eyes, Joe agreed to provide horses for the party and not to take riders up the left fork until he was given permission to do so.

Shirley had called home and spoken to Allison in the interim, explaining that they'd have to stick around awhile.

"You found them?" the lieutenant asked. His name tag identified him as H. R. Ohlman. His hair was tan, also his skin, also his uniform, a monochrome broken only by cold, blue-green eyes surrounded by nets of sun-squint wrinkles.

"I did," said J.Q.

"What were you doing out there?"

Shirley explained about the spade.

"Was that all of it? You just wanted your garden tool back?"

There was a sneer somewhere under the words that Shirley pretended not to hear. "It wasn't just a garden tool, it was a birthday present, and after Joe told me their

28

car was still here, I was worried about them. They're . . . they were only kids, and they were staying with us."

Joe had saddled two more horses. The lieutenant mounted one of them with unpracticed awkwardness as one of his men, obviously a rider, got onto the other with easy grace. The two followed Shirley and J.Q. as they rode out once more, to the extreme annoyance of the black horse. When they took the left fork, the lieutenant rode up next to Shirley and asked, "When you came up here before, did you see anything on the trail that might indicate who had been here?" His eyes fastened on her face like suckers. The look felt unclean, and she fought down the urge to brush his glance away, like a spiderweb.

"Hoofprints," she said. "Going up and going back. Joe had a group of about fifteen, and they went up before the kids were killed and came back after. When J.Q. and I were riding back down after we found the bodies, I looked at the trail, and I didn't see anything but hoofprints."

"I'm trying to figure out how the murderer got up there," he said, eyes still intent upon her face.

"It wouldn't be too steep to walk up the canyon from the bottom. Or he could have come on horseback."

"From the stables?"

"More likely on his own horse. I think Joe would have said something about a lone rider renting a stable horse. So far as I know, Joe doesn't rent to riders who want to go off on their own. The liability would be pretty high. Besides, Joe doesn't own the land. It's national forest, so anybody can ride in it. Anyone could drive in at the bottom of the canyon—there are Jeep ruts there, if you'll notice on your way back down. Then one could walk or ride horseback up the canyon bottom, in among the trees, without being observed by anyone at the stables. A person could leave the same way." She bit further words back, realizing she was babbling.

"Is that how you figure it?"

He was challenging her, disbelieving her, making her justify herself. Perhaps this was his standard practice with anyone who discovered a body, or perhaps he was just that type. Whichever, she didn't like it.

"Hell, Lieutenant! I don't figure. Maybe somebody followed them there, or they ran into someone who was already there. From the looks of the spade, I'd say the boy might have been struck with it. I don't know how the girl was killed. Whoever killed them must have untied their horses and chased the horses down the trail. They'd have kept going on their own."

"You believe they'd have gone back to the stables by themselves?"

"Horses aren't dumb—that is, most of them aren't. They know where the oats and hay are."

"Then the killer did what?"

"God knows, I don't. Did like the horses, maybe. Went home!"

Ohlman frowned, took off his hat, and set it over the horn of his saddle while he wiped his forehead with a crumpled handkerchief before returning to the attack. "Were they from around here, the victims?"

Shirley turned to ask J.Q., "Someplace in California, J.Q.? I don't remember which city."

He shrugged. "West Coast somewhere. I can look it up when we get home."

"Los Angeles," Shirley said, suddenly remembering the labels in the clothes. "I think it was around Los Angeles."

They had reached the white-capped stone. Shirley tied her horse and waited for the others to do likewise, then she and J.Q. led them down the slope, past the ledge of stone, and through the thicker woods to the clearing where the bodies were. The lieutenant walked around the edge of the clearing to the point nearest the bodies, then stepped back into the trees.

"I'm going to want a forensic team here," he said to his sergeant. "We're not even going to step into that clearing." Turning to Shirley, he asked, "The spade that killed them is where?"

Shirley led him there.

"You touched it?" It came out as an accusation.

"Not today. I *have* touched it, of course. It's mine. But this morning the blood had attracted flies and we could see what it was. If it had been out in the open, the rain would have washed it clean. The blood is what made us go on looking for the kids."

"You knew they were dead?"

"Of course not. I knew there was blood on the spade, which might have meant one of them had been hurt. J.Q. and I thought maybe they could be around here somewhere needing help."

The other officer said, "We've got a guy who helps us out sometimes, Harry Begay. He's one hell of a tracker. Do you think it would help to bring Harry out here?"

J.Q. examined the duff beneath his feet, a thick blanket of pine needles, shaking his head. "Maybe down at the end of the trail. I don't know if he could do any good here."

Shirley said, "A dog might be able to track, if he had a scent, but pine needles don't take footprints. They're almost impossible to track on."

"How would you know?" Another challenge from the lieutenant.

She bit her lip and counted slowly to ten. "When I was a kid, my father had a cousin of his living in a little shed on our place, and the old guy used to tell us all about his adventures as a hunter and trapper. He told me dried pine needles make the toughest surface there is to track on. Tougher than rock, even, because on rock you can look for lichens that are disturbed, or stones that've been turned over or kicked out of place. Rocks are usually paler on top, and if they get turned over, you can see the difference. But pine needles are always being burrowed in by chipmunks and squirrels, they don't take a footprint, they're uniform in color."

Ohlman looked unconvinced, but he contented himself with, "We'll need the spade."

She made a face involuntarily. "You can have it and keep it. I wouldn't want it back. Also, you'll probably want to come over to the ranch and go through the house the kids were occupying." She dug a card out of her shirt pocket and handed it over. "There's a little map on the back that tells you how to get there. Okay we leave you to it?"

He nodded. "Stay out of the house they were in!"

Without explaining that she'd already been in it, she nodded agreement. As the lieutenant went down the hill she and J.Q. started up the steep slope, bending forward to get a grip. Almost at once Shirley cursed and put a wounded finger to her mouth. "Damn. Something sharp there."

J.Q. examined the slope. "Piece of rock? What?"

She scuffed the soil with her boot sole, dislodging a shard of broken pottery. Black. With a sharp edge. Only a couple of inches long. She turned it over, wondering fleetingly whether it might be of Anasazi origin. It had that look. There was another one right next to it. Shaking her head, she pocketed the two bits and went on climbing.

Two hours later she stood in the door of the Garden House, having opened it for a team of technicians who would search it for whatever they could find. Still later she and J.Q. sat in the kitchen while Lieutenant Ohlman finished his report.

"How did they intend to pay for their stay?" he asked.

"They sent a money order for the deposit," J.Q. replied, shoving the sheet across the table. "They could have paid the balance by check or cash or credit card."

"The boy had fifteen thousand dollars in his wallet," said Ohlman, with a suspicious glance at Shirley. "Thousand-dollar bills. That strikes me as a little odd. Do your . . . customers carry that kind of cash?"

J.Q. shook his head. "No wonder he was so casual with money."

"That would not be typical of our guests," Shirley replied. "Someone with that kind of pocket money would be more likely to stay at the Inn of the Anasazi, or one of those exclusive little gourmet inns that seem to be springing up here, there, and everywhere."

"So they were from Los Angeles."

She tapped the sheet. "That's where I sent their confirmation."

"Well, ma'am, their driver's licenses were issued in Colorado." He took two licenses from his pocket and placed them in front of her, thumping them down as though to say, 'Gotcha!'

Shirley frowned at the licenses in front of her, then

passed them to J.Q. "I have no idea where they actually lived. I never saw their driver's licenses until now. She made the reservation, and she gave us that address. We don't ask for ID. We don't take anyone off the road. All our reservations are made in advance. By the time a person ends up here, we've got an address and phone number and usually a credit-card number, or if not, we've recorded information from their check to give us a bank reference. I feel quite free to tell people there's no room available if I don't like the sound of them, and I think we've had a total of two bad checks, and both of those were made good."

"Is this date when they made the reservation?" he asked, pointing.

"Right. She called the first of July. Normally August would be filled up by July first, but we'd had a cancellation that they fit into. We sent the confirming letter to that Los Angeles address, and I know she received it, because they had it with them when they arrived. That's the phone number she gave us, though we never had to call it."

"Why do you ask for a phone number?"

"If people leave stuff behind, we phone them to see where it's to be sent."

"Why would you do that, if you have the address?"

Shirley traded a glance with J.Q. This guy wanted to be a prosecutor *sooo* badly. Maybe he should go to law school.

"Because Mrs. Brown makes the reservation from an address in Oregon, but they're with Mr. and Mrs. White from Palo Alto. Somebody leaves a pair of shoes. We don't know who the damn shoes belong to, Brown or White, so we call to find out. Or, if we get a bad check or a credit-card transaction is denied, or if our well gives out, or a roof falls in, we need to be able to cancel from this end."

"Does that happen often?"

Shirley shook her head. The man had no sense of humor and he was just going to keep pushing. "Not yet, but it might. As today proves, anything might happen."

"Are you finished with the house?" J.Q. asked. "May we clean it up?"

"There are still two men out there packing up and making an inventory. When they leave, you can do what you like. You haven't noticed anything out of the ordinary?"

"Just their odd insistence upon a light in the closet," J.Q. remarked.

The lieutenant frowned. "You wouldn't need a light. It's a shallow closet. You open the door, you can see anything that's in it."

Shirley said, "Right. That's why it was out of the ordinary."

He didn't understand. She didn't explain it. If she mentioned a dog not barking in the night, he wouldn't get it. She said, "We'll call you if anything else occurs to us."

He shook hands with both of them, as though required to do so by some standard of conduct he obeyed only reluctantly, and when he departed he drove too fast for the surface, slinging gravel in all directions.

"He's paranoid," said J.A. "He wanted us to be suspects."

"Well, if we were, it might make his life easier."

"That's one guy I don't want to make his life easier. I didn't like him. That's the kind of guy will kick your dog when your back is turned." He fumed for a moment. "I don't know about you, but I didn't have any breakfast, or lunch."

"Nor me," she agreed. "Let's pretend none of this happened and start the day over."

"Starting over is fine, McClintock. Pretending it didn't happen? I know you too well to agree to that."

2

AFTER THEY HAD lunch; after J.Q. had gone off to pick up some milk from the dairy; after Allison returned from her ride on Beauregard, was filled in on the morning's happenings, and departed once more to take a walk with Ultimo; after the crime team departed from the Garden House; after all this coming and going, Shirley found herself in the quiet kitchen at least momentarily alone. The Buscovitch reservation sheet lay on the desk like an admonition. It was Labor Day, the rates were cheap, no one was home to tell her to mind her own business. She dialed the number, presumably Buscovitch's. Twelve rings and no answer. She hung it up, telling herself that the police could obtain the address that corresponded with that number, even if it differed from the address Shirley had been given. Besides, it wasn't her business. The state police would handle it.

She was dissatisfied with that. A moment's reflection

convinced her it was because the victims had seemed so young. Children. Her own daughter hadn't looked much younger when she died. Her son hadn't been much older. The death of children was simply worse, somehow. She found herself brooding over it, and went out to sweep the patio. It wasn't her problem!

Nonetheless, after J.Q. and Allison returned, the three of them went to the Garden House to assess the damages. The crime team had taken with them everything belonging to Jones and Buscovitch, plus a copy of the reservation sheet that Shirley had made for the lieutenant. What remained in the house was merely a cluttered vacancy, with towels and bed linens thrown about amid a general disorder.

"Ultimo says we're lucky," Allison offered in a gloomy voice as she stared around the messy room. "For all the dead bodies we've come across down here, we're lucky nobody's actually died on the place."

"You're forgetting the man Mama Swales shot in the driveway," said Shirley.

"He wasn't a victim!" Allison objected. "He was a perp. And he was going to shoot you."

Shirley shrugged. It was quite true. She hadn't felt a bit sorry for him and she'd been extremely grateful to Mama Swales.

"They left the phone book open," said J.Q. from the desk by the phone. "Yellow Pages, Nurseries. Red marks next to some of them."

"Of course they wouldn't close the phone book and put it away," Shirley murmured. "From the looks of this place last night, neither of them ever hung anything up or closed anything they'd opened. It was a pigsty."

"You came out here last night?" J.Q. asked.

"I woke up. They weren't here. I thought maybe they'd packed up and left."

"You think somebody was in here, looking for something?" Allison asked.

"No, Alli. It wasn't purposeful disarrangement. It was just messy, like a kid's room. Or someone terribly spoiled or slobbish."

"What makes people like that?" Allison asked, opening the drawers one by one and peering into the corners. "I get myself into a mess like that, it makes me itchy until I clean it."

"Me, too. I've wondered if people who live like that have turned their perceptions off. Though maybe they never had any."

"Maybe they tell themselves messiness doesn't make any difference."

"Oh, I'm sure they do. They go through life breaking things, dirtying things, destroying things, making things ugly. If they don't have someone else around to fix and clean and mend, they just live in squalor." Shirley frowned and bit her lip. She had a thing about squalor.

J.Q. had opened both closet doors and stood before the shallow space, brows furrowed. Inside, the ironing board leaned against one end wall, an iron stood on the closet shelf; extra blankets and pillows took up one corner of the shelf space, leaving plenty of room for hanging or stacking garments. "Why would they have needed a light?"

He ambled over to the window, pulled the curtains shut, then turned on the lamps, one by one. The lamp nearest the closet was on the bedside table, and it didn't come on. J.Q. unscrewed the bulb and regarded it with puzzlement. "This looks like a new bulb. Allison, your legs are younger than mine. Run on over to the supply room and bring me another, will you?"

Allison departed while J.Q. switched off the lamps, then sat on the edge of the bed, staring at the closet. "It doesn't make sense."

"You won't get anywhere thinking of them as sensible," Shirley remarked, stowing the phone book in the desk drawer. "They weren't sensible. They were like little children, totally unaware of the rest of the world, as though it had nothing to do with them, like puppy dogs, running around with their noses to the ground, not noticing the grizzly bear across the clearing. You know what I mean."

"Most twenty-year-olds—" he began.

She interrupted. "That surprises me, that they were that old."

He gave her a reproving look. "It surprised me, too, but their driver's licenses gave Jones's age as twenty-two and hers as twenty-one. And most people that age have learned to be at least slightly aware. It's almost as though they'd been raised in some totally foreign environment."

"Perhaps at an isolated lighthouse on the shore of the Bay of Fundy?" Shirley suggested. "Or by scientists working in Antarctica? Or on Mars?"

Allison came in and proffered J.Q. a new lightbulb, which he screwed in with no more success than previously.

"Something's wrong with the lamp," J.Q. announced. "Which is why they couldn't see into the closet."

He unplugged the lamp, drew his multipurpose pocket-knife-cum-screwdriver-cum-pliers from his pocket, and began to take apart the socket fitting.

"How in hell," he muttered, drawing it out all by itself, unencumbered by wire. "How did the wire get loose?"

40

He turned the lamp over and began to feed the cord into it from the bottom. Shirley and Allison both looked up at his exclamation and saw him staring at a fat roll of bills that had dropped from the lamp onto the bed.

"Wow!" Allison exclaimed, joining J.Q. on the bed. "Look at all the money. *Lots* of money!"

Shirley came to join them, eyebrows raised. "Really!"

J.Q. took the rubber band from around the roll of bills, spread them flat, and began to count. "Fifty thousand," he said when he'd done it twice. "Fifty thousand dollars."

Shirley shook her head in disbelief. "Plus what was it? Fifteen thousand in his wallet?" And all those clothes, she reminded herself. And the fancy little car, which, in light of all this wealth, might not be a rental.

"You know, there was this movie the other night," Allison offered. "A week ago, I guess. A TV movie. This guy hid some stuff, photo negatives or something, in the closet of his apartment, you know, in the light fixture, the box where the wires go, and then he got killed. And it took everybody the whole two-hour movie to figure out where he hid the stuff."

"This room has no ceiling or wall fixtures," Shirley mused. "Only lamps. But Jones expected there to be a light fixture. He complained that we didn't have one."

"There's a ceiling fixture in the bathroom."

"One that takes a stepladder and a tool kit to take apart, if I recall. And the kitchen lights are all under the wall cabinets, to light the counters."

"So maybe he saw the same movie and he used the lamp instead." Allison turned the pottery base over and pushed the cord until it emerged from the top of the lamp base. "That could have happened."

"It could," Shirley agreed, wandering into the kitchen

41

while J.Q. resumed work on the lamp. The sink was dry and shiny, unspotted, obviously unused, though Jones and Buscovitch had spent at least two full days in the house. The dishwasher was empty, as was the refrigerator.

"They didn't even use the kitchen," she said, returning to the larger room with the contents of the kitchen wastebasket. "There's nothing in the wastebasket but soft-drink cups, two hamburger containers, and two stale doughnuts. I think we'd better call the lieutenant. Fifty thousand dollars could be a motive for murder." She went into the bathroom and returned with the plastic liner from the wastebasket, adding the one by the desk. The bathroom basket had only tissues. The one by the desk was empty, but beneath the plastic liner, in the bottom of the basket, were a few scraps of paper with writing on them. She laid them on the desktop, turning them this way and that. Most of it was missing. She saw the word *barn*, the words *burn it*.

"What've you got?" J.Q. demanded.

"You got me," she said. "Looks like a page from a yellow tablet, lined on both sides, and it's not all here." She tucked the scraps into her pocket.

"Okay," said J.Q., screwing in the bulb once more. "Plug it in for me, Allison." He set the lamp back on its table, from which point it clearly illuminated the inside of the closet.

Shirley stared around the room. "Weird. We've got a kid carrying over sixty thousand dollars in cash—assuming he put the money in the lamp—married to a child bride with no sense at all. Neither of them seemed capable of reason, but maybe they saw the same movie Allison did, and maybe she's right about it: since they didn't have a light fixture, they chose the lamp instead."

"All of which raises some very interesting questions," J.Q. opined. "You want to call Jenny from here? Let her know the place is empty and ready to be cleaned."

Shirley shook her head. "She's taking today off. Jones and Buscovitch had planned to leave tomorrow, and Jenny's planning to clean it then. There's no hurry." She led them out the door and locked it behind them. The visit to the house had stirred up her earlier dissatisfaction and curiosity. Back in the kitchen, she tried the phone number once again, turning her back on J.Q.'s skeptical expression. After ten rings, an impatient voice said, "McCreary's!"

"I'm sorry," Shirley said. "I was calling Helen Buscovitch."

"Not here," snarled the voice. "Hasn't been here lately."

"Forgive me," Shirley murmured in her most conciliatory tone. "But did she live there?"

"Roomed here. Paid me two months, July and August, plus a deposit that she will not get back. You've never seen such a mess. Not that she spent much time here. And when she was here we wished she wasn't. Messiest kid I've ever had the misfortune of cleaning up after. Ten minutes, she could make a swamp out of the bathroom. Her and the little prince."

Shirley warmed up to the voice, wondering briefly if it was male or female and then deciding it didn't matter. "You mean Alan Jones."

"Alan? I thought she said something else. Maybe not. They come and they go."

"This is Los Angeles, right?"

"More or less."

"And why was she there, did she say?"

"Oh, sure. I got this long story about how her mom is in prison in China or somewhere, and how Helen was here to see the people at the embassy about getting her out. Then she told one of the other roomers she was here on an art scholarship, that she had paintings in a show in San Diego, then she told the janitor that she was dying of an incurable illness and she wanted to spend her last months traveling around, seeing things. Like a soap opera; a new story every day!"

"What about Alan? What was his story?"

"Damned if I know. I saw his cute little matching car and his expensive clothes, and I didn't need to know more than that. Spoiled rich kid, just like her."

"Why do you say that?"

"You can tell. She left the soap in the sink, so it melted. She ruined towels right and left. She walked all over her clothes, expensive clothes! Rich kids."

"So she got mail there, and she could use this number to get calls."

"She paid two months in advance, plus her deposit. She's got a few more days before I clear the room out. She got mail here, yeah. And she could use this phone to *make* calls. They're not supposed to monopolize it or get calls on it, but she was on this thing night and day. I tell the boarders not to give the number out, it's a pay phone, and I'm not about to drop everything and run to answer the damn thing. I answered you because I was going by. You're sure nosy. Who are you, anyhow?"

"I've got a few rental places, here in New Mexico."

"Well, she got a thing from New Mexico."

"Yes, I sent her a letter about her reservation here. She arrived okay, but she left some loose ends of trouble behind, so I'm trying to find her."

The person's voice warmed immediately. "Loose ends of trouble would be just their style. She got you, too, right?"

Shirley chuckled. Nothing built rapport more quickly than being a fellow victim. "You could say so."

"Well, personal, I think both of them are cuckoo birds. I had a sister went crazy. She was just like those two. You'd ask her what the weather was, she'd tell you it looked like watermelon. My name's McCreary, Salome McCreary, by the way, and my personal phone is 555-9205. You want to give me your name and number in case I hear from 'em, which I won't?"

Shirley did so, spelling it out clearly. "If they get any mail, or if they've left anything, or if anyone calls, let me know."

"I'd be glad to. And you're not the only one interested. Just a couple days ago there was a guy here, looking for them."

"A guy? Did he give a name?"

"He said he was the kid's uncle. Maybe he gave me a name, but I didn't listen."

Shirley hung up, more confused than before she'd called.

J.Q.'s ears were quivering. "So, what did you find out?"

"Buscovitch rented for two months, though she wasn't there much, and she did receive some mail and used the phone a lot. She had a boyfriend whose name might have been Alan, the little prince, who drove a cute little car and wore expensive clothes. Helen was messy and wasteful. She told lies. Or, putting it more kindly, she wove stories about herself. And somebody else is looking for them."

"Somebody who's maybe missing some money?"

"That's possible."

"You going to tell Ohlman?"

"It would be nice of me, wouldn't it?" She snorted and looked up the number. "I believe in being nice."

"Sometimes," muttered J.Q. "When it doesn't get in your way."

Shirley gave him a reproving glance. Lieutenant Ohlman had just come in, and Shirley repeated the information in as terse a form as she could manage, starting with the discovery of the money.

"I'll be damned," he commented. "Give me that number again."

She did so, continuing, "The landlady, Salome McCreary, says she had a rich boyfriend."

"Salome? What the hell kind of name—"

"I have no idea. By the way, Lieutenant, how was the girl killed?"

He said, as though unwillingly, "Strangled. He was hit with the shovel, back and side of the head. She was strangled."

"Manually?"

"The pathologist says some kind of cord or belt. We'll know more when the autopsy's done." His tone told her to back off.

She decided to push him. "I'm too inquisitive not to dig around."

"This is police business and you stay out of it. And if anything shows up, I'd suggest you make it a point to let me know."

"I would do that, of course."

"I'll be sending a car for the money."

"If you like. We could bring it into town, tomorrow."

"Fine. Do that. Be sure to get a receipt. Since you counted it, I suppose you handled it?"

She shook her head. Boy, you couldn't get away with anything with this guy. "Right. Sorry."

"Well, whoever counted it should get fingerprinted when you come in, for elimination purposes."

She hung up and turned to find J.Q. and Allison watching her like a pair of hungry cats watching the can opener.

"You heard," she said.

"Not what killed her," said Allison.

Shirley told them, noting Allison's troubled frown and feeling slightly ashamed of herself. "Hey, forget it. It's not really our business. Let's set all that aside and think about something else."

"Think about the mushrooms we picked," said Allison. "There's a whole sack of them, and we didn't even bring them in from the car."

"Let's dry them," Shirley agreed. "It'll only take a few minutes to clean and slice them."

J.Q. fetched in the sack, and all three of them washed the mushrooms, pared off the bits eaten by bugs or squirrels, sliced them, and spread the slices on pads of newspapers covered with paper towel in the sunny kitchen window and on the oven racks. They were just arranging the last of the slices when the phone rang.

Allison answered it. "Yes, ma'am?"

Rustle, rustle of the calendar pages.

"No, sir, no one by that name."

"I'm sorry, we only have the names of people who've made reservations. . . ."

"If they're bringing guests, they don't necessarily tell us. . . ."

"Thank you."

"Who did they want?"

"Some Japanese person. Yukio? Jaime Yukio?"

"Somebody called for him a week or so ago," said Shirley, musingly. "I told them he might be here as a guest of someone else, but I didn't have a reservation for him."

"Could be that guy with the Ortiz woman," J.Q. offered. "His name is Jimmy and he could be part Asian."

"Should I go ask him?" Allison offered.

Shirley laid a restraining hand on her shoulder. "No, Allison. You should not. It's none of our business who Ms. Ortiz's guest is. If Ms. Ortiz or her guest had intended us to know his name or take messages for him, they would have told us. And if the person who called had wanted us to search the place, he'd have given us a reason and a description. Such as, his mother just died in a traffic accident; he's a baldy, five-feet-eight with big ears. We may thank our stars the caller gave us neither reason or description, thus limiting our choices."

"She means it would be indiscreet," J.Q. told Allison.

"We're not some kind of hot-pillow place, are we?" Allison demanded.

"Where on earth did you pick up that language?" Shirley asked, astounded. "I thought hot-pillow clubs went out thirty-some-odd years ago along with sexual liberation."

"Well, are we?"

J.Q. drawled, "Since our average guest makes his reservation at least three months ahead, since many of them show up not only with children but with dogs, I'd

48

be inclined to believe the pillow could be at best no more than lukewarm."

"Sometimes I don't understand you," Allison complained. "Don't you care if somebody comes here with somebody else's wife, or husband?"

"If I had my choice of guests," Shirley said as she washed the knives, "it would be a couple in their forties, madly in love for at least a dozen years, with two children, both well behaved and articulate, plus a well-trained dog. We would invite them to join us on the patio to discuss politics and world news, the latest scientific discoveries, and the best recent books and theater, meantime drinking a good wine while the children would romp quietly but energetically with the dog. They would all wipe their feet before entering their house; they would never get car grease or face makeup on the towels; they would not wash our white towels with their red swimsuits, thus turning the towels pink; and their children would not destroy the china, tear the curtains, or break the lamps. Since many of our guests fall short of that exemplary attainment, however, I think it best that we let, as it were, sleeping dogs lie."

"There was a pun in there somewhere," Allison said suspiciously.

"Nonsense. There was a very mild double entendre."

"So when people call for a sleeping dog that doesn't have a name on the calendar, I don't know who they are?"

"Right. At all times walking the fine line between complicity and discretion."

"You're crazy, you know," said Allison, with a very slight smile.

"Always has been," said J.Q., who had unfolded the

morning paper and was examining the movie ads. "Would you two like to join me at the movies?"

"What?" asked Shirley suspiciously. J.Q. had a fondness for odd, usually ancient movies, with indecipherable subtitles.

"Animation. Wallace and Gromit in a new movie. You remember *The Wrong Trousers*."

"When? Tonight?"

"Why not? As Allison says, we need to do something familial."

It was traditional for the family to eat out after evening movies, but the choice of place proved to be difficult on this occasion. Pizza was a no, so was Chinese. Thai didn't ring a bell, nor did New Mexican (green chilies), Old Mexican (*mole*), or Spanish (Mediterranean). All the French-type restaurants were too expensive for a casual meal. Shirley finally said either sushi or sandwiches at home, and they agreed on a Japanese restaurant, where they ended up having tempura since Allison wasn't into raw fish. J.Q. had met the restaurant owner somewhere or other, and they stood near the table chatting while Shirley was waiting for her receipt.

". . . matsutake," said J.Q. "I saw some the other day."

"Very early for matsutake," the Japanese gentleman commented. "I have a friend who goes every year hunting matsutake. He has his own secret valley in the mountains where he always finds it. He will share his harvest, but he will not tell us where he finds it."

"What's matsutake?" whispered Allison to Shirley.

"It's a mushroom the Japanese people are very fond of. It has a definite aroma and a rather strong flavor. I remember up in Colorado, Japanese families made pilgrimages every fall to the pine forests up around Ward to harvest matsutake. The Pacific Northwest has a lot of matsutake, and up there they actually have mushroom wars, the local residents against the commercial pickers who come in from California."

"Maybe that's why the newlyweds got killed," Allison suggested. "Maybe they were trespassing on somebody's mushroom grounds."

Shirley started to say she thought not, but then remembered all those shining disks in the glade where the bodies lay. She hadn't examined them, but they had looked like matsutake, armillaria. They could also have been large agaricus, or even poisonous chlorophyllum. "Maybe," she conceded. "It makes as much sense as anything else."

Allison was intent on her subject. "Are there a lot of Japanese people in Santa Fe?"

Shirley looked around the dining room, spotting only three Asian couples. "I shouldn't imagine so. There are quite a few in Colorado, because after the Japanese attacked Pearl Harbor, the government sort of assumed the Japanese citizens in California were a security risk, so they were interned, sent to camps in Wyoming and other places without much protest from anyone. They were American citizens; there was no proof that any of them were security risks; but the government did it anyhow. Their homes were lost, their businesses, everything they owned.

"Governor Carr, in Colorado, thought it was shameful and unconstitutional and he said so. He invited the internees to come to Colorado as soon as they were released, and since they had very little to go back to in California, a lot of them did move down around Denver.

When the Japanese community built Sakura Square in Denver, they included a monument to him."

"Of course," said J.Q., rejoining them, "the wages of virtue were ignominy. He didn't get reelected."

"He would rather be right than be governor," said Shirley, signing her receipt and pushing her chair back. "To paraphrase. Let's go home, people. School, tomorrow, Allison. A junior? Good Lord, you'll soon be seventeen."

"It's a pain," Allison confided. "It's not old enough to really do anything, but it's old enough to want to."

"Want to what?" Shirley asked, alerted to this unspecified danger.

"Oh, you know. Travel, which I can't afford. Get a job, which I'm not qualified for yet. Now that I've got my license, get a car, which I also can't afford. Do all the grown-up stuff I'm not ready for yet."

Shirley relaxed. "Well, you can tell yourself that none of those things are unmitigated delights. Travel is tiring, jobs are often boring, and cars are a constant pain in the ass unless you have someone like J.Q. around who's a compulsive maintenance type."

"I'll start looking for one now," Allison commented.

"A car?"

"Someone like J.Q."

"Impossible, dear. He's one of a kind." Shirley cast an appraising glance in J.Q.'s general direction.

When they arrived home, J.Q. sat down to check the phone-message service, jotting rapidly. "Two Easterners asking us to call back, and Sofia, the one who's having the wedding here next week," he said with a sigh. "She wants to bring her wedding coordinator out tomorrow."

Shirley exploded. "For God's sake, J.Q.! She spent one full day here with the groom. Then a day with the groom's family. Then a day with her family, except for her mother, then another day with her mother, who never dismounted from her high horse throughout the visit. Then a half day with her caterer. Then another half day with the new caterer after she fired the first caterer. Then the bandleader—wasn't it? Or was it someone from the rental company? I'm sure I've seen both! And last, but not least, one almost full day with her astrologer!"

"I didn't realize she'd been here that much," J.Q. confessed.

"Whenever she brings someone, they take over the place for hours. One time she monopolized the pool and our guests complained; last time she held a loud conference in the garden while the people in the Garden House were trying to get their baby to sleep. One time she stood out in the driveway with her family for half the day! We advertise this place as being private and peaceful, and she has descended on us repeatedly like a flock of magpies! My heavens!"

"There's an easy solution."

"Don't have weddings. I know. Well, this one is the last!"

"You said that last year," Allison commented. "Why did you let them have this one?"

"They begged," Shirley confessed. "I am not resolute with people who get down on their knees and kiss my feet."

"They didn't!"

"Almost. They whined. They whimpered. They said they couldn't be married in church for some reason or other, that it's difficult to find anywhere to throw a wedding bash in Santa Fe. The hotels are fabulously expensive. Private homes won't hold fifty or a hundred people or two hundred. Though why people who have been living together for several years need to have a ceremonious wedding is beyond me!"

"Maybe their parents demand it, just to prove to all the parents' friends that the kids are no longer living in sin," remarked J.Q. "Shall I call her back and tell her yes?"

"Call and tell her no. I don't need her wandering around here getting in my hair tomorrow."

"You have something else planned?" His eyebrows went up skeptically.

"I do. I want to get out the brooder and clean it up and put new skirts on it."

"We can still do that tomorrow or first thing the next morning," J.Q. remarked. "The chicks aren't coming until Thursday. And if Sofia can't come tomorrow, she'll have to come later. She will show up eventually."

"Oh, hell, let her come tomorrow."

Shirley simmered. She'd broken her own rule, one made in the cold light of day, perfectly sensibly, after weighing all the advantages and disadvantages, pro and con, and now she was ruing it. Her father would have pointed his finger at her and shaken it, saying, "You see! What have I told you? You've got to stick to your better judgment!"

J.Q. was on the phone, making appropriate noises. Allison, yawning, told Shirley good night and went back in the direction of her bedroom. J.Q. hung up the phone, poured a small Scotch, and set it before Shirley, where she fumed at the table.

"Settle down," he said. "The wedding'll be over in another week, and you need never do it again."

She sipped. "It isn't just Sofia. It's everything. I keep thinking my troublesome years are over, I can relax and be peaceful, but then I do something stupid like finding another corpse. Now they're coming in pairs. Juvenile pairs. It's really upsetting." She found her eyes moist, and wiped angrily at them.

"You didn't find them. I did."

"You, me, Allison, what's the difference? They keep cropping up. I've felt sort of agitated all day." She sipped again.

"You needn't concern yourself any further with these particular corpses. Lieutenant Ohlman seems very capable."

"Right. Quite right, J.Q. He seems very capable. He seems very . . . something else, too, but I'm not sure what. I can tell you one thing. I wouldn't invite him to dinner."

"Still . . ."

"Right. I don't need to concern myself."

He, observing a well-known glint in her eye, was not at all convinced she meant it.

She woke for no particular reason at six in the morning, lying drowsy for a long moment until reality began to percolate through the haze. Tuesday. Something psychologically urgent about Tuesdays, something left over from the old days in D.C. when the first days of the week meant heavy matters hanging upon what she did or did not do. Mondays often meant a conference with Roger, Tuesdays meant research and coordinating among various subgroups, the beginning of a push that, by the end of the week, would have produced a product, either finished or on its way. The week's work. See, here, this is what I did. Of course, there had been weeks when nothing jelled, when everything liquefied and ran off in all directions. The problem with working for a quasi–think tank was that the tank wasn't always leakproof.

But all that was a long time ago. Years and years. All that was way back when she was married the first time. And the second time. When she was a mother. When she wasn't a mother anymore. Before her second husband died and she had returned to the West, to the family ranch, which, like her other loves, had not proven immortal. She didn't even do special reports for Roger anymore, as she had when she'd first left Washington. And here in New Mexico, weekdays mattered not at all except to Allison. People came, people went. Days passed. Only the seasons seemed noticeable, and the slow turning of what Xanthy called the floral clock.

"Winter jessamine blooming in February, crocuses and aconite in March, early tulips and daffodils in April, fruit trees and peonies and early iris in May," Xanthippe Minging chanted. "Then poppies and more iris and fox-tail lilies in June; monarda, daisies, daylilies, and delphinium in July; coneflower and aster in August, along with hummingbird mint and echinops and phlox; and then in September, sunflowers and late asters and chrysanthemums. And in October and November, the last roses of summer and, probably, frost."

It was almost a litany, the way Xanthippe said it. Or a prayer. And all the time, if the weather had been kind, the slow ripening of fruit, apricots and apples and plums and pears. Though this year the weather had not been kind. A dry winter and spring—not a drop of precipitation between February and June—plus a late-spring freeze had killed too many trees and flowers.

The pace of the place wasn't one she'd grown up with. Despite the paying guests, it was more leisurely, more tranquil than the Colorado ranch had been. More mañana. J.Q. accused her of having a hard time finding things to be mad at, which there'd never been any shortage of in Colorado. And even down here there were daily outrages reported in the papers. A drunk driver, arrested nine times and let go each time until he finally killed a family of five, a drunk driver whose family now claimed he was being persecuted because of his race, whatever his race happened to be. If an Indian killed a Hispanic, he was prosecuted because of his race. If a Hispanic killed an Anglo, he was prosecuted because of his race. The death didn't matter. Only the ethnic disparity. Only when victim and killer were of the same tribe was justice invoked instead of ethnicity. Drunk drivers, one of whom had killed her daughter long ago, still had the power to infuriate her.

If that source of fury failed, there was always the Forestry Service, which was going into contortions trying to figure out a way not to sell grazing leases to environmentalists who were outbidding the cattlemen because the environmentalists wanted to save the riparian lands the cattle were ruining. Or the Bureau of Indian Affairs, whose mishandling of Indian funds had lately proven egregious. There was plenty of stuff to be mad at. She yawned, however, unable to summon ire. Maybe it was too early in the morning to pick a fight.

She rolled out of bed, got herself dressed, and went into the kitchen to start a pot of coffee. This morning she'd beat J.Q. getting out of bed, a rare feat. While the coffee brewed, she walked down to the barn and found the brooder in a dusty corner, covered with spiderwebs. She brought it back with her to the patio outside the kitchen door, washed it off with the hose, then fetched a

57

large mug of coffee, a large towel—washed, but too stained with some idiot's shoe polish to use in a guest house—a roll of duct tape, and the shears. The brooder had been made by a local sheet-metal man: a thirty-inch-square roof that slanted up on all four sides to an eight-inch-square hole in the top, a six-inch sidewall all the way around, and stout four-inch legs at each corner, joined by a raggedy skirt of dirty fabric fastened on with duct tape. She peeled off tape and fabric and threw them in the garbage, then replaced the skirt with five-inch-wide strips of toweling, taped lengthwise to the sides so they hung to the ground all the way around. The last step was to cut the cloth at three-inch intervals, making a kind of fringe at the bottom.

With a reflector bulb suspended in the hole at the top, the temperature inside would stay around ninety, which is what baby chicks needed for a few weeks. A small feeder and waterer would go underneath, and the chicks could stay as warm as under their mothers' wings, protected by the brooder roof from being stepped on by the grown hens. The cloth fringe made no corners, preventing a pileup of little bodies that smothered the ones on the bottom. Mama hens had no corners, either.

"You're up early," said J.Q. from behind her.

"I woke up," she said unnecessarily.

"Still fretting about those kids?"

She shook her head. "No. I'm ashamed to say I wasn't thinking about them at all. I woke up thinking about days of the week and how peaceful everything usually is and Xanthy's floral clock. We ought to be seeing rabbitbrush and roadside asters any day now."

He took her cup and went in, returning a moment later

with full cups for both of them. "You've got it ready for chicks," he remarked, examining the brooder.

"Hmm," she agreed. "I ordered fifty."

"Fifty! My lord, woman. You'll have eggs piling up like coal."

"Only twenty-five layers, brown leghorn pullets . . ."

He sipped, nodding approval. "They seem to survive the coyotes better than any others we've had. They fly like crows, and they roost in the trees, like the peafowl. We've still got over half of last year's."

"I also ordered twenty-five straight-run sweep-the-floor."

"What kinds?"

"No idea. Whatever they've got left over. I thought it would be kind of fun to have some different kinds. Nothing so boring as monotonous poultry."

"They'll all turn out to be roosters."

"Statistically, only half should be."

"You can't tell me the hatchery doesn't foist off the roosters on straight-run orders. They're supposed to take hatchlings at random, but every time we've ordered straight-run, we've ended up with three-quarters roosters."

"Well, the roosters are good-looking."

"And loud. And useless. And hungry."

She agreed, with an unapologetic smirk. "Like a lot of menfolks we know?"

He snorted.

"Sorry, J.Q. You're right, of course. Still, it'll be fun to see what we get." She picked up the brooder, preparatory to taking it back to the chicken house, but was forestalled by the arrival of a car. It was too early for guests, or business. Not even seven-thirty yet.

59

"State police car," said J.Q., peering over the wall.

"Oh Lord," she muttered. "Now what?"

"It's not Ohlman," said J.Q. "It's Raul Griego, the sergeant who was with him when we rode up to the site. I'll get another cup and bring out the pot."

"Maybe he drinks tea."

"A cop drink tea? You're out of your mind."

The man who came in was starched and neat, but battered looking from the neck up. His eyes were red. "Griego," he said, offering Shirley a hand. "Raul." He thanked J.Q. for the offer of coffee, took a large mug, and drank quite a bit of it before saying anything beyond good morning.

"Ohlman decided I should come out and get the money."

"We'd have brought it in."

"Right. Ohlman decided that wasn't good enough."

"I'll go get it," said J.Q.

"Sit," said Griego. "I need this coffee worse than I need money, even. Besides, you probably'd like to know what we've found out, right? If you don't let on I told you?"

Shirley grinned at him. No love lost between this man and his boss, obviously.

He returned her grin. "Well, we checked with the Motor Vehicle people in Denver." He set the cup down and stretched, yawning uncontrollably. "Turns out the kid's driver's license is a phony. Both of them are."

"Why am I not surprised?" said J.Q., offering milk and sugar.

"They needed IDs to get married," said Shirley with sudden conviction. "They were too young to be married legally."

"The medical examiner says you're right about their age," Griego said. "He says the boy was maybe sixteen, seventeen. He says he can tell from the bones he hadn't even stopped growing yet. The girl wasn't any older."

"They were schoolkids!" Shirley sighed. "God. I knew something was weird and wrong about them."

"There's more. We towed the car into the police lot. We figured it for a rental car, but it isn't."

"It has New Mexico plates," said J.Q.

"Right. But it's not a rental car. Not a local one, anyhow. The sticker is current, but the plates should be on a ninety-three Plymouth station wagon. No one reported stolen plates, so maybe they came from a junkyard. We're having the engine number checked, but it'll take a while."

Shirley mused, "The girl, Buscovitch, paid rent at a boardinghouse, rooming house, what have you, in Los Angeles, but she didn't really live there. So? What was she doing? Acquiring a mailing address?"

Griego took another large swallow of coffee, rubbing at his eyes with his free hand. "If we forget about the money for a while, we could say the kids were just running away to get married. Say they were too young to get married legally in whatever state they lived in, and say they didn't think about going to some state where they *could* get married legally, so they decided to establish new identities for themselves, identities old enough to do whatever they liked. The first step would be a birth certificate."

"How . . . ?" J.Q. asked, puzzled.

Griego interrupted him. "Oh, hell, over the last two or three years I've seen half a dozen TV stories on how scam artists and terrorists get fake IDs so they can buy guns or get passports. Anybody with half a brain can do it: just go to the cemetery or read the obits in old newspapers to find a death of a child or young person who was born the year you want as your birth date, then send for the birth certificate. Then, using that birth certificate, you get whatever else you need, a Social Security card, a credit card, a bank account, a marriage license. But you do have to have a mailing address, maybe even a phone number."

Shirley said thoughtfully, "And they'd want the mailing address or the phone number not to be connected to their real identities. Which would explain the two months' rent at the boardinghouse. You really don't need any motivation beyond that." She poured the last of the coffee into her empty cup. "Two romantic kids who want to get married and who're willing to do almost anything to do it. The thing that doesn't ring true, however, is that they honest to God didn't seem bright enough to go through all those complications."

Griego nodded. "Like I said, TV has spelled it out, more than once: *60 Minutes*, *48 Hours*, *Dateline* . . . I think they've all covered it."

"If they got it from TV, it fits with where they hid the money," said J.Q. "Allison said hiding stuff in a light fixture was in a recent TV movie."

Griego said, "The biggest complication is the money. Where did they get it?"

"I suppose it's remotely possible they earned it," suggested J.Q. "If either of them was a well-known juvenile actor or musician. Ah, maybe one of them could have inherited it. One or both of them could have stolen it."

"Safe-deposit box," said Shirley. "All those thousand-dollar bills. Doesn't that seem like a safe-deposit box to you? Emergency money. Getaway money."

"Or a safe," J.Q. agreed. "And the money they had with them could have been only a part of whatever cache they got it from." He rose to his feet. "Since we're talking about the money, let me get it for you now." He went off toward his quarters.

Griego stared after him, murmuring, "That money thing bothers me. Say it was in a safe, or a safe-deposit box belonging to Dad or Mom or Uncle Joe or the family business. Who gives a kid the combination, or the key?"

They were silent for a time, considering how a seventeen-year-old might come up with sixty-some-odd thousands of dollars. J.Q. returned with a sealed envelope, opened it, and counted out the bills to Griego, who got out his notebook and gave J.Q. a receipt.

"I have a problem with the phony driver's license, too," commented Griego. "If they got birth certificates and Social Security numbers, why couldn't he get a real California driver's license in the name of Jones?"

"Maybe he couldn't pass the test," Shirley said. "Or maybe he didn't want to bother." She thought a moment, then added, "Or, maybe he couldn't leave home, wherever that was, long enough to go get one."

"He couldn't, but she could?" asked J.Q., eyebrows rising. "Didn't the boardinghouse woman say he was there, too?"

"She didn't say he stayed there. She said she saw his car, and his clothes. Maybe he could get there on weekends, but not when the licensing bureau was open. So suppose Jones was with Buscovitch when she rented the place, but not after that?"

"Why would she be able to stay there and not him?"

"Maybe she was supposed to be somewhere else, or had run away from her family. Maybe she didn't have any family. Maybe he still lived at home or was in boarding school, for instance. My guess would be, they really wanted out-of-state licenses. I don't know why, but it seems to fit in with the other silly stuff they did."

"Too early to tell." Griego yawned, rising. "I've been up all night over this, and now all I want to do is drop off this cash and head home."

"How come the state police?" Shirley asked as they walked with him toward his car. "I thought the sheriff's office would handle it."

He laughed shortly. "You didn't hear it from me, but in that particular county, the sheriff got fired for buying department supplies from his brother and taking kickbacks. The guy who's acting as sheriff could probably do all right with a stolen car, but anything more complicated than that, he's not going to stick his neck out. He wasn't about to be responsible for investigating a double homicide. Some of these little tiny counties, all the sheriff has to do most of the time is pick up drunks and run down speeders. They don't have the money for much training or staff, but they don't have much crime, either, so it usually works out. We're there to back them up when it doesn't." He yawned again as he opened the car door. "Lord, I'm tired. I'll give you a call if we find out anything, okay?"

"We appreciate it," Shirley said. "Sometimes law enforcement would rather we'd butt out."

"Yeah, well, that's how Ohlman feels. He'd like the world to butt out, but I figure you did us a favor, finding the bodies and then not tramping all over that crime scene." He gave them a grave salute then departed slowly, his car seeming to take the mood of its driver, a weary engine dragging itself away.

"Nice guy," said J.Q.

"Who?" asked Allison, popping out of the kitchen, neatly dressed and combed. "The policeman?"

"Sergeant Griego, yes."

"What did he have to say?"

"Jones and Buscovitch were probably just about your age."

"Wow," she said. "Romeo and Juliet. How did they find that out?"

"Something about their bones." Shirley glanced at her watch. "They hadn't stopped growing yet. You weren't planning to walk this morning, were you? If you're walking, you don't have time for breakfast. I can drive you, if you like."

"I would like! I've got things to put in my locker, gym shoes and notebooks and my just-in-case-it-rains coat and stuff."

"You're leaving me here alone to face Sofia and her wedding consultant?" J.Q. objected.

"I'll be back by the time she gets here. Come on, Allison, let's fix some breakfast."

J.Q. took the brooder and went off in the direction of the barn. Shirley and Allison had scrambled eggs and toast. J.Q. was returning to the kitchen as they got into the car, ready to leave.

"You look sort of frazzled this morning," Allison said. "You feeling all right?"

"I woke up at the crack of dawn. Actually, I was thinking about Xanthippe and her floral calendar. At one time in my life, weekday mornings were a kind of crisis time, something to gear up for. And I was thinking how

65

peaceful things are now, by comparison, and feeling sort of guilty over that, and that brought Xanthy to mind."

"She says she's going to tutor me, this year and next, for the SATs. She says it'll help if I decide I want to go to a college where it matters."

"She mentioned to me that she thinks your schooling needs some help."

"Well, it isn't Los Alamos. If I were going to Los Alamos, I wouldn't need to worry. The schools up there are probably the best ones in New Mexico, but you know how it is down here. The dropout rate is around fifty percent. Most of the kids around here don't even think about college, and education isn't high on their list of priorities. It isn't that they aren't smart—they are—but the boys would rather work on cars than on science or math and the girls would rather flirt with the boys. They don't get a lot of push at home."

"You're very vocal about all this."

"I've been listening to Ultimo. He gets really mad about it. He says most of our schools aren't doing a good enough job teaching math and science, and if we don't do it better, there won't be any jobs for our generation. He says local people have been farmers and mechanics and craftsmen for generations and they aren't thinking enough about getting their kids educated to use computers, and they've got to have more math and science skills to get better-paying jobs or go into the professions. Ultimo says a better life doesn't just drop in your lap while you go on with the same old habits."

Long silence while Shirley stopped at a traffic light to let four lanes of north- and south-bound vehicles crawl on their way.

Allison added, "He wants to be a mechanical engineer."

"You mean Ultimo?"

"He wants to go to MIT. Not right away. He doesn't think he could get in as an undergraduate, but he wants to go to graduate school there."

"What about you? What are your life's goals?"

"I haven't the least weeniest idea." She laughed, an unamused, slightly defiant sound.

"You're good with animals."

"I don't want to be a vet. I'm not that crazy about blood and guts."

"I was thinking more in terms of zookeeping, or wildlife management, or whatever."

"Maybe." She stared out the window, suddenly moody. "How did you decide what you wanted to be?"

Shirley echoed Allison's mocking laugh. "Love, I never decided a thing! I took business and secretarial courses because my mother said it was a practical thing to do. I moved to Washington because I wanted to get away from home and see different parts of the country. I started out sharing an apartment with three other women—which I never, ever want to do again—while I worked as a secretary. I found I had a talent for research. I got promoted into a research-associate kind of work. Roger, my boss, found out I could put things together, spot trends, foretell what people would be thinking. A syncretic mentality, he called it. It's a small talent, but it was valuable to Roger, and he said it was valuable to the bureau, though I was never as sure about that as he was. Anyhow, a few years went by and I found myself moved into a neat corner office with access to the executive dining room and my own staff and a little prestige, and except for the tragedies, I really enjoyed the life, for quite a long while."

Allison didn't comment on the tragedies. She knew about them all. Shirley's daughter killed at twelve, in '76. In '81, her son gone, presumed dead. In '83, her husband, Martin, died. Eight years later her second husband, Bill, dead of cancer. All long ago, Shirley said. Past grieving.

"Why did you decide to leave it when Bill died?" Allison asked.

"Actually, I didn't think of leaving it until a few months after that, when my father died and left me the ranch in Colorado. I was having a late midlife crisis about then. . . ." Too many deaths. No one left for her to care for. No one left to care for her! She cleared her throat. "Washington seemed stale and oppressive. Prestige seemed overrated. The executive dining room no longer served anything I liked." She laughed again, ruefully. "I got this nostalgia for the bucolic life. Roger told me I could go on working for him, at a distance, and that gave me a kind of lifeline. I did work for him for a while, you remember. I was doing that when I met you. Reports. Projections. What's wrong with our society and how to fix it in six impossible steps."

"So you didn't plan your future when you were my age."

"Nope. Guilty as charged. I just tried to make the best of what came along."

"Well then, I'm not going to worry about it just yet."

"Don't worry about it at all, child. But don't just take what comes along, either. I lucked out, but not everyone does. Try now, soon, to put yourself well onto a path you can enjoy walking. It will save you an enormous amount of grief later on."

They finished the drive in companionable silence. Allison, heavily burdened with notebooks and sacks of supplies, got out of the car, then leaned back to say, "Thanks, Shirley. I love you, you know. I will think about it."

And she was gone.

Shirley sat for a long moment, warmed by the words. Strange how things worked out.

When she returned home, J.Q. was waiting in the driveway, his normally pleasant expression replaced by one of distress, as when he had overdosed on green chilies or was coming down with a cold. When she pulled up, he opened the passenger side and got in beside her.

"What?" she demanded.

"Listen. Turn off the motor. Take a deep breath. And don't say anything for a minute."

Her immediate impulse was to hit him, but she obeyed, not quite in the order he had commanded, taking the deep breath first.

"Don't say anything," he cautioned again. "I've got a message to give you. I'm going to give it to you, all of it, and I don't know anything except the message. Don't boil over with questions, because I don't have any answers. All right?"

She stared at him. "All right, J.Q."

"A man called. He did not give me his name. He asked for you. I said you would be back in a little while. He said to give you a message. He's coming here, this afternoon, about two, to talk with you. He believes he may know where your son is."

The world went into a tiny cone of awareness, a buzzing quiet, narrowing to a tiny light, infinitely distant, the end of a long, long tunnel. Something whined inside it—a fly, or a lonely bee, or the faint crackle of electricity. The sound of her own blood in her ears.

"Marty?" she said wonderingly. "Marty's dead."

"He didn't say alive or dead, Shirley. Listen, dear, please don't hope, don't get any kind of feelings going. He hung up after those words, so don't interpret."

"How on earth . . . ?" Pain stabbed at her, familiar pain, long ago subdued. She shook her head, feeling a sudden flush of anger. If this was someone's idea of a joke. Someone's idea of being funny . . . Whose? She didn't know anyone capable of this kind of cruelty.

"Come on into the kitchen," J.Q. said. "Have another cup of coffee. I'll take care of Sofia when she shows up."

"I can't imagine," she said. "How would anyone—"

"Marty wasn't alone when he disappeared," said J.Q. "I've often wondered what happened to the person he was with. If that person returned, or if that person was seen by someone else, there might be a link."

"Glenn Beardsley," she said.

"Who?"

"The boy . . . the young man who disappeared when Marty did. His name was Glenn Beardsley. I met his mother. She came to Washington to talk to me, to see if I knew any way we could . . . search for them. I told her Roger had already . . . pushed the State Department, as a favor, to work with the Brazilian government. But that was all jungle, where they were. There weren't any roads into that area. There were still tribes that hadn't been contacted by outsiders. There were crocodiles. Jaguars. Snakes. Oh, they told me what the difficulties were, and I

70

told her. We cried. She stayed for several days. We talked. We told one another about our sons. We decided there wasn't anything else we could do."

"What was she like?"

"Lovely. Very sad, of course. Her daughter was with her, Glenn's sister, Marguerite. She'd met Marty at the university, at a dance. She said she'd enjoyed meeting him. I told Mrs. Beardsley . . . Janice . . . I told Janice to be glad she still had a daughter. Oh God, J.Q., it's all so long ago! Sixteen years ago!"

"It may be a hoax. It may be a mistake. It may be real but not . . . significant. Someone may merely have found . . . found where he was."

"Found where he died. Say it! Someone might have found where he died. That's possible. That whole area is opening up. The tribes are being moved onto government-assigned lands; the jungles are being cut down. Someone might have found where he died. One of the tribes may have remembered him, or have kept something of his." She was shaking. She gripped the steering wheel and insisted that her body obey her. Gradually, the shivering stopped.

He tugged her out of the car by one lax hand and propelled her through the gate and into the kitchen, where she collapsed like a rag doll.

"You'll have to talk to Sofia," she murmured. "I can't."

"Sure. You get yourself together. I wish Xanthy were here."

"God, so do I. She's so . . . sensible."

"What can I get you?"

"Nothing, J.Q. I don't . . . I . . . I need the bathroom." She rose, totteringly, and ran, out and across the patio to

71

the nearest toilet. The morning coffee came up, and the morning eggs. She washed her face. She retched again, drank a glass of tepid water, and leaned on the basin for a long time, waiting for the internal turmoil to subside.

When she had herself in hand, she went back out, paying little attention, almost running into the cluster of people when she turned the corner by the kitchen door.

"Oh, Ms. McClintock," Sofia gushed. "I want you to meet my wedding coordinator, Jane Gardener. And you know my mother, Mrs. Caravel."

Through stiff lips, Shirley managed to acknowledge the introductions. Mrs. Caravel was a robust woman with fiery eyes, pinched lips, and a great deal too much, too black hair, worn à la Liz Taylor. Shirley bowed slightly and attempted to go around them.

"Mrs. McClintock," wailed the bride's mother. "I know you'll understand. They"—she waved dismissively at the other two women—"don't understand at all. You are a mother. You know how much your only daughter's wedding means!"

J.Q. tried fruitlessly to derail her. "Mrs. Caravel, you wanted to see the terrace—"

"Please!" The mother cried imperiously. "Let me have my say. You know, Mrs. McClintock—"

"It's Ms. Ms. McClintock. Neither of my husbands were named McClintock. It's my family name."

The dramatically arched and augmented eyebrows went up. The fiery eyes narrowed. "*Miz* McClintock," she said with only a hint of a sneer. "Perhaps marriage does not mean to you what it means to people of my culture. . . ."

Shirley grated, "I married until death did us part. My first husband died of heart disease. My second husband died of cancer. I have no idea what marriage means to people of your culture, and I doubt it would be significant to me if I did know." She felt the familiar fire at the base of her skull, the tenseness across her scalp. Oh, she was working up into a fine old fury. "Do you have a point to make, Mrs. Caravel?"

"There is no panache!" she shouted, throwing her arms wide. "No panache. This place. It is . . . rural. It is like a farm."

"It *is* a farm," Shirley said. "So it's not unusual it should be like one."

"But it would take such little effort on your part. The animals. They could be kept in the barn so there would be no sounds. The house where the caterer will serve, surely it could be repainted, something gay. . . ."

"The house is adobe," said Shirley, achieving a completely expressionless voice.

J.Q.'s face lost color. He knew that tone. He took Mrs. Caravel by the arm and forcibly pulled her away, chatting about nothing in a mild voice as he led her around the corner of the house.

Sofia cried, "Mother! She can't repaint the house."

"I fail to see why not. It would be at my expense! If she does not like the colors we like, she can paint it again, afterward. You have paid for this place, darling. It should be done to our liking!"

"I'm afraid not," said Shirley. "I will not repaint anything, and certainly not an adobe house. I will not keep the animals in the barn. I will not do anything at all except allow your daughter to be married here and house her guests here, which is absolutely all she's paid for."

"*My* guests," cried mother. "And I would not want *my*

73

guests to be in a place where there is so little refinement, so little attention to how things should be done."

"Very good," Shirley announced, holding open the door. "Please come in."

They followed her inside, stunned for the moment by her imperious tone. She went to the desk, took out the checkbook, referred to the ledger, and wrote a check. "Three thousand four hundred and thirty-two dollars," she said, proffering the check to the bride-to-be. "I am returning your rental. Find somewhere else to be married."

"You can't. . . . This is abominable. . . ." cried Mother.

"I quite agree," said Shirley. "It is abominable. It is probably the most abominable situation I have encountered in years. May I show you out." She stalked to the door and held it open. "I have work to do. If you please."

"Mother!" screamed Sofia. "Now see what you've done!"

"I? What I have done?"

They went out, screaming at one another like a pair of parrots. They had come in two cars. Mother got into hers and left, flinging gravel in all directions.

Daughter, wiping tears, came back to the place Shirley was standing, leaning against the wall, shaking.

"Please," she said. "The invitations were mailed weeks ago."

J.Q. and the coordinator emerged from around the corner, looking guiltily about themselves, as though in fear of an ambush.

Shirley said in her softest voice, "Sofia, do what you like about your plans. However, don't come out here again until your rental of the place begins. You've already been out here ten times or more for lengthy

74

visits; you've cluttered the landscape with your caterer and your consultant and your costume designer, and for all I know, your minister of protocol. My patience is not unlimited and you've used it up. I don't want to lay eyes on you again until your wedding day, and I don't want to lay eyes on your mother even then. You'll have to figure out how to keep her somewhat subdued, because if she makes any further demands that we alter our usual routine or redecorate in any way, I'll set the dog on her. When your relatives arrive, make sure they know that this house is off-limits."

"You're angry," sobbed Sofia. "I don't blame you. Mother always makes people mad."

The wedding consultant offered, "Maybe your father can talk to her, Sofia. I'll talk to her. Even now while she's angry—"

"Daddy gave up years ago. He says it's easier to let her blow up, then she cools off for a while and it's easier for us."

"What will she do now?" J.Q. asked.

Sofia sniffled. "She'll scream at Daddy. Then she'll call my brother in Fort Worth and scream at him. Then he'll call me. Then he'll call Daddy. Then Mother will call my sister-in-law, and my sister-in-law will call me. Then they'll fly in for a couple of days, and we'll all take Mother to dinner and try to calm her down."

"What about the groom?" J.Q. asked, fascinated.

"He stays away from her. That's why he didn't come today."

"I sincerely hope that once you are married, you are moving far away," said Shirley.

"Hawaii," sobbed Sofia. "We decided that after the wedding shower. My aunt gave it. And Mother came. My cousins had given me some silverware as a wedding gift. It was the pattern I'd picked, and I loved it, but they said they got it wholesale, and Mother screamed they were cheapskates for buying it wholesale and not giving me an expensive enough shower gift. And now *they* aren't talking to me. I don't know if they'll even come to the wedding."

Shirley felt herself sag. "Sofia. Tell your father he's going to have to keep a lid on things until after you're married. Then take the next boat for Hawaii, and if that isn't far enough, move to Rangoon."

She went back inside, tears on her cheeks. Lord, all that ire, boiling up, and it wasn't even aimed at this child or her stupid mother. She glanced at her watch. Only ten o'clock. A full day's fury spent, and it wasn't even noon.

She collapsed in a chair and stayed there, without moving, even when J.Q. came in.

"I told them," he said, "that your only daughter had been killed, and that Mrs. Caravel's comment about your feelings concerning a daughter's wedding had been unfortunate. Here's your check back. Sofia begs you to take it."

She waved him away. "I wasn't that mad at her."

"I know, old dear. You picked a bad moment to join the party. I was going to drag her all over the place for a couple of hours until she ran down."

"Which she would have. I'm sorry, J.Q. I just . . . I can't believe this. Sofia and her mom were just the last straw."

"I wish you had a Valium or something."

"It would only delay the inevitable. I can't believe there's any truth to this thing about Marty, but still it

76

made me throw up my breakfast. I think I'll have some toast. Then I'm going to call Xanthy."

She had toast, two pieces, lightly buttered. She called Xanthy, was told Xanthy wasn't there but would be back momentarily, waited momentarily, and received a return call. J.Q. left the kitchen, deeply troubled, while Shirley was on the phone. When he returned in half an hour, she had calmed down.

"She says the information can be only that Marty is dead or he is or may be alive. If he is still alive, or may be, either his location is known or it is not. If it is known, I will, of course, seek him out. If it is not known, I will, of course, try to find him."

J.Q. contented himself with saying, "She's right, Shirley. She's perfectly right."

Xanthy was right, but the situation wasn't. He had heard the trap in Shirley's last few words, one he'd been worrying about since the call that morning. What a perfect game for some credible-seeming con man, finding a much-loved son who'd been lost for sixteen years. What a perfect forum for building hope and stringing it endlessly along.

3

Somehow the next few hours worked themselves out. The phone rang often enough that Shirley had no time to fall into an emotional swamp. J.Q. insisted that she come with him to look at the Frog House where a door frame had pulled away from the adobe behind it. She thought it over, quite mechanically, and said she'd call Ben Salazar, a handyman/carpenter they'd used a few times recently for minor repairs.

"How will he fix it?" J.Q. asked, with a completely specious interest in detail.

"He'll bury some wood blocks in the wall and foam them in," she said. "Whoever built this house originally didn't plan a door at that point or they would have put wooden blocks to fasten the door frame to. This door must have been put in during remodeling."

"Now, there's a window over in my quarters that needs replacing. . . ."

He had gone a step too far, and she bridled. "Cut it out, J.Q. I'm all right. You don't need to distract me."

"There really is a window—"

"And has been for the last five years. I ordered the new ones two months ago."

"More than one?"

"Well, it's a row of four windows. One different one in the middle would look kind of silly, wouldn't it? And if one is completely rotten, the others are sure to be partly rotten." For a moment she seemed actually to care about the matter, but the distraction didn't hold her attention long.

J.Q. fixed lunch. Shirley picked at the food on her plate and finally fed most of it a bite at a time to Dog. J.Q. read aloud from the "pets for sale" column in the paper. They were looking for a trainee dog, the previous one having proven unreliable when he first insisted upon killing chickens and then, when punished—humanely—for this infraction, ran off with a tribe of coyotes. "Either with or inside of," Shirley had said at the time.

"How about a shar-pei?" he asked.

"Too many skin diseases," she said. "No wrinkly dogs, no white dogs. The sun's too strong at this altitude. No fuzzy dogs that collect burrs, no great big dogs. A medium-sized dog, maybe a chow-shepherd mix with a smooth coat. Chow for territoriality, shepherd for good sense."

"You want another one like Dog."

"Don't you? Oh God, J.Q. Stop all this. I don't care about dogs right now."

He refused to give up. "Did you read the newspaper account of the deaths?"

"Jones and Buscovitch? No. I hardly looked at the paper this morning."

"It gives their ages as twenty-one and twenty-two, describes them as a vacationing couple, but gives no names pending notification of next of kin."

"I think Ohlman is withholding information. He hasn't given the press their real ages and the fact that their licenses were phonies." She gritted her teeth. "Damn, J.Q. I don't even care. . . ."

He shook his head at her, finally giving in. "It's one-thirty. Only thirty minutes to go."

"If this isn't somebody's idea of a joke. If it isn't some kind of con . . ."

"So you thought of that."

"Of course I thought of it! That's the first thing I thought of. But I can't think that, can I? I can't set aside any willingness to believe. . . ."

"Just hold on to your old irascible self, that's all I ask. Don't go all icky on me!"

She started to reply, then stopped, head cocked. A car was coming down the drive. She rose, smoothed her trousers, tucked in her shirt. The car stopped outside.

"He's early," said J.Q. "You? Or me?"

"Both," she said. "I need the support."

The man getting out of the car looked harmless. Average size, average build, dressed in slacks and a casual shirt, a high forehead and thinning hair, pleasant though rather squinty eyes in an unremarkable face. He came to the gate and extended his hand across it.

"Ms. McClintock—who was Mrs. Fleschman?"

"Yes."

"My name is David Littlepage. May I come in?"

She gestured him in, led him across the patio to the

table under the umbrella, and seated herself in one of the chairs, gesturing for him to do likewise.

"I'm John Quentin," said J.Q., holding out his hand to have it shaken firmly. "A family friend."

Mr. Littlepage seated himself, fished in a breast pocket for a Lucite envelope, which he turned between his fingers and then presented to Shirley.

She stared at it. A Social Security card. Burned around two edges. Bearing a number. Bearing Marty's name. Not Engmar Titus Fleschman, which was the name Shirley had given him, after a brother who had died, but E. Martin Fleschman, which was the name he'd chosen for himself at age eighteen, in defiance of the Jewish custom of not naming children after living people.

"You didn't name me after Dad," he'd told her, when he'd adopted the name legally. "I did. Engmar is all well and good, but I think I'll stick with Martin."

"May I tell my story?" Littlepage asked, watching her narrowly.

She nodded, unable to speak.

"I'm a journalist. I do special-report kinds of things, a lot of travel writing at crisis times, conditions in postwar situations, refugee-camp interviews, you know the kind of thing. I'm a congenital coward; I stay out of shooting wars whenever possible; and I do my own photography." He fell silent, examining her.

"And?" she said impatiently, taking the card from the bag and turning it between her fingers.

"And, last year I got a commission to do a series on the Brazilian rain-forest situation, or I should say, situations. There seem to be as many different situations as there are informants. I was particularly interested in the resettlement effort, moving Stone Age migratory rain-forest people into settlements, mostly to make way for the timber interests and the ranching interests. Well, you know the story. It's the same here. Ruin the world so long as it creates jobs." He grimaced, shaking his head briefly.

"Anyhow, through an interpreter I interviewed elders and leaders of several different tribes. The young people are already turning to drugs and liquor, the old people are lost. It's not a happy situation. We exchanged gifts. I gave them T-shirts and cooking pots and axes, and they gave me carvings and feathers and animal skins. Well, one of the animal skins was sewn into a little pouch, with some leaves inside. The headwaters of the Amazon are in Peru, even among isolated tribes there's always been some trade back and forth, or so I'm told. I thought the leaves might be coca, and I had no idea how American customs officials would react to that, so before I flew home, I emptied it out. Down in the bottom, I found that."

"This?" Shirley held up the card.

"That. It meant nothing to me, but I have a storyteller's curiosity and a few good friends in useful places. The card was traced to a passport, the passport to names, Martin and Shirley Fleschman, of Washington, D.C., who lost a son in 1981."

"You probably looked up the newspaper accounts?" J.Q. asked, with a troubled look at Shirley's white face.

"I read them. I also took the skin bag to the Smithsonian and had it identified. It's an animal found in the upstream jungles, not in the area currently occupied by the tribe who gave it to me, though who knows where they might have been over the last sixteen years. I wrote to my interpreter, asking him to try to find out where the skin bag came from and offering to reward him for any verifiable information. And then I found out where you were, and I flew out here."

"Marty . . . Marty disappeared only a few days upriver from the coast. The place they were going wasn't . . . upstream, so far as I know," said Shirley.

"What's your interest?" demanded J.Q.

Littlepage glanced at him. "I said, I'm a journalist. I sell stories. This is a story."

"If it is," Shirley murmured, "I have no part in it. I have no idea where my son is or was. Martin and I held hope for some little time, but then we gave it up as fruitless."

"There was also another young man who disappeared."

"Glenn Beardsley," Shirley said mechanically. "I met his mother, Janice, and his sister. Her name was Marguerite. She was about fourteen at the time, a very sweet child."

"She's now a Mrs. Orr, with two children of her own. I called Alexandria to talk with her and her parents."

"For a story?" asked J.Q., narrow-eyed.

"It depends." He shrugged again. "So far it's no story. If we could find him, either or both of them, it would be."

Shirley, ashen-faced, took a deep breath, rose to her feet, and excused herself. Littlepage rose to his feet with a murmur, watching her go.

"She took the card," he said in a slightly worried voice. "I'd really like to keep that."

"She probably just wants to make a copy," soothed J.Q. "Or maybe she forgot she had it in her hand."

Littlepage sank back into his chair and turned his attention to J.Q.

"This is certainly a lovely place. A little Eden."

"People do call it that. I think it's all the animals. It's half zoo, half botanical garden."

"You rent the little houses, is that right?"

"To vacationers." J.Q. leaned back, willing to make innocuous conversation.

"What kind of people do you have here?"

"Families, mostly with young children. We try to make it a safe place for children, a place they enjoy."

"I should think you'd get couples."

"In the winter," J.Q. agreed. "Retired people. The rates are cheaper then."

"Honeymooners," mused Littlepage. "I'd market it to honeymooners."

J.Q. did not intend to discuss honeymooners. His face was impassive as he replied, "When we do get honeymooners, they tend to be mature. I think younger couples have another picture of honeymoons, don't you? Champagne and music and dancing and a lot of room service? The only service we provide is peace and quiet."

"Nice enough, in itself," Littlepage murmured, looking slightly frustrated as he peered at the door through which Shirley had disappeared.

She's his quarry, thought J.Q. His benefactor to be. His funder of Amazonian exploration. Along with the Beardsleys, if they are playable. How could one tell whether this man was sincere or a consummate con man?

Inside, Shirley was leaning on the basin in her bathroom, staring at herself in the mirror, full of the same questions. She looked haggard. At the corners of her mouth there were tightly pinched lines, little brackets that came from pinching her lips together when she was in pain or trying not to ask, not to scream, not to react, not to feed him anything he could use if that's what he was after. She drank a glass of water, washed her face, dried it, combed her hair, then took a deep breath and returned to the patio.

"Mr. Littlepage," she said pleasantly, laying the card back on the table. "What kind of animal did the Smithsonian say it was?"

He looked up, momentarily startled. "I thought it was a monkey skin, but it's not strictly a monkey at all. It's a marmoset. The pygmy marmoset. If you'll give me a moment . . ."

He rose, went out the gate to his car, opened the trunk, and burrowed inside it for a time, returning with a scrap of fur in one hand and a small spiral-bound notebook in the other.

He handed her the scrap of fur with a tiny tail protruding from it and then leafed through the notebook, back and forth, finding what he wanted only after some time.

"*Cebuella pygmaea,*" he said. "Pygmy marmoset. Five to six inches long, tail of equal length. Tawny fur, darker head, orange belly. The tail is ringed, as you can see. There's only one species in the genus, according to the primate expert I spoke with."

"Tiny," she commented, stroking the fur, turning the bag in her hands. It was made of the entire skin, minus the head. Legs had been severed, and the resultant holes sewed shut. A lacing around the neck let it be opened or closed. "Surely too small to serve as a food animal."

"The local tribes . . ." He searched through the pages. "Oh hell, I have the names but they're in an earlier notebook. I can get them for you. Anyhow, the man at the Smithsonian told me the rain-forest people use them as delousers. A person will put one of the little guys on his head, the marmoset clings there. The lice leave the human because the marmoset skin is softer, and then the marmoset delouses itself, or its family does, through grooming. This skin could have been from a pet that died or from an animal that was found in the forest already dead. They don't do well in zoos, my informant said, and the tribes that know this critter are up at the headwaters, in Peru and Ecuador as well as western Brazil."

"I see there are leaves in the bag. Do they help narrow the area down?" She smiled calmly at him, turning the rustling skin between her fingers, pulling the sack open, spilling the leaves onto the singed Social Security card, taking the resultant pile into her hands to sniff at it.

He took a deep breath. "When I found that card, I put the leaves back in the bag and buried the bag in the middle of my camera gear. Luckily, customs didn't even look at it. A botanist colleague of my primate expert said the leaves are indeed coca, but not freshly picked or even freshly dried. They're old. I'm afraid that doesn't narrow the area much."

Slowly, she put the card into its Lucite envelope, then into the skin bag, dropped the leaves in on top of it, tightened the pull string once more, and laid it on the table, saying in that same calm voice, "Certainly the entire Amazonian basin, including the headwaters, would be an impossibly large area to search."

"It would be impossible, yes. And if my interpreter can't come up with any information as to where the bag came from, or who put the card in the bag, it'll be a dead end. On the other hand—"

"On the other hand, if you get some definite and verifiable information, you must get in touch with me," Shirley said.

"The Beardsleys," he said. "They mentioned they might want to finance further inquiry. . . ."

"I'll call Janice," she said. "On the basis of what you have so far, I don't think financing anything is warranted. However, as I said, if you come up with something additional. Something verifiable."

"You don't seem at all eager," he said almost petulantly. "I thought you'd be—"

"Are you married?" Shirley asked.

His jaw went rigid. "Ah, not currently, no."

"Do you have children?"

He shook his head. "No."

She spoke calmly, holding herself in check. "If you had had children, Mr. Littlepage, you might understand. My experience was that grieving for a child was not like grieving for an older person who has lived his life. Not like grieving for a parent, or even a husband. We expect to leave our children behind us. They are our link with life and the earth. I had two children and I've lost them both. I've talked to other people who've lost children, either through death or because they joined a cult or because they became estranged, and we all agree it's a different kind of grief. Grieving for a child, your own child, is like a cancer. It metastasizes throughout your life. No part of your life is free of it, not work, not play, not love, not duty.

"It doesn't go away with time. Even years after their deaths, even when I returned to my old family home, the grief was there waiting for me. It lurks and slithers and puts itself in your way, like a serpent sunning itself on your doorstep. Grief over our dead children killed my husband. If I had let it, as he did, it could as well have killed me. I think one must either learn to subdue it or die of it.

"I'm not going to turn all those emotions loose without good cause. I'm not going to start a bonfire of false hope that I'll burn up on. You understand me?"

He nodded, mouth pinched. "I'm sorry. I guess . . . I didn't realize."

"No," she said angrily. "I've observed that journalists don't realize. They thrust themselves in people's faces after tragedy, demanding to know about feelings, reactions, and grief. They don't realize."

She took a deep breath. "I'll talk to Janice Beardsley. I can't speak for her, but as for me, there'll be nothing financed at all on the basis of this." She held up the skin bag, rustling with the dried leaves inside it, and handed it to him.

"But you'll talk with me if I find something more."

"Oh, of course. Even if you find nothing more, I hope you'll let us know."

"While I'm here I'd really like to take some pictures of the place. Some of the guest houses, the grounds . . ."

"I'm sorry. That would be an intrusion on our guests. I can't permit you to photograph the place or use anything about it in anything you are writing."

"But I told you I'm doing this for the story. . . ."

"If there is a story, it's yours. If there is news, you can report it. I can't stop you. But this place isn't part of any story concerning Marty. Marty was never here; it would have meant nothing to him; and I won't let you use my name or Marty's to concoct a fiction. So far, that's all we have, isn't it? An interesting fiction."

"He could be alive!"

"I doubt that. If my son, Marty, were alive, he would have gotten in touch with me one way or another."

"He could have amnesia."

She snorted. "So convenient, amnesia. One encounters it all the time in soap opera, but rarely in fact. However, if my son had really forgotten who he was, then he wouldn't have been my son anymore, would he? If he's still alive, not knowing who he is, then he's lived almost half his life as another person."

"Maybe he remembers, but he just put it off, getting in touch with you."

Her face tightened. "If there is a person walking around in my son's skin, someone who let me grieve and let his father grieve as we did, that person is not my son. When Marty disappeared, I didn't grieve for his body. I grieved for his personality. Only if *that* survived would I consider that my son was still living, and there is no way *that* could be alive for sixteen years without somehow having gotten word to me." She gripped her hands together, willing them to stop shaking. "The form isn't the person, Mr. Littlepage."

Just for a moment anger flickered across his face, then he shook his head and extended his hand, saying in a conciliatory tone, "The last thing I wanted to do was upset you, Ms. McClintock. I'm sorry. I guess this is upsetting no matter how I go about it, but I've destroyed your peace, and I'm sorry. This is such a peaceful place. Mr. Quentin was telling me about it. About the kinds of guests you have. I was surprised you didn't have more honeymooners here. It's the kind of place I'd like to honeymoon in."

J.Q. interrupted. "I told him the only honeymooners we get are likely to be mature couples."

She fixed her eyes on J.Q.'s face and murmured, "That's true. Young people ... prefer more entertainment than we can provide."

There were a few more words, not important ones, then Littlepage went away, dissatisfied. Shirley leaned on the table rigidly, almost panting.

"Okay," said J.Q., putting his arms around her, feeling her shake. "You're cold! I'm going to get you a hot drink."

"Whatever," she said between her teeth. "Why that business about honeymooners?"

"He was too interested in possible honeymooners, that's all."

"You mean those kids."

"He was just too interested."

"Oh God, J.Q., did I do the right thing?"

He lowered her into the chair, patted her clumsily. "What else could you do?"

"I don't know. Do you think the guy has a source in the state police? You're right about his interest in honeymooners. It seems ... out of place unless he's heard something about our guests being murdered. That could be another story, of course. He wants a story. Where could he have found out? The local papers didn't mention us."

"Which I thought was kind of the lieutenant."

"I'm sure he didn't do it out of kindness. We're probably reacting to nothing at all." She took a deep breath. "After I call Janice, I'm going to call Roger and ask him to find out what kind of a guy this Littlepage is. I want to send the card to a lab, somewhere, Roger will know. To find out if it's genuine."

"The card? You put it back in the sack."

"No. I put my first husband's card, Martin's card, back in the sack. It was right there in his wallet, in the little box he always kept his cuff links and studs in, which has been on my dresser for the last fourteen years."

"But the other one was burned!"

"I burned the card around the edges with a match when I went in to wash my face. I kept one of the so-called coca leaves, too. I dropped it in my lap when I was sniffing them."

"And here I thought you were falling apart."

"I was, J.Q. I am." She gasped, feeling the world bank and sway around her. "I am. But not without a battle."

J.Q., feeling decidedly out of his emotional depth, thought it sensible to call Xanthippe Minging, who was staying with a cousin in Baltimore. He went back to his own quarters and used his own phone, not wanting Shirley to think he was as worried about her as he genuinely was.

"When I spoke to her about it, she sounded quite calm," Xanthy said.

"It's the calm at the eye of the storm, Xanthy. And please don't tell her I called you. She'd be furious at my spoiling your fun."

"Well, it may be fun and it may not," she replied tartly. "They're all so set on entertaining me that they're wearing me out. All I wanted to do was sit on the porch and watch the children play and talk about old times, but they're determined I shall be wined and dined and taken to events of one kind or another. I'm beginning to dread the smell of restaurants."

"That being the case, I honest to God think Shirley could use your company right now."

"I'm also thinking about Allison," she said in a

troubled voice. "If Shirley is really emotional about all this—and who can blame her, really?—Allison may think it puts her in a strange position."

"It wouldn't change her position at all," J.Q. said, startled.

"You know that, and I know that, but Allison is very sensitive to the fact that she's a foster child. I think it's time for me to come home. I'll call you as soon as I get a plane reservation."

Satisfied, he went back into the kitchen, where he found Shirley on the phone, talking to someone in Roger Fetting's office. She hung up as he came in.

"No luck?" he asked.

She shook her head. "His aide says he's unavailable. He's out of contact for the next two days, which means he's doing something secret for the Oval Office or the Pentagon or some other Very Important Place. The aide says if he calls in, he'll get the message. When I met the Beardsleys, they lived in Maryland, but Littlepage said they were in Alexandria. I figured he meant the Alexandria in Virginia, and I got their number from information."

"What are you going to say to them?"

"What I'm saying to me. Don't panic, don't be gullible, don't get your hopes up."

He hugged her, or tried, but her stiff shoulders were unyielding, so he sat down at the table, pulling the morning's *Wall Street Journal* over to stare at it without seeing a word, wishing he could hear both sides of the conversation.

"Janice?"

"It's Shirley McClintock. I was Shirley Fleschman, Marty's mother?"

Long pause. "Yes. As a matter of fact, he just left."

Another long pause. "No. He says he's asked someone down there to find out where the bag came from, who had it, who might have put the card in it. Until he gets that information, there's nothing we can do."

Short pause. "I don't think money will help, Janice. I think at this point money would be the wrong thing to throw at the situation. The idea that there's money involved might encourage someone to fake something, just to keep us on the hook."

Very long pause at Shirley's end. Her face grew troubled. "He may be perfectly reputable, Janice. He may have done work for half the newspapers and magazines in the country, but if you pay for information, you'll never know if it's real or not. If you and Bob are determined to do something, make the reward contingent upon results."

Short pause.

"No, I mean, don't pay out any money until there's proof it means something. If this is a con . . ."

Short pause.

"Janice, there's *always* that possibility. And if it's a con, you'd be feeding right into it."

Long pause.

"That's unkind and untrue. You do not have a lock on tragedy, Janice. There are all kinds of tragedy in the world. Just this weekend we had one here, a young couple killed, younger than our sons were. Newlyweds."

Brief pause. "Janice, I'm sorry I bothered you."

She hung up and turned, tears in her eyes.

"What?" demanded J.Q.

"Oh, she's all up in the air. She's been talking about nothing else for the last two days, ever since Littlepage called. The whole family has been in constant conference, including her in-laws. She *just knows* Glenn is alive somewhere. Amnesia, she says. Inability to reach civilization, she says. All the unlikely scenarios Littlepage was feeding me, she's swallowed. Littlepage didn't ask her for money, not right out, she says, but she offered to pay him to investigate further. She's agreed to pay for information."

"That wasn't worth crying over."

"No. But she got angry and said I didn't care about Marty the way she cared about Glenn. That I don't know what tragedy is. She seems to feel that any effort we might make to avoid being conned is equivalent to a death sentence for our sons, either or both. She kept saying, 'We can't just do nothing,' as though it were a law of nature." She dabbed at her damp cheeks with the backs of her hands, smearing the tears without drying them.

"Which makes you feel like an ogress," he murmured, fetching her a wad of tissues. "You're right, Shirl! You're right. Just keep telling yourself that. As for the Beardsleys, if they lack the strength of character to hold out for proof, it isn't your responsibility."

"She says Littlepage lives near Washington, that he's done work for *The New Yorker* and *The Washington Post*. That may be true. God, I wish Roger had been in his office. I'd really like some top-level advice about now."

"It's been sixteen years. Two more days isn't going to make it or break it."

"Right. Now, if I could just figure out a way to get through them . . ."

Blessedly, the phone rang, and when Shirley answered,

it was Xanthippe, announcing her imminent return. J.Q. left in the middle of Shirley's exposition of the latest— with Xanthippe playing possum, as though J.Q. had never called—and went out onto the patio to lean against the wall while he digested his own discomfort.

If the card could be identified as a forgery, the whole thing could be forgotten. If the card was genuine, if Littlepage was sincere, then how long would this take? It could be years! And the end result might be exactly what had always been assumed, that Shirley's son was dead, had been dead for sixteen years.

"Hell," he muttered to himself angrily. At their time of life, peace and quiet and pleasant routine were infinitely desirable. Uncertainty and trauma and grief were not. Old ghosts, rising from uncertain graves, were not. As Shirley herself had said, bonfires of hope were not. People did get charred and burned out by hope. He'd seen it happen to friends and to relatives, people who would not give up, who would not write finis to any chapter, who were determined to hold on to hope regardless of the effect on their lives. A nephew who would not cut his losses in a failing business and ended in bankruptcy and suicide. A widowed daughter, who would not admit that her son was an ingrate and a con artist, who kept taking him back, taking him back, impoverishing herself trying to meet his needs. A former wife with too little talent to be a successful artist, who refused any other employment and had been living for years in disappointment, raging at those who tried to convince her some other interest would be more rewarding. His ex-wife's sister, who would not accept that her husband was dying, who made his last months an agony of travels from doctor to doctor, clinic to clinic, a tortuous journey from this touted nostrum to that rumored miracle, and who, since his death, had worn herself out endlessly ruing all the other clinics and doctors and miracles she should have tried.

Hope, springing eternal, and laying waste all around it.

And if Marty was alive?

He heaved a sigh, started to go in, then stopped, hearing voices on the drive.

It was Allison, being escorted home by Ultimo, her blond head even with his shoulder, his dark, ponytailed one bent toward her, both of them laughing. J.Q. opened the gate and went down the drive to meet them. Better he tell Allison what was going on. And good to do it with Ultimo there, to provide sensible support and an attentive ear.

Ultimo was invited to stay to dinner, not for the first time. He helped in the kitchen with practiced ease, got Shirley to talking about her children, when they were children, told some stories about his many nieces and nephews, and afterward went with Allison to pay a visit to her horse, Beauregard, with every intention (J.Q. thought) of helping her realize the current crisis made no difference in Shirley's or J.Q.'s feelings toward Allison herself.

"That kid," said Shirley, over her evening coffee, "has more poise and sensitivity at seventeen than most people do at forty."

"Ultimo? He's not your typical adolescent."

"Scares me a little."

"You mean Allison? And him?"

"If he were a little more gauche, I'd be less worried.

Then Allison would have the good taste not to fall for him."

"But he might then have the bad taste to hurt her in some way."

"Right. Depending." She sighed deeply. "God, J.Q., what a mess! I feel like I've been riding a tractor on rough ground all day, all shaken up. I'm so glad Xanthy's coming back!"

"Xanthy's coming home?" he asked, in spurious surprise.

"Tomorrow. She got a flight out of Friendship early in the morning. She'll be at the Albuquerque airport about three tomorrow afternoon. One of us should meet her."

"Why don't you. I'll hold the fort."

"Right." She scratched her chin meditatively. "I won't sleep tonight. I can feel it. I'm all churned up inside."

"Then pick something to do and do it. Rearrange the books in the library. You keep saying you're going to."

"That's not a one-person job. I'll do it this winter, when Jenny's available to help me. You know, it's the funniest thing. I haven't thought about Jones and Buscovitch all day. . . ."

He snorted. "Well, neither have I, woman. Not since what's-his-name called."

"But this morning, early, before all this hooraw, I had a thought. Something we'd overlooked."

"And what was that?"

"I can't remember. I was going to talk to you about it when I got back from driving Allison to school, but this other thing drove it out of my head. I've been sitting here trying to remember what it was. Something we overlooked."

"It'll come to you." He took out his pipe, filled it,

97

tamped it, then went to the door. "Come on outside while I have a pipe."

She rose, taking her coffee with her. They sat in the evening, watching the sky turn from blue to rose to purple through the smoke cloud J.Q. emitted, watching the first stars come out. It was growing dark when the young people returned from the barn.

"I was telling Ultimo about Dr. Osinsky and her kids," Allison said.

"Little terrors," Shirley said feelingly. "Most children like little animals, little furry animals. They may be rough out of ignorance, but they don't deliberately try to hurt creatures. These two little monsters were quite deliberate about it."

"How old?" Ultimo asked.

"Well, the younger one was about four, and the other one was six or seven. They seemed to be unable to do anything but throw, break, and hurt."

"And scream," offered J.Q.

"Right. While Mother stood helplessly by, smiling a little *Mona Lisa* smile and saying she couldn't control them."

"A little woman?" Ultimo asked. "Boys can kind of dominate a little person."

"She is five-foot-ten, a hundred eighty pounds, and she moves like a halfback," said J.Q. "It isn't that she couldn't. It's that she doesn't want to. She's one of that 'let children grow up naturally' school."

"Don't remind me of her," Shirley grumped. "Change the conversation."

Allison laughed. "All right. I was telling Ultimo about the dinner we had the other night," Allison said cheerfully. "At the Japanese restaurant. He's never had Japanese food. Can he go with us sometime?"

Ultimo added his bit. "I was telling Allison she's lucky to have folks who do so many interesting things. I doubt I could get my family even to try raw fish!"

Shirley nodded. "Ceviche is raw fish, Ultimo. That's Mexican."

He grinned. "My mom would be offended if anybody took her for Mexican. She's all the time telling me her family was here before the gringos."

"Well, it was part of Mexico then."

"Sure, but it's been American longer than most gringos have. So when did you get to like Japanese food?"

She leaned back, thinking. "It must have been almost forty years ago, in Washington. I was new to the town, and some young man took me out. Funny. I can remember the occasion but not the person. He'd been attached to the Japanese embassy or had served there with the military, something of the kind. He talked about Japan. We had hot sake and sukiyaki, fixed at the table. I was so impressed. I was silent and adoring."

"You, adoring?" J.Q. muttered.

"Well, I was young. Relatively, shall we say, inexperienced. He was enough older to seem a proper object of adoration."

J.Q. grinned and changed the subject. "Your folks weren't big on fancy cookery?"

"Mother was a professional cook before she married Dad. She produced marvelous meals, but she never tried her hand at anything very exotic, so far as I remember."

"Japanese food is supposed to be healthful," Ultimo commented. "Very little fat. Lots of fish and rice."

"The fish is getting harder to come by every year," murmured Shirley. "And damn it, they've got to stop stripping the seas and killing whales."

"They should concentrate on matsutake," Allison said, turning to Ultimo. "That's a kind of mushroom they like—"

"That's it," Shirley said suddenly. "That's it!"

"What's what?" demanded J.Q.

"That's what I remembered this morning. The thing that didn't make sense."

They looked at her, two confused faces and a slightly irritated one.

"Shirley," J.Q. said threateningly. "For heaven's sake . . ."

"I'm telling you," she protested. "Matsutake. Mushrooms. There were mushrooms under the trees where we found the bodies. Finding things, that's the point. We found my spade, we found the water jug, we found the sack the tree was in. Where was the tree?"

J.Q. pursed his lips, thinking. "We were in the middle of a grove," he said. "There were trees everywhere."

"Not little ones," she said. "Remember! We were in a small clearing among big trees. There were mushrooms all around. The two bodies were lying against one of the trunks. The jug was there, at their feet. The sack was there, folded up. But I don't remember any sign of digging. Where was the tree?"

The resultant conversation, which went on for at least an hour, ranged widely and arrived at no conclusion. Three of the participants did everything they could to extend it. During the time it went on, Shirley almost forgot about David Littlepage.

* * *

Allison went off to school in the morning and Shirley went with J.Q., at his insistence, back to the Silver Saddle Stables, where they once again borrowed horses from Joe Cisneros—far less trouble than trailering their own from home—and rode up the canyon to the point above the clearing where the bodies had been discovered. They tied the horses and clambered down the hill to the clearing, crisscrossing it, walking through the trees around it, spiderwebbing outward in all directions. They found signs of mushrooms, possibly armillaria, now too dried and insect-eaten to identify surely, but no search pattern turned up any sign of planting or digging or any tiny tree. There was no small tree, potted or unpotted, anywhere that they could find. Indeed, there were no seedlings of any kind among the ponderosa pines that gathered thickly at the bottom of the canyon.

"You'd think there'd be some little ones," J.Q. said, after a fruitless half hour.

"As a matter of fact, no," Shirley responded. "Back before my father died, a big piece of the mountain land on the Colorado ranch had accumulated a lot of small trees and brush, and he felt it was a fire danger, so he decided to sell some of the timber on it. A man from the state forestry department came out to help him select the trees to be marked as keepers. When Dad commented on the fact the youngest trees seemed to be thirty or forty years old, that there weren't any seedling ponderosas, the forester told him ponderosas only germinate on bare ground. All the younger ones had sprouted right after the most recent fire."

J.Q. leaned against a convenient trunk and took his pipe from his pocket. "That's why we always see forests of little ponderosas along new road cuts, where the ground is steep and bare."

"Right. That's why there are all kinds of seedlings in Yellowstone since the fire, and up west of us, where the Dome fire burned part of Bandelier National Monument last year. Ponderosa won't germinate on ground that's covered with duff or grass, and there aren't any bare places here except for rock outcroppings. There's a thick layer of fallen needles everywhere."

"So, Jones and Buscovitch didn't dig here," J.Q. agreed. "How about where the spade was, up the hill on that rock ledge?"

"We haven't looked there."

Wordlessly, they slogged up the hill to the exposed outcropping. Here the ground between the stone was steeper, but no more bare. Rocky surfaces underlay the shallow soil deposits that were uniformly grown up in grass or bushes.

"Mushroom hunters have been here," said J.Q., pointing at a boulder up-canyon from the outcropping. "Somebody sat there and cleaned his harvest."

The sun-warmed rock had a small pile of dried fungus at its base. Shirley spread them with the toe of her boot, cut off bases of stems with the dirt still on them, as well as complete specimens too wormy to take home.

"Was this here when we found the bodies?" Shirley asked. "Or when we brought the police?"

"I have no idea. We went up and down this slope on the other side of the ledge both times."

They went on with their search, what J.Q. thought of as fruitless perseverance in action. He was just on the point of suggesting they give it up when Shirley called:

"Here. Look here."

She stood at the edge of a half-buried and lichen-covered boulder, about five yards from the mushroom hunters' rock and closer to the ledge. Beside it was an irregular bare area, a couple of square feet of dark earth. Nearby lay several small stones, their stained undersides making them darker than the surrounding outcroppings. J.Q. turned them over. The bottom sides were clean and pale and bore similar patterns of lichen. He picked them up and set them onto the bare spot, shifting them until they fit exactly. Two on the bottom, one slightly overlapping. Even the lichen patterns lined up.

"So the kids came here, and they looked for a spot to dig," she said, musing. "They moved the rocks, but they didn't dig in the soil."

"Maybe they tried and it was too shallow," said J.Q., taking out his multiple-purpose knife, opening the longest blade, and stabbing it down. "Nope. It's deep enough to get a spade into, certainly large enough to hold a quart-size plant."

"Baffling," she said, shaking her head. "Though I suppose some animal could have eaten the tree, or dragged it heaven knows where. There are elk droppings down in the clearing." She leaned over, inspecting the area closely. "There's another piece of that pottery."

She picked up the black shard and showed it to J.Q. "I cut my finger on one like this the other day." She fished the earlier pieces out of her pocket and compared them with the one she had just found. "Anasazi, you think?"

He looked at them, grunted, and gave them back. She dropped them in her jacket pocket, and they scrambled up the hill once more.

The trip, though unfruitful, had served to take up a good part of the morning, which was precisely what J.Q.

had intended. When they arrived home, J.Q. went off to his own quarters to pay some bills, so he said, while Shirley checked the message service. There was a message from Roger, with a number where he could be reached, and there was also a note from Jenny, the housekeeper, saying she'd "found something" in the Garden House the day before.

A call to Jenny's quarters brought her over immediately, bearing a small, wine-colored book with a shiny lock. "It's a diary," she said, handing it to Shirley. "It fell out when I stripped the bed. It was in the sheets, clear down at the bottom of the bed—along with some underwear." She looked quite disapproving, though whether at the location of diary or underwear, Shirley couldn't tell.

"No key," Shirley commented.

"Nope. You can open 'em with a hairpin, though. My brother always used to open mine."

"I may do that. Or give it to the police. Or both, one after the other. Thanks, Jenny."

The lean woman arranged herself comfortably, arms folded, hip aslant. "Do they have any idea who killed those two?"

"Not that I know of."

"Poor babies." She shook her head sadly.

"Babies is right. The medical examiner says they were just teenagers."

"Mr. Quentin says they had all kinds of money on them. Where would two babies get that kind of money?"

"From somebody who resented their taking it, maybe. We can't think of any other motive for their being killed."

With an expressive *tsk* and a shake of her head, Jenny went back to the soap operas and fancywork with which she passed most of the hours not spent shining the ranch houses to a high gloss. Shirley, after a long look at the diary, put it in her jacket pocket and called the number Roger had left.

"This is hard to believe," he said, after she had told him of Littlepage's visit. "A little too good to be true."

"He had the story down pat, Roger. Why he was in Brazil, who he talked to, how he found the card, what the bag was made of, how he happened to empty it, all the little circumstantial details. If it's a scam, it's not your garden-variety con artist at the bottom of it."

"You want to send me the card? I shouldn't think Social Security cards would be hard to fake."

"True. The results may not be definite, but I'd like to explore all avenues."

"And his name, again?"

"David Littlepage. The Beardsleys, in Alexandria, Virginia, have offered him money to continue the search. Their son, Glenn, was with Marty when they disappeared. Littlepage told them that he's done work for *The New Yorker* and for *The Washington Post*."

"That should be easy to check."

"So should his trip to Brazil. If he went into the interior and talked to resettled tribes, someone at the what?—maybe the ministry of the interior?—should know about it. Now that the area is opened up, maybe they even have government people who can investigate."

"I think we'll not ask that question, Shirley. Tribespeople who would talk to an interpreter or a wandering journalist might draw the line at a government man. I don't want to draw a curtain over information before we've tried to get it in other ways. We've got Americans in Brazil who are involved in the resettlement, people doing research. Some of them are people I know."

"Littlepage mentioned amnesia. I pooh-poohed the idea to him, but I suppose it's a remote possibility. We could perhaps ask, through whatever means possible, if there's a white man living with some tribe upriver."

He laughed. "Shirley, the rain forest is going to be gone within decades, along with the last rain-forest natives in the world. It's probable that every tribe there has at least one anthropologist living with it, and maybe more. I don't think that will get us anywhere."

"Only a thought," she said.

"Let me see what I can do with what I have. And until I do get some information, try not to let this get to you."

"Afraid it already has," she murmured.

He said a few soothing words and hung up. Shirley, now at loose ends, took the diary from her pocket and was just preparing to pick its lock when J.Q. stuck his head in the kitchen to inquire:

"Are you going to have lunch before you leave for Albuquerque? Xanthippe will be coming in at three. Of course, you could have something at the airport."

Shirley flushed, looked at her watch, then put the diary back in her pocket. She'd forgotten all about Xanthippe.

"I think I'll eat in Albuquerque, if at all. The drive will clear my head."

"Remember that brake's started grabbing to the left," he yelled after her as she went out the door.

She nodded, not really paying attention to what he said until she had the car halfway down the driveway.

Once through Santa Fe, the road to Albuquerque was dull. Desert and highway, highway and desert, the Sandias off on the horizon, the highway signs and exits mere mileposts, without significance. Shirley tried to think about Jones and Buscovitch, but ended up thinking about Marty. All the things she'd thought about sixteen years ago. The venomous snake, striking out of underbrush: the fer-de-lance, the South American rattlesnake, the *jararacussú*, the *tamagasse*—called the jumping viper because it actually left the ground when it struck. She had looked them up. She had made a special trip to the zoo to see them, staring into their flat eyes, wondering if her son had died because of their fangs, their poison.

Or perhaps it had been a hostile tribesman, thrusting a spear. She had looked them up, too. A few such tribes were still there, or had been, sixteen years ago, territorial and suspicious, liable to attack first and ask questions later if at all. Or maybe there had been a hole that opened at their feet, into which they plunged and stayed, bones broken, unable to get out. And if these scenarios failed, there was always the jungle itself, into which they wandered and became lost, either separately or together, and which they lacked the skills to survive.

Even while at the zoo, staring at the unblinking eyes of the serpents, she had never been able to convince herself that any of these scenarios was the right one. She'd thought of the Amazon itself, in those seasons in which it ran over its banks, back into the forest. One could fall into it and become enmeshed in roots or weeds and drown. One could be eaten by piranhas, though that wasn't likely, so she'd been told, not down where Marty and Glenn had disappeared.

The boys could have been taken captive. They could have been mistaken for a prey animal and shot with a poisoned blow dart. That, at least, would have been quick and sure. None of the mental pictures was convincing. She'd never come up with one to which she could assent emotionally. In the end, she had had to accept "I don't know." It was a wrenching acceptance, one she hadn't liked then and didn't like now. My son is gone. I don't know where. I don't know how. I don't know whether alive or dead. I don't know.

Forget it. Think about Jones and Buscovitch. Think about the missing tree. What kind of tree was it? It had been Sunday morning when they set off to buy it. The local nurseries who did business on Sundays opened late on that day, ten o'clock or later. The newlyweds were due for their ride at ten, so . . . where did they get their tree? Now, that was interesting, why hadn't that occurred to her before?

They had to go all the way through Santa Fe to get to the Silver Saddle Stables, so wherever they stopped in Santa Fe, they didn't have to go far out of their way. The phone book had been open to Nurseries. There had been red marks in it, according to J.Q. Now, why hadn't she looked at it?

(The anaconda, dropping from a vine-draped tree . . .)

Because it hadn't seemed important. Besides, the phone book was still there. She could look at it when she got home.

(The jaguar, most muscular of the big cats, quite able to take a human as prey . . .)

Find out where they got the tree and what kind it was, that might lead somewhere. Though probably not. Murder wouldn't depend upon that. Murder depended upon emotion: wrath, fear, lust, maybe. Though Jones and Buscovitch seemed young to stir up wrath, or fear, or lust.

(The dark jungle. Wandering. Drinking polluted water from the river. Trying to find food without knowing where to look. Pain, sickness, weakness . . . eventual death . . .)

And here was the turn off to the airport. She braked, felt the car pull left, compensated for it. J.Q. said he'd made an appointment for the following week to have the brakes fixed. Until then, they'd just have to remember about them.

(Being lost among endless trees. Being unable even to find the river. Being only twenty, and having your life's ending there, before you . . .)

And pick up a parking ticket, and park, and put the ticket in the pocket of the jacket, and go inside. She glanced at the airport restaurant, finding herself without appetite. She'd buy a candy bar, something to give her a sugar rush if she needed one. She'd buy a couple of paperbacks, too. Just in case there were more sleepless nights coming up . . .

(Crocodiles. There were Amazonian crocodiles. There were poisonous plants. . . .)

"Are you going to say hello, or just stand here like a statue forever?" someone asked.

She came to herself with a shock of surprise. "Xan-thippe! It isn't time for your plane yet!"

"Well, actually, dear, it is. How long have you been standing here, staring at the floor?"

Shirley glanced at her watch, flushing. "About twenty minutes."

"This is all very upsetting, isn't it?"

"Very," Shirley barked.

"Well, my dear, I have no idea if you're hungry or not,

109

but I could not face the airline food. My seatmate told me it was rubber chicken and rice, with paper lettuce and plastic tomatoes. If you wouldn't mind dreadfully, could we stop in the restaurant for a bite before we start back?"

"Of course," Shirley said, contrite, taking Xanthy's carry-on bag and leading the way. "Of course we can. Allison will be so glad to see you. She's been wishing you back for the past few weeks."

They sat, they ordered, or rather Xanthippe ordered for both of them: a salad for herself, a Reuben sandwich for Shirley (who had gone off into never-never land again), reasoning that if Shirley got the sandwich in her hand, she would take bites from it automatically, which was good, because J.Q. said she wasn't eating. Xanthippe prodded gently, getting the story, then getting the story again, with frills, then still again, with addenda and extrapolation and Roger's ideas as well.

"It sounds terribly wearing," Xanthippe said, putting down her fork and glancing with satisfaction at Shirley's plate. The sandwich was entirely gone and heavy inroads had been made into the french fries as well. "Well, if you're finished, dear. I've several bags to pick up downstairs if you'll bring the car to the baggage."

Surprised, Shirley examined her almost empty plate. "What was I eating?" she asked.

"A sandwich, dear. It looked very nice. Baggage?"

"Of course. You go ahead. I'll pay for this and bring the car."

The drive home was almost silent. Shirley had said everything she had to say, several times, with cathartic effect. She felt drained, for the moment.

"What's this you mentioned about some of your

guests being killed?" Xanthippe asked as they approached Santa Fe.

"The newlyweds," Shirley answered. "I'll tell you all about it," which she did, concluding, "And I've got the diary in my pocket. Just haven't had a chance to look at it yet."

"Wonderful. Let me dig it out. I think I have a hairpin . . . yes. Now, let's see if I remember how this is done."

She fiddled with it, talking to herself, then saying, "There. Got it."

"Read it to me."

"Well, let's see. The first half of the book is blank. The first entry is in June. My, oh, my, this child never learned to spell. She never learned to write, either. Let's see, if I allow for misspellings, cross-outs, and smears, and if I concentrate really hard on the execrable writing, I think I can make it out.

" 'June third, 1997. We want to get married and his father won't let us. He's such a pig. It all has to be his way, and other people don't even matter! He doesn't care what we want or how we feel. He's like . . .' What is this word? P-r-a, no, it's an e, and that must be meant for an h. 'Prehistoric! We have to figure out a way to just go!

" 'June twelfth, 1997. We're going to run away together. We will change our names and everything, and we need enough money to live on for a long time. He says he is going to finish school. He says he'll get plenty of money he knows where he can get it. He says we have to leave a false trail. Weekend after next vacation starts but his dad is going to be gone so we can go rent us a place to use.' "

Xanthippe laid the book facedown on her knee. "I've

had children just like her in my classes. I know exactly what she's thinking. Poor little thing. All that lust and romance boiling around inside her and no place at all to go with it." She shook her head and looked sadly out the window for a moment before taking up the book once more.

" 'June twenty-third, 1997. We drove all around Hollywood. He says he knows that part of town pretty well because his folks used to live near there. We rented a room in a boardinghouse. It's not very nice, but since I'll be there mostly weekends, we didn't want to spend too much. I have to be at school during the week so nobody gets suspicious.' Spelled s-u-s-s-p-i-s-h-u-s. Honestly. Don't the schools teach spelling anymore?"

"Read on. You're doing fine."

" 'He doesn't want to get the money until just before we leave, and we had to pay for July and August in advance. We'll get married by then. His father will go through the roof about the money, but we'll be gone, so let him. We went to the library and read the old newspapers on the computers until we found two people we could be. Their names are Alan Jones and Helen Buscovitch. From now on, we have to call each other Alan and Helen.

" 'June twenty-fourth. We went to the bookstore and bought magazines on different places. We got *Arizona Highways* and one from Nevada and one from New Mexico and one from Hawaii.' Something heavily crossed out. 'Alan's dad will look in Hawaii, because of how Alan hates it anyplace he can't surf. We'll find a place to stay while we find a place to live.' Cross-out. 'Alan says I can pick. Arizona is really hot and Nevada is all gambling. We should stay away from there. Besides, we need a place Alan's dad won't look for us. Like in that mystery movie.

" 'July first. I moved in today. I only took one suitcase and hardly any clothes. Alan will come back next weekend. I only have to share the bathroom with two other people. That's better than school. We called a place in Santa Fe and made a reservation for the end of next month. The birth certificates came in the mail, too.' "

Xanthippe sighed. "She spelled certificates starting with s-i-r." She read silently for a time. "There are other entries following, none of them significant, dealing mostly with Helen and Alan's erotic life and their weekend wanderings in and around Hollywood."

"Where did they wander?"

"Mostly Rodeo Drive, where they patronized expensive restaurants and purchased expensive clothing."

"Nothing cultural, I suppose."

"No. Why would they? Here's something. On the thirtieth of July, they received driver's licenses in the mail. Driver's licenses? Or driver's license. I can't tell which. What's that about?"

"They both had fake Colorado licenses. My guess is they wanted out-of-state licenses—I mean licenses from a state where they didn't reside—and didn't have time to go out of state to get them. Alan was seldom at the rooming house, according to the landlady."

Xanthippe turned to the book once more. "On the tenth of August, Alan bought a car, 'like his other one.' And the last entry is the fourteenth of August, the day before they left California to drive to New Mexico."

"No reference anywhere to their right names?"

"Not that I see."

"And no reference to where they lived or who their folks were."

"None. In fact, this diary defeats the very purpose of a diary, doesn't it? It isn't a welling-up of confidences. It conveys few personal feelings, except for a spot or two of violet prose concerning their lovemaking."

"Which you skipped over," Shirley charged.

"Well, yes. In my day, one did not use those words outside the boudoir. I'm not sure they were even used there."

"I'll have to peruse it myself, just to get the flavor."

"The flavor is similar to chocolate truffles. Very rich and luxurious and habit-forming. I wish adolescence could revert to the 1800s. Back then, girls didn't reach maturity until they were fifteen or sixteen, they could marry at eighteen or nineteen, so families only had two or three years to worry about. Now, with everyone popping their zippers at eleven and twelve, it's simply too much to cope with."

"Every time I look at Allison, I know what you mean. J.Q. and I were saying the other day that we don't know whether to be glad or not that Ultimo is so mature in his attitudes. We can rely on his good sense, I suppose, but on the other hand, that may push the relationship more quickly than we'd like." Shirley, made the turn off the highway that would take them home, once again correcting the pull to the left.

"Allison is sensible."

"You said it was like chocolate, Xanthy. Even sensible people can be chocoholics."

Silence. When Shirley glanced sideways, she saw

Xanthy's face, calm and relaxed, peering ahead through the windshield at the approaching gate.

"Home," she said. "Oh, Shirley, I am glad to be home."

4

SHIRLEY MADE A copy of the diary pages before calling Lieutenant Ohlman to tell him about finding the book.

Irritated, he snarled, "How did my people miss that?"

"Not their fault," Shirley assured him. "It was all tangled up in the bed linen. They wouldn't have found it without stripping the bed."

"Which is exactly what they should have done," he growled, unmollified. "I'll send Sergeant Griego to pick it up this evening. He lives out near there."

"Ah . . . about what time?" Shirley queried.

"He'll call you."

Which Griego did, so promptly that Shirley suspected he had been in the room with his boss during the earlier call.

"We'll have finished supper by seven," she suggested. "Unless you'd like to have it with us."

He spoke formally. "Thank you, but my wife says I'm not home enough as it is. Excuse me a moment. . . ."

There was conversation at the other end, the sound of a door closing. When Griego came back on the line, he sounded friendlier, more casual.

"Tell you what, though. If they feel up to it, would you mind if I brought my wife and her sister along. They'd enjoy seeing your place."

If they felt up to it? "Wouldn't mind at all."

"My wife's sister, she's . . . she's in a wheelchair."

What did one say to that? "I'm sorry to hear that."

His voice dropped almost to a whisper. "She had a spinal injury. They say she's getting better, but she gets discouraged."

"We'll keep things cheerful," Shirley promised.

She and Allison made supper. Two pounds smoked or Polish sausage. One large can kidney beans, drained. One large can whole tomatoes, tomatoes broken up. One can garbanzo beans. Carrots, already peeled and shaped for the lazy cook. Additional water or tomato juice as needed. All simmered for half an hour or so, with mushrooms and shredded cabbage and a handful of pasta added shortly before eating. Garlic bread. Red wine.

"So you couldn't find any trace of a tree?" Xanthippe asked, over her share of the one-bowl meal that Shirley called *ragoût andouille* and J.Q. called sausage stew.

"Not a twig," J.Q. replied.

"I had a thought," Shirley said, selecting a spoonful of spicy beans and tomato. "It was Sunday morning that they went looking for a tree, and there aren't that many places open on Sunday, at least not early. Weren't there some nurseries marked in the Yellow Pages?"

J.Q. took another chunk of garlic bread, dipped it in his stew, and took a bite, chewing ruminatively. "In the

Garden House phone book, right. I'll collect it when we've finished supper."

"Does it make any difference where they got it?" Allison asked.

Shirley replied, "It's just a detail, Alli. It may not mean anything at all, except that anyone they met on Sunday might be able to tell us something more about them. Did they have anyone with them, for instance. Come to think of it, they had some clothing with local labels, fancy stuff. Someone in those shops might remember them, too."

They cleaned up the kitchen and adjourned to the patio, where they chatted briefly with a carload of wedding guests who were just taking up residence in the Ditch House. When the arrivals took themselves off, J.Q. fetched the phone book from the currently unoccupied Garden House, and they looked up the nurseries section in the Yellow Pages. There were four red-ink checks next to large display ads.

"I know for a fact these three aren't open before ten or noon on Sundays," Shirley said, tapping off three of them with a dismissive finger. "This one might be. Oh, look here, J.Q. Here's an ad for the man I met Sunday when we were mushrooming. Mr. Akagami." She turned to Xanthippe, remarking, "A very nice man who asked me about mushrooms. He was collecting seedling trees."

Xanthy looked confused. "I thought you said there *were* no seedling trees. . . ."

"Not where the young people went riding, no. That was southeast of town, out of Silver Saddle Stables up toward the Pecos Mountains. I'm talking about where J.Q. and Allison and I were, picnicking up the Santa Clara Canyon. Mr. Akagami seemed to find plenty of seedlings up there. He had a nice little bundle of them, the roots all wrapped in moss and plastic wrap. I sometimes wonder what we all did before plastic wrap. At any rate, he gave me his card."

"The ad says bonsai," murmured Xanthy. "My great-niece, the one I stayed with last month, collects bonsai. She has about twenty of them in a special little yard at the back of the house. The deciduous ones shed their leaves in the fall and they bloom in the spring, tiny little things, only a few inches high. She told me the pride of her collection, a plum tree, was over a hundred years old. Amazing. I've been wondering—"

Her wonder was interrupted by the arrival of the sergeant's car and the confusion attendant to getting Mrs. Griego's sister, Rena, out of the car and into her chair. The two women resembled one another in skin and hair, though not in features. Lupe Griego was voluptuous and jolly looking, with laugh lines around her eyes, dressed in bright trousers and shirt, extravagant earrings tinkling as she moved. Rena was pale and thin, wearing dark glasses and a limp cotton dress that covered her legs almost to her ankles. As she was wheeled onto the patio Shirley noticed the cupped shadows at the ends of her mouth, those same brackets of pain she noticed from time to time in her own mirror when either her knee or her memory was acting up.

Lupe laughed and joked and commented on the beauty of the place. Rena smiled weakly, nodding agreement, saying little. Raul Griego was courtly as he settled the women and chose from J.Q.'s menu of refreshment. He and J.Q. opted for coffee; Allison brought soft drinks for herself and Rena; Shirley fetched out a dusty old bottle of Madeira to share with Lupe and Xanthy. They chatted about nothing while the sergeant leafed through the diary, looking alternately puzzled and embarrassed.

"Xanthy and I read it," Shirley confessed. "A couple of things struck me as odd."

"Like?" the sergeant said, putting down the diary and taking up his coffee.

"Like Helen's statement that they should stay away from gambling and the desert. It's an odd statement."

"Meaning?"

"Connect it to the remark that Alan's father would be really mad about the money."

"I saw that, yes."

"So, Alan must have stolen it from his father. Large amounts of cash suggest several things. Gambling among them."

"Or drugs," Raul said. "Drug money doesn't usually come in thousands, though. When we find it, it's mostly huge stacks of small bills."

"Even when it's for a buy?"

He looked at her thoughtfully. "You mean some high-level buy? By a dealer? I've never been in on any of that. I guess you're right, though. That could be large bills, probably would be. Nobody'd want to hold up the deal counting a lot of little money."

"Helen didn't mention drugs," said Xanthy. "But she did mention gambling."

"There's a lot of it around. Did you hear why we had that drought last spring?"

They looked expectant.

"All the Indians were too busy running casinos to do rain dances."

Shirley smiled. The quip had gone the rounds the previous year, along with a factual one noting that the five-month drought had finally broken on the day the Hopi finally did perform a rain dance. Of course, the Hopi were too religious and conservative to run casinos.

"If you won a lot and cashed in your chips, you might get thousand-dollar bills," commented J.Q.

"Possibly," Shirley agreed, turning to Griego once more. "I take it you've had no luck finding their real identities."

Griego shook his head. "Nope. We've had the usual calls, people looking for relatives or friends who've disappeared, but the bodies don't fit the descriptions anyone came up with."

"I noticed the newspaper account gives the ages as twenty-one and -two," Shirley commented. "Maybe if the papers said the victims were teenagers . . ."

Griego frowned. "The lieutenant likes to keep his cards close to his chest. Even though we're looking for them in national computer listings of missing kids, H.R. doesn't want to list their real ages. He says if we do, we'll be answering the phones every thirty seconds for the next six weeks."

"He might be right," Shirley conceded, with a glance at the two women. "And I'm sure Rena and Lupe are bored to tears with all this. Your wife probably gets quite enough cop talk at home."

"Rena does, too," Lupe said. "Sometimes I think policemen don't talk about anything else. Football, maybe."

"You're also married to an officer?" Shirley asked, turning to the pale woman.

"Rena is married to my boss," Griego said, in a slightly strained voice. "To H.R."

"Yes," Rena agreed, without inflection. "We've been married almost six years."

Shirley glanced at Lupe, getting an unmistakable message from her face: anger in the clenched teeth, hate in the eyes, pity in the little softening of her lips when she turned to her sister.

"H.R. sort of wears out wives," Lupe said flatly. "Rena is his third. She needs a little nursing right now, and H.R. can't take the time, so she's staying with me and the kids."

"I suppose a lot of your friends must be other officers and their wives or husbands," Xanthy said sympathetically. "It's the same with doctors, I think. They and their wives tend to run in flocks."

"Lawyers, too," said Shirley, concentrating on defusing Lupe.

"How did you hurt yourself?" asked Allison, refilling Rena's glass.

Wrong question. Rena's face went ashen, her sister went red, Shirley stood up and looked out toward the road, saying urgently, "I heard a bang from out there. Is that the kids who have been beating in the mailboxes? J.Q., if we could catch those little sons-of . . ."

J.Q. rose, peered, Raul Griego at his side as the tension dissipated.

"No, I guess not," said Shirley. "There for a moment I thought it was." She seated herself, smiling on the company. "We lost three mailboxes to kids going along in a pickup truck, bashing them with a baseball bat. We ended up buying one of those indestructible steel boxes out of a catalog."

"Did it work?" asked Lupe cautiously, one eye on her sister.

"Well, they broke off the flag right away, but they haven't been able to dent the box. Every now and then

J.Q. carves another flag out of a plastic milk bottle and paints it red."

"They still tear it off, but they have to stop and get out of the truck to do it. If nothing else, it spoils their rhythm," muttered J.Q.

"And we don't use the flag that often," Shirley continued. "We lost some outgoing mail a time or two, and since then we haven't left anything in the box for the mailman. I think the same kids go through outgoing mail."

During this deliberate exchange, Allison had retreated to her chair, where she sat watchfully poised. J.Q. asked where the Griegos lived and turned the conversation to the status of local real estate between Nambe and Chimayo. They finished their drinks, then stood a few moments chatting in the driveway before the guests departed.

"All right, what?" demanded Allison. "What did I say wrong?"

"Nothing, darling," mused Shirley. "You weren't sitting where you could see their faces. When Raul mentioned his boss, his wife got this expression, as if he'd mentioned bedbugs or maybe sewer rats, and she turned toward her sister instantly with her mouth all ready to say 'poor dear.' Meantime, sister herself went absolutely white."

Allison thought about it. "I asked how she hurt herself. You think her husband did it to her?"

"A woman doesn't usually wear dark glasses after the sun's gone down," said J.Q. "Unless maybe she's got a black eye."

"Does Sergeant Griego know?" Allison asked.

Shirley shook her head. "I don't know. Maybe he sort

123

of knows but isn't sure. The women might be keeping it from him."

"Why?" Allison asked plaintively. "Why not tell him?"

"To protect him. Ohlman is his boss. If he knew, beyond doubt, he might say or do something that would endanger his job."

"Or his life," said J.Q.

"Well," Shirley murmured, "maybe that's going a bit far."

He made a snorting sound. "Listen, old dear. Any man who will put his wife in a wheelchair isn't going to draw the line at a little accidental homicide."

Roger Fetting called Shirley early Friday morning with an interim report.

"Littlepage is perfectly respectable, though he's tenacious about getting the story, if you care about the distinction," he told her. "Seems he'll keep at it to get an interview or a story, but he won't make stuff up. He's written for *Smithsonian* magazine and *Natural History* as well as the periodicals you mentioned. He's well regarded by the editors we've talked to, and he has made several trips to Brazil.

"On the matter of the card, the lab won't have a report for a few days, so you'll have to be patient. On the basis of what I've heard about him, my guess would be that if the card isn't genuine, David Littlepage didn't create it. On the remote chance it is forged, I confess to being unable to think up a reason for anyone doing it."

Shirley furrowed her brow, thinking. She'd worried over this same question for some hours the last couple of days. "Roger, when Martin died, he left everything to me, but he had a life-insurance policy payable to Marty. His instructions were that the money was to be held for Marty during my lifetime unless I needed it for my own care."

"Aha."

"It wasn't a huge policy, but the money's been collecting interest for fourteen years. During part of that time, the interest rates were double digit."

"Enough to be what one might call a tasty morsel?"

"If anyone knew about it, but so far as I know the only people who might have known about it are the people who were involved in probate and some of Martin's family."

"Would you suspect any of them?"

"Not of doing it, no. But they might have talked about the policy where someone heard them."

"So, if it's a scam, it isn't necessarily Littlepage's scam?"

"He could be a cat's-paw. He could be the guy who gets handed the ball after the play is in motion. He's supposed to get us all stirred up to go looking, and then, whoopy-do, here's the long-lost son rising from the Orinoco or some such."

Roger made a grating noise in his throat. "Who, since you were looking for him, not him for you, would be almost above suspicion. Sort of, 'Hey, look, lady, you came after me, not the other way around.' "

"Right."

"I'm glad you haven't lost an iota of your native suspicion, hostility, and paranoia."

"J.Q. says I mustn't."

He laughed sympathetically, not really amused. "I'll call you when I learn anything more, Shirley."

"Right, Rog. Thanks."

She turned to find J.Q. staring at her from the doorway.

"Roger says Littlepage is legit," she told him. "Though not necessarily nicey-nice about ethics."

"The card is real?"

She shrugged. "He doesn't know yet. Where's Allison?"

"I heard her down the hall, talking with Xanthippe. Has that coffee finished making?"

She leaned over to peer into the space between filter and pot. "It seems to be. Pour me a cup, too."

"And one for me," said Xanthippe from behind J.Q. "Allison and I have been discussing the shrubs you were going to put in but didn't get to, and we've agreed to take the matter out of your hands. We don't feel you need horticultural concerns on top of everything else that's going on."

Allison offered, "I said I'd dig and Xanthy could show me where. Today's only a half day of school."

"A half day off so soon?"

"The teachers have to have a meeting. There's some new stuff the legislature has decided they have to teach us. You know, along with drug awareness and child-abuse awareness and alcohol awareness and racial-harassment awareness and sexual-harassment awareness and tobacco awareness and all the other awarenesses. Mr. Patterson says it's a pity there's no time to teach us mathematics awareness or science awareness or anything that might help us make a living. Anyhow, teachers need Friday afternoon to learn about whatever it is. So, I'll dig and Mingy can put in her bushes."

"I thank you," Shirley muttered. "I really did mean to do it, Xanthippe."

"I know. And I did return sooner than planned, so I'm not holding it against you. I'm sure you have a lot to do."

"Not really," Shirley said defensively. "As I've been reminding myself all night, the Jones-Buscovitch thing isn't my business, and the Littlepage thing shouldn't be fooled with. Either or both will ripen in due time."

"Well, then, you and I can do it this morning instead of my waiting for Alli's help this afternoon," Xanthippe remarked tartly. "Providing nothing ripens out of season."

They settled to the business of breakfast, Allison opting for a bagel with cream cheese and marmalade before heading for school. Jenny arrived briefly to check the calendar and see what houses were to be cleaned that day. Shirley tried to keep her face uncreased and all thoughts flowing smoothly across the surface of her mind, letting nothing thrash about and kick up mud, no lurkers or dwellers making ripples or eddies, an attempt she defined to herself as "keeping the monsters down." The day was warm, seasonal, a good day for any kind of outdoor work, and the morning passed productively.

By noon, all the new shrubs were in, with wide earth saucers formed around their bases to hold irrigation water, a necessity come spring when northern New Mexico would be unlikely to have April showers but would have a peculiar season that Allison called the sizzling breezes. The combination of wind, heat, and drought that passed for May in northern New Mexico was often the year's severest test of gardeners' perseverance. Once the hurricane season set in on both coasts, the vast swirls of tropical moisture usually brought much-prayed-for rain to New Mexico, a true case of ill winds that blew somebody good.

"Now," Xanthy said, when they had cleaned their tools and had a bite of lunch. "I want to buy a thank-you gift for my great-niece, and your comments about bonsai gave me the idea of giving her one. She has some very nice examples, so I don't want to buy something ordinary."

"I have no idea whether Mr. Akagami has extraordinary ones or even good ones," Shirley commented. "But since we do need to go to town to pick up some fresh fruit and vegetables anyway, let's find out."

On the way to town, Xanthy added to her shopping list. "Next year we really should have a vegetable garden."

"I haven't even got the hang of the flower garden yet. You'll have me canning, next."

"Your mother always canned food."

"My mother did the washing by hand, too. That doesn't mean I intend to follow her example."

"I remember her spiced peaches."

"So do I." For a moment Shirley was lost in nostalgia, tasting cloves, ginger, cinnamon, and fresh peaches. The family had made an annual pilgrimage to the Western Slope, over near Grand Junction, where they had picked their own peaches, ripe, fetching them home in bushel baskets to be put up within hours of their arrival. There were peaches sliced in syrup for winter cobblers and pies; peaches preserved as chutney to eat with lamb and pork; as peach butter and peach jam for breakfast muffins. "All the good peaches are shipped east now. All we can get are the rock-hard ones."

"Peach cobbler," said Xanthy. "I want to make a peach cobbler for supper."

"If we can find any ripe ones."

"If we can't, we'll ripen some in a paper bag and I'll make the cobbler when they're ready. Tonight I'll make apple betty."

"With brown sugar."

"And butter and spices and thick cream . . ."

Both of them sighed simultaneously, then broke into laughter.

Mr. Akagami's place, located on one of the small twisting side streets evidently laid out along cattle trails by original Santa Feans, was too residential in character to be called a shop. The house was like every other house within sight, stuccoed in earth tan with protruding vigas making a covered portal before the door. They knocked and were admitted by a young woman in jeans and a T-shirt who ushered them into a side office that opened onto a fenced and graveled yard.

"Feel free to look around," she said. "Grandfather will be with you in a moment."

She disappeared as Xanthy moved through an open sliding door into the graveled area. The board fences served as a backdrop for tiers of shelves, each of them holding a row of tiny trees. Most of the pots bore faded price tags, though one shelf was labeled in large, bright red letters NOT FOR SALE.

At one side of the yard a door opened into a potting shed with shelves of empty shallow containers, square, oval, round, or rectangular, in dark matte colors or shiny oxblood or celadon. The floor held sacks of soil, gravel, broken pottery, and interesting-looking stones. An elderly man turned from the potting table, inspected them briefly, then returned to his workbench and his trees. In a pot of loose soil on the table were a number of seedlings like those Shirley had seen the previous Sunday, none of them more than a few inches tall.

Shirley watched, fascinated, as the man trimmed the roots of a tiny treelet, anchored it with a carefully placed stone, filled in around it with soil and gravel, then began shaping it, wiring the trunk into a tortured curve, then wiring each branch and twig into a particular configuration.

"It takes great patience," said a voice from behind her.

She turned to see her acquaintance from the canyon. "Mr. Akagami. I'm Shirley McClintock. We met the other day, in Santa Clara Canyon. You were digging seedlings, and I was hunting mushrooms."

"Of course." He bowed, something between a nod and an obeisance. "How nice of you to come."

"This is my friend Ms. Minging. She wants to buy a very nice bonsai as a gift for her niece, who collects them."

Xanthippe bowed slightly in her turn. Mr. Akagami led her away down the rows of shelves, telling her about each plant, its variety, its style, its history. Shirley's eyes wandered back to the "Not for Sale" shelf, which was centered by a long shallow clay planter, no deeper than a tray, which held a rock outcropping planted with a dozen tiny pines, the tallest about fourteen inches high, the others diminishing to a six-inch specimen at the far end of the miniature forest. Each tree seemed to have been shaped by wind around the rocks. Heavy moss covered its base. It was a perfect high-mountain grove in miniature. An elfin glade.

"That is not for sale," said a voice.

She looked down on the man who had been working in the potting shed. His eyes glared at her.

Momentarily taken aback, she bowed. "One would

130

never wish to sell such a beautiful thing. Is it very old?" She gazed admiringly at the little forest, smiling.

He relaxed only gradually. "Very old. Yes. I am the fourth generation of our family to care for it, and before us, it was three generations in another family."

A couple of hundred years. Lord. What perfection over all that time.

"Does it change, ever? Do you still work on it?"

He smiled slightly, and his face grew animated. "Of course. It must still be repotted from time to time. The roots must be trimmed, so slightly. It must be fed. The branches must be trimmed also, and trained."

She nodded, then turned to the other trees on the shelf, fixing on the next pair, in matching pots, each holding a single tree, its trunk diameter huge in comparison to its height. They were identical except that one had greener moss. "What are these tiny ones?" she asked.

He took one of the pots in his hands and turned it almost reverently. "This is a pine tree planted by a long-ago ancestor. This one is three hundred years old. The other is not so old, but it is trained in the pattern of the other."

"Ah," she murmured, remembering her conversation with Akagami. "It has great . . . character."

He glanced at her, surprised. "True. Of all the trees here, this one has the greatest character." He set it down, bowed slightly, more to the tree than to her, and went back into the shed, disappearing around the corner while she remained staring at the tiny tree. Now she could see the difference between them. The one with the greener moss had a thicker trunk, as thick through as her wrist and as tortured as foxtail pines she had seen along the tree line at ten or eleven thousand feet, every branch twisted away from the wind. At its foot, its gnarled roots bent around and into the stone, anchoring itself, indomitable.

"That one is the pride of my brother's collection," said Mr. Akagami, at her elbow. "Very old. Very great work. It has been through the hands of the greatest artists. It is one of the few things remaining to my brother from happier times."

"The gentleman I just met?"

"Yes."

"I'm sorry he has experienced . . . unhappiness. Tragedy."

"He was . . ." He moved farther away from the potting shed, lowering his voice. "Do you know of the Wyoming internment, during the Second World War?"

"Yes. I'm from Colorado. It was our Governor Carr who invited the internees to settle in Colorado."

"Some of our friends did so. During the internment, however, our family lost everything. We were loyal Americans; we had been in California for three generations; still, we lost all we had. My brother, too. His business gone, his wife who died of grief and humiliation, so he is convinced, his children who became estranged in the camps, his home, most of his trees. A few of the best he put into the hands of non-Japanese friends before he left California, and he recovered those that survived after the war. This one he kept with him. It was his companion in adversity. It has its own name, in Japanese. In English it would be called, 'Warrior Against the Wind.' "

"It looks . . . fresh, somehow."

He cocked his head, considering. "Ah. Well, it has been repotted recently and the moss is new and bright. The moss doesn't live as long as the trees, and sometimes it dies out and must be replaced. It will darken in a week or so to seem more natural."

Xanthy approached from across the room, bearing a tiny treelet in her hands. "Mr. Akagami, I'd like to buy this one for my niece."

The shiny-leaved tree was, like the very ancient one, thick through the lower trunk but heavily leaved higher up. It bore a single blossom, like a precious stone.

Akagami said, "This is one I would sell only to a collector, someone who knows how to care for it."

"It will be safe with my grand-niece," Xanthy agreed, digging out her address book. "Please feel free to call her and talk with her about it."

He nodded, pleased. "If you will give me your niece's address also, I would prefer to pack it myself."

They moved back into the office area, in lengthy conference. While they settled their business Shirley went back to the little forest. In a small country like Japan, overflowing with people, with little room left for real nature to exist, such representations of nature might be all one had of the natural world. There might come a time when even in America, all that was left of nature would be miniature trees, planted in trays, a pretense of a world long dead. Companions, as Akagami said, in adversity.

"A very pleasant person," Xanthy remarked as they were driving toward the market.

"His family has evidently suffered a good deal. They lost most everything in the forties when they were interned in Wyoming."

"One of our more shameful bits of history." Xanthy sniffed. "I'm pleased that they seem to have recovered. Julie will love the little tree I bought, and though I don't know a lot about bonsai, I'd say that Mr. Akagami is an exceptionally skilled practitioner of the art."

"Him and his older brother."

"Was that the gentleman in the potting shed?"

"Um," Shirley agreed, turning off into the parking lot. "Tell you what. You take one cart and get the vegetables. I'll take another one and get the other stuff." She looked over Xanthy's list and tore off the bottom part for herself. "Meet you at the checkout counter."

Thus expedited, they were on their way home within thirty minutes, only to be stopped in the driveway by the emergence of a Santa Fe party rental truck.

"Damn," Shirley erupted, with feeling. "I forgot about the dratted wedding!"

"Wedding?"

"Sofia Somebody is marrying Jorge Somebody Else. They are setting up a dance floor out by the pool—that's what the truck is for. They're also setting up their wedding ceremony on the terrace. They are taking all the houses for their guests from out of state—some of whom you met when they arrived last night. The festivities take place tomorrow. They are having a caterer, a band—or maybe two bands—and a bar. That means at least one or two guests getting very, very—"

"Like the teenagers, that other time?"

"Well, that was just silly! You don't put all of an extended family's teenagers in one house, by themselves, and give them access to unlimited champagne! Not unless you want several young bulls having a fistfight in the kitchen which results in a very large bill for damages. Which they paid without demur, I will say to their credit. Money seems to be no object when it comes to weddings. For this one, the bill for rental tuxedos alone will be in the thousands!"

"Is this really going to be the last one?"

She snorted. "The very last. You may rely upon it,

Xanthy. From our point of view, this weekend is going to be a circus, but it will be the very last one!"

Xanthy shook her head. "Can we go somewhere else?"

"We could go camp out in the wilderness, but I really don't want to leave the place with people swarming all over it."

"Maybe we'd best just circle the wagons and hunker down."

Shirley laughed. "J.Q. would approve of that. We'll probably find him cleaning his rifle."

Xanthippe mused, "I always tell Allison we must turn adversity into opportunity. We can observe from the house all that occurs. We can take notes. We can write a scholarly monograph on regional customs vis-à-vis ceremonial occasions."

"Right, Xanthy. Go to it."

J.Q. met them at the gate, sans rifle, wearing his stiff-upper-lip expression.

"What?" Shirley demanded, before even getting out of the car.

"More," he remarked. "Come on in. I've got something to show you."

They went in, each carrying a sack of groceries. J.Q. directed them to sit, then put an open copy of an old *Smithsonian* magazine in front of Shirley. Xanthy leaned over to take a look as well. The magazine was open to an article on the resettlement of rain-forest people that Shirley halfway remembered reading. The author was David Littlepage.

Shirley sat back, her face very white. Xanthy pulled the magazine in front of her and scanned the story. It was written in simple, compelling language, and the accompanying pictures were dramatically composed and well

135

shot. One, a photo of the author, showed him in a dugout between two tribesmen who were totally naked except for T-shirts. The author had a lean, craggy face topped with an aureole of light, very curly hair.

Xanthy looked from J.Q.'s face to Shirley's, both displaying an odd mix of emotions in which anger had a considerable part.

"What?" she demanded. "Shirley, for heaven's sake, what is it?"

Shirley laid her finger on the picture of the author. "If that's Littlepage," she said, "then the man who came to talk with me was someone else."

Pressing her lips together to stop their trembling, she skimmed the article. David Littlepage had traded T-shirts, cooking pots, and axes for animal skins. David Littlepage had received a skin bag made from pygmy marmoset. David Littlepage wrote of the use of this little animal as a delouser for the natives.

"The man who was here got it whole cloth from this article," Shirley snarled, tears in her eyes.

Xanthy tried to be soothing, with little success. It was too late in the day and the week to reach Roger in his office. In any case, there would be nothing he could do about the impersonation. They had no picture of the false Littlepage to send him, and the false Littlepage had handled nothing during his visit from which fingerprints could be lifted. The Lucite case, yes, but she'd given that back. The card, maybe, but Roger already had that.

"If he wasn't real," said Allison, over a hastily put-together supper, "then his story wasn't real either."

"Unless the card turns out to be real," Shirley muttered, pressing palms to either side of her forehead, which had been threatening to explode. "In which case, his story wasn't entirely real, but some parts of it may be. I should have known."

"Why should you?" J.Q. said in his "there, there, let's be calm" voice.

"When he started to talk about the tribes he'd lived with, he couldn't remember their names. He said the information was in another notebook. If he'd been with a particular tribe for a while recently, if he'd just written about them, he'd have remembered the names. Any author would. I thought at the time it was odd, but there was so much else to think about—"

She was interrupted by loud noises in the parking area, someone shrieking, a babble of voices.

J.Q. got up and looked out the window. "It's the bride's mother," he said in a disbelieving voice. "Having a fit."

"I'm not going to talk with her," said Shirley. "The mood I'm in, I'd probably end up in jail for assault."

"Let me," said Xanthippe. "I have some experience with hysterics."

"She's not hysterical," Shirley retorted. "She's just temperamental. She wanted me to repaint the Ditch House, some cheerful color or other."

"It's adobe," Xanthy said. "You couldn't paint it. Such a request is ridiculous. Totally inappropriate."

"Tell that to Marie Antoinette out there. I have a hunch the people around her have experience with doing three or four inappropriate things before breakfast, or else."

"Off with her head," suggested J.Q. "Let her eat cake."

"I'll see to her," Xanthy said, moving toward the door. "Is she supposed to be staying here?"

"No. Not that I know of. All the houses are occupied

137

by relatives, and she has a perfectly good home in Santa Fe. I don't know why she's here tonight."

"Rehearsal," suggested J.Q. "A walk-through of the rites."

"Of course." Shirley subsided. "Go to it, Xanthy. See what good you can do."

Xanthippe went out into the driveway, approaching the gesticulating group as she might once have approached an unruly group of subteens. She said something, they said something, she said something else. She smiled. Someone took the bride's mother's arm and led her away.

She returned to the kitchen. "A very silly woman," she said. "Having a crisis over nothing."

"Dares one ask what?" Shirley demanded.

"I think it had something to do with the menu for tomorrow's bridal supper. Santa Fe authenticity was the buzzword."

"There's very little authentic about Santa Fe," J.Q. remarked. "Its architecture is as neo-orthodox as its cuisine. Delightful, but certainly not authentic. To get authentic, you have to get beyond the city limits."

"Well, the bride's mother believes she has the lock on authenticity, and the recipe used by the caterers is not it."

"How did you shush her?"

"I told her she was probably the only person present with sufficient taste to know the difference, that we all deplored the merely derivative, but inasmuch as the groom's family would no doubt be looking for opportunities to feel superior to the bride's family—weddings always bring out such rivalry—perhaps an attitude of impenetrable poise would be less assailable."

Shirley shook her head in wonder. "If my hair were white, I could get away with that."

"You could never get away with it, my dear. You have to adopt an expression of infinite wisdom and kindly concern, and it's not one you've ever mastered."

"She has too," said Allison from the door. "She sounds very kindly concerned about me, lots of times."

"I was referring to the use of the ploy on nonfamilial occasions," said Xanthy. "When confronting idiocy, Shirley is inclined to foam at the mouth."

"I do not foam. I merely fizz a little."

"You fizz at the top of your lungs," said J.Q. "Now that we've dealt with that topic, what about clearing this table?"

"I don't suppose we could leave for the evening, not with all these people about," Shirley offered, hoping to be contradicted.

"I don't suppose we should," J.Q. affirmed. "This is the kind of group about which accidents gather, waiting to happen. They have already climbed about, stringing little twinkly lights through the trees out near the pool. Somebody is going to fall out of a tree and drown. They have kerosene heaters standing about on the lawn, in case it turns cold tomorrow evening. Somebody is going to light one and set himself afire. They have a bar being set up in front of the Ditch House. Depend on it. There will be people who consume more than is appropriate. I think we stay here for the next two days, glued to the windows, binoculars at the ready."

Shirley felt herself summoning up arguments, but was sidetracked by the phone. Salome McCreary from Los Angeles, wanting to chat.

"Their rent ran out, so I cleaned out their room today," she said. "Those kids?"

"Right. Did you find anything?"

"They had a pile of magazines and papers, plus a few odds and ends. What I want to know is, you want me to send them to you? If I kept all the stuff people leave, I'd have no room for roomers, but you said to let you know anything about them."

"Salome, I'd consider it a favor, and I'd be glad to pay for the postage and your time."

"Oh, it'll take no time. I've already dumped it all in a box, and I'll send it UPS collect. I guess the guys didn't take anything."

"Guys?" Shirley asked. "What guys?"

"It was a couple weeks ago. Long before you called. Back around the middle of August? These two guys showed up with pictures of this kid in his matching car, not the one he had when he left, another one, and the guys said he was a runaway and so was his girlfriend, and could they see the room. Well, the kids were gone. They'd left the day before, suitcases and all, so I didn't see any reason why not let these guys look. Besides, one guy looked like a banker, or lawyer. I stood right in the door seeing they didn't take anything, and they didn't. They just walked around, looked at this and that, leafed through a book or so, stared at the clutter, and left."

"Did the kids tell you they were leaving for good?"

"No. That's why I kept the room vacant until their rent ran out. They could've come back."

"You said 'guys.' Was this the same visit as the guy you mentioned before? The one who said he was an uncle?"

"Ah. Hey, no, I forgot about him. No, the two guys came the day after the kids left. The other guy, just one, another banker, lawyer type, he came later, just a day or so before you called. He looked more at the stuff the boarders wrote on the wall than he did the room."

"Stuff on the wall?"

"You know. By the phone. The way they do."

"Do you have any idea who any of them were?"

"Well, you know, the one who said he was an uncle, he didn't much look at the room, like if he really was an uncle, he'd have looked for a note or something, right? And the others, the ones that did see the room, like I said, one looked like a banker or lawyer—gray hair, nice tie— and the other could've been his driver or his assistant. I suppose they could've been police. Who else would they be? Maybe private investigators, hired by the kids' folks? That could be, I suppose."

"So what you're sending me is whatever the couple left in the room when they left around the middle of August."

"Right."

"Salome, I do appreciate it, and I thank you a lot."

"They must've really left you with a mess."

"Well . . ." She toyed briefly with the idea of telling the truth and decided against it. She didn't want to scare Salome off, which the mention of murder might well do. "They did. But it'll all come right. Thanks for your help."

She hung up and turned to meet three pairs of avid eyes. "Somebody was looking for the kids in Los Angeles. Two guys turned up there the day after the kids left, and another one turned up there a week ago."

"What's she sending you?" Xanthy asked.

"Whatever they left lying around. Magazines. Paper. Any old thing they didn't think worth packing. Probably no help, but then, something might click."

"You said something before about their clothing labels," Allison commented. "That would be kind of fun, to go to the shops and see if anybody remembers them."

"If you and Shirley would like to do that," Xanthippe remarked, "J.Q. and I will hold the fort tomorrow morning."

"Maybe," Shirley said doubtfully. "If it doesn't become a mob scene here."

"Let's do," Allison begged, coming to throw her arms around Shirley. "You and me. Let's go detecting."

Xanthippe caught Shirley's eye above the girl's tousled head and nodded, very slightly, almost an admonition. Go with her. Reassure her. It'll do you both good.

As it would. Shirley returned the hug. "If you'd like to, Alli, that's good enough for me."

That night, before she went to bed, Shirley jotted down the names of the shops she remembered seeing named on Jones and Buscovitch's clothing labels. A pair of ostrich-hide boots had borne the label of Pied-Panache, a Fort Worth, Rodeo Drive, Santa Fe chain offering ostentatious footwear. Le Vêtement was one of the hand-weaving places, with stores in Santa Fe and Tucson. Why did places in Santa Fe give themselves French names? Maybe the shop started in Tucson and came east later. Some such shops might conceivably be named after their founders. This one was no doubt begun by Xavier Vêtement et Fils.

Then there was Doña Ana's for the hand-beaded stuff. Probably the beading was done by ten-year-old Mexican girls for fifty cents an hour or less. Shirley had never been in any of these shops, but she recognized the names from the stunning ads that appeared in each issue of the

Santa Fe Guest Book, a thick, slick prestige marketing tool that was distributed to every high-priced hotel room in the city. Gorgeous designer jewelry, marvelously arty clothes, handmade furniture, and top-price artworks. All mouthwateringly portrayed.

Well, so hell, she'd wear something decent. She had a cashmere jacket or two and a really good hat with a porcupine-quill band. And her good boots were not to be sneered at.

She stared out the dark window with burning eyes. Sleep seemed as far away as the Sahara. Damn and double damn the man who called himself Littlepage.

Was there any possibility he was real? One could allow for the fact that the *Smithsonian* could have printed the wrong picture. It had been known to happen, even in respectable, careful publications. If the picture was correct, however, then what was Littlepage (false) up to? Would it do any good to get in touch with Littlepage (true)? Littlepage (false) had acted like a real writer, very snoopy and pertinacious, eager to take pictures of the place and of her. Perhaps (false) Littlepage was someone (true) Littlepage knew or knew of. Perhaps (false) had felt free to borrow Littlepage's identity, because (false) knew (true) was out of the country. That issue of *Smithsonian* had been three years old. She would never have remembered it, but J.Q. kept everything. He was a pack rat. Every so often, Shirley and Jenny had to decoy him away from his quarters and dig them out, putting magazines in boxes for indeterminate storage elsewhere, throwing away stacks of old newspapers, and uncovering pair after pair of long-lost socks and parts of machinery that had been fruitlessly searched for.

She closed her eyes. Somewhere in all this tangle, sleep had been detoured. She hadn't admitted it to herself, but she had hoped. She had hoped. Admit it. But if Littlepage was false, then so was the Marty story. What was she feeling? A grudging relief? Rising out of an unwillingness to be hurt again? Or grief, which she had thought long gone until today? Or both, inextricably mixed, tortuously entwined.

One couldn't close doors, of course. So, let it play out. Don't fall into it, don't refuse to listen to it, let it play out. And be sure, tomorrow, to let Allison know that she was much loved, no matter what happened, ever.

She lay staring into the darkness for what seemed hours. Somewhere among the quiet hours, she fell asleep.

The next morning, Shirley and Allison drove to town to enter the boot store as soon as it opened. Shirley introduced herself to a salesman so overwhelmingly godlike she thought immediately of plastic surgery. She produced a card and a brochure, explained that it was necessary for her to locate two young guests who had (she said) disappeared, and in order to do so, she was backtracking their actions in Santa Fe. They had bought boots here. She described the boots and the couple while Allison listened, her eyes fixed on the incredibly handsome face.

"I remember them," said the salesman, for a moment forgetting to radiate. "Sure. Money falling out of their ears."

"Really?" breathed Allison, stricken.

He grinned. He had a slightly cocked front tooth, which reduced him to mere demigod status. "Left ear for bills, right one for coins! Not really, hon, but he had plenty, and he acted like there was plenty more where that came from. All told, he dropped about five thou, and ended up tipping me five hundred because sweetie-face told him to. I mean, I don't work for tips, but I wasn't turning that one down."

Shirley nudged Allison to be sure she was still breathing, then glanced around the store to verify that they were alone and not taking up time needed for other customers. "Could we sit down a minute and you tell us about it?"

"Sure. It was . . . must have been Thursday or Friday week before last, the twenty-seventh or twenty-eighth about. It was dead. This is the in-between season, and I was bored, looking for any kind of amusement. They came down the street loaded with packages, like Christmas and birthday and the Fourth of July. She stood out in front looking at the ostrich boots, and then they came in. The tag is on the boots in the window because it gets tiresome telling people the boots are two thousand a pair. She didn't blink an eye, just sat down and asked if I had them in her size."

"And did you?"

"Not that pair, but another pair even pricier. She tried them on along with a few pairs of imported shoes and told the boyfriend she wanted them. He got out the wallet and began counting off thousands, and he's due five hundred change, which she says he should give me as a tip. Then he tells me they're just married and these are wedding presents from him to his wife."

"And that was that?"

"Not quite, no. See the golden boots over there under the dome? Those are Pied-Panache's trademark. There's a pair in each store. Rare leather embroidered in gold thread, with real gems, all handwork, God knows how much they cost to make, and not for sale, so when they head out, she sees those and she has to have them."

"You told her they weren't for sale."

"Sure. And she says how much. And I say, no, honestly, not for sale. And she gets kind of a frozen look on her face, like a kid about to have a tantrum? You know? My sister's kid, two years old, he looks just that way before he throws himself on the floor and starts turning blue. Anyhow, he real quick says how much, how much, she really wants them, and I was afraid we were going to have some kind of scene, when in comes a guy I know who's a policeman. He's in uniform and he wants to sell me some raffle tickets."

"Which interrupted the tantrum?"

"It did something. She got quiet, and the two of them just sort of oozed out the door. I show my friend the tickets I've already bought; we talk a minute; my friend leaves, and the door sticks on a wrinkle in the doormat and doesn't close. So, I go over to shut it. I kneel down to straighten the doormat, and there they are just outside, and she's saying, 'So next time just drop some money on the counter and take what you want, Jimmy. Don't let people push you around.' "

"Jimmy?"

"I thought it was Jimmy. It could have been 'Dummy.' Anyhow, she sees me looking at her, and she gets this uptight expression and they go off down the street."

"Where else had they been?" Shirley asked.

"Oh, she had shopping bags up both arms, like bracelets. At least one from Doña Ana's. I remember thinking he'd better stay away from the jewelers."

Shirley fell silent, pondering. In a moment she came to herself, thanked her informant, and went back out onto the street with Allison. "Are you breathing?" she asked. "Or are you in a state of permanent paralysis."

"He was . . . really good-looking," Allison admitted.

"Right. From the neck up."

"Shirley!"

"He had shoulder pads in his jacket and he was wearing a girdle."

"He was not!"

"He could have been. You can't tell a book by its cover."

"I wasn't going to throw myself at his feet," she said indignantly. "He was just very good-looking."

"Um," Shirley said, distracted.

"You thought of something!" Allison challenged.

"I thought of jewelry," Shirley admitted. "If the groom bought the bride some really expensive jewelry, and if she was idiot enough to wear it or carry it on that trail ride, we might have a motive. She wasn't wearing any jewelry when J.Q. and I spoke to her that morning, but she went back to the Garden House before they left—"

"If somebody killed her for her jewelry, it would almost have to have been somebody who saw her leave," Allison commented. "I mean, from our place. Otherwise they wouldn't know she had it, would they?"

"Anyone on the trail ride would have seen it. You know, we never did verify Joe Cisneros's account of what happened. Because we know Joe, we just sort of took it for granted he was telling the truth."

"Don't you suppose the police checked?"

Shirley shrugged. "I wish we knew if she'd bought jewelry."

"So, we've got all day. Let's ask."

They did ask. Shirley picked up a copy of the *Santa Fe Catalogue* from a friendly concierge at La Fonda, they picked out the half-dozen jewelers and designers they considered most likely, and spent the next two hours in a frustrating attempt to find out if Jones and Buscovitch were known to any of them or their salespeople. The clerk at the last place they went told them, reluctantly, that the young couple had looked at a ring but left without it. That ring was no longer in stock, so maybe they'd come back and bought it, but not when this clerk was on duty. The clerk said Shirley would have to ask the other clerks, but she declined to tell Shirley who they were.

"You'd think they all worked for the CIA," Shirley grumped, when they were outside. "Or that they subscribed to some unwritten policy of jeweler-customer confidentiality."

"I don't think the kids bought anything from any of them except maybe that ring," Allison offered. "She was my age. If I won the lottery or something, I wouldn't be afraid to buy clothes, or boots, but I would be afraid to buy jewelry. I'd be afraid I'd do something stupid. Clothes and shoes you can try on and if you like the way you look, that's okay. And a wedding ring, that would be okay to pick yourself. But real jewels are things other people know about, like wine or yachts. I don't think she bought jewelry."

"She spent five thousand on shoes!"

"But look, five thousand bought the best boots they had. In the jewelers, even fifty thousand wouldn't buy the best they had. Don't you sort of figure, the way she

148

acted she wouldn't buy anything unless it was the best?"

Shirley nodded, convinced. Right. Buscovitch wanted nice things. Probably the only way she had to judge "nice" things was by price. If she couldn't buy the best, she wouldn't buy.

"So, if she didn't buy the ring, wash one possible motive. I thought it was too good to be true."

"You want to try some of the clothing stores?"

"Doña Ana's. It's the one place the boot guy was sure of."

The clothing store was on San Francisco Street, one floor up, a saltillo-tiled expanse with carved vigas and tall windows overlooking the street, with half a dozen comfortable chairs scattered about. Several outfits arranged on display racks were the only clothing in evidence. The only person was a dark and slinky miniature who made up in hauteur what she lacked in stature.

"I'm Gloria. May I help you?"

Shirley went through her explanation again, describing the couple. "Blond," she said. "And he was dark, with a little mustache."

The saleswoman sniffed. "She is no blonde. Her hair is naturally dark, almost black. At the back, here"—and she touched the back of her head—"when I buttoned her into the Sebastien dress, I could see roots. And she asked me where to go to have her hair done."

"Where did you suggest?"

"My friend Clare at La Fonda. Clare is very good with color. The young woman used my phone to make the appointment."

"What did she buy from you?"

The woman frowned. "Two blouses, silk, one with silver and turquoise buttons, one beaded. There was a leather outfit she liked, but he, the husband—who told me three times he was her husband—he did not like the color."

"And what did you think of them?" Shirley asked.

"I?"

"Yes. You serve a lot of people. You're observant. What did you think of them?"

Gloria snorted, amused, and climbed down off her high horse. "I thought they were children, playing at being grown-up. I thought she was the one who made the rules, and he was the one who supplied the money. I thought they did not know the worth of money."

"Why is that?"

She shrugged, smiled. "There are good things in this shop, things one could wear for years. And there are faddish, expensive things that aren't worth the money. Things one will wear once or twice, then no more. That's the kind of thing she liked. The really good things she ignored."

"You think they were playing a game?"

"She was. It's a game I see young women play sometimes with rich men, though usually the men are older. Adore me. Spend money on me. Show me how much I am worth. You know."

"She didn't love him?"

"I would be surprised if she loves anyone. She buys expensive things so that she can claim to be loved. In her eyes there is this expression ... she does not believe anyone loves her."

Shirley dropped into one of the armchairs, fascinated.

Alli took up her post at her shoulder, equally fascinated. "Tell me more."

The woman laughed. "I am a fortune-teller? All right.
He's well educated, good schools, probably private schools,
and probably a good family at least in terms of wealth. He
speaks well; foolishly, but well. She is what we used to
say, 'not quite.' "

"How could you tell?"

"From listening. Her voice is common. Her vocabulary
is common. She is very ignorant about quality. People
with old money, they may not have good taste in dressing
themselves, but they are usually knowledgeable about
the quality of what they buy. With her, it was the opposite. She knew what made her look good, but she didn't
care about the quality. Only the price. Between two
things, she would choose the higher-priced, even if it was
not as well made."

"And she had dyed her hair."

"Yes. Definitely. She was naturally dark."

Shirley held out her hand. "Gloria, you've been very
helpful. Thank you."

Gloria smiled with conscious charm. "I tell the truth,
as I see it. For example, the jacket you're wearing. It's
very good, but the cut is dated. I have a very nice one that
would suit you and is more in fashion."

Shirley grinned. "In my size?"

"I carry tall."

Gloria brought out the jacket. Shirley bought the
jacket, plus a new pair of trousers and an elegant shirt.

"Wow," Allison said, when they were back on the
street. "She got to you."

"She appealed to my vanity," Shirley admitted. "I

151

haven't bought any new clothes in seven or eight years. Besides, she was helpful. Let's find a phone. . . ."

She found one and called Griego's office.

"Raul? Listen, the girl victim, it's possible she wasn't a natural blonde, and she may have dyed her hair recently. Did your medical examiner pick up on that? Oh, he did. Well, yes, that *would* raise the question. Thanks."

She turned to Allison, slightly flushed. "The medical examiner noted a difference between head and body hair on the girl. Evidently she didn't change color all over."

"Why did she change at all?"

"They didn't intend to be identified. Which means they thought they might be seen by someone who knew them. You know, I never asked Salome to describe them?"

"Are we going home now?"

"Wouldn't you like some lunch?"

"Can we go someplace fancy?"

"Sky's the limit."

"Okay. Let's have lunch."

They went to Nellie's and lunched in quiet splendor. When they had finished everything, including a whipped-cream-topped chocolate mousse rolled in almonds and decorated with coulis of raspberries and apricots, Shirley remarked, "I suppose we'd better go home."

"J.Q. could probably use some help watching everybody," Allison said. "Except the ceremony should be pretty soon, and once that's over, maybe everybody will settle down."

"I wouldn't count on it," Shirley remarked. "But you're right. J.Q. could use some help."

They drove home, encountering another roadblock at the driveway, an officious young man who told them all guests had to park in the little pasture down the road and be picked up by a van.

"Young man, I'm not attending the wedding. I own the place."

He looked shocked at the idea. "She didn't tell me about anybody owning the place. . . ."

"Did you think it was just lying here, vacant?"

"Well, no, but—"

"Just get out of the way. If anyone fusses at you, refer them to me."

He stood in the middle of the drive, looking disconsolately after them as they went down into the parking area and parked in their usual spot, beside the gate.

"You can't park there," said a bustling woman. "We're keeping this area open."

"Keep it however you like it." Shirley smiled. "I own the place. I always park here."

"But I understood my clients had rented the entire place. . . ."

Shirley smiled again, grimly. "They rented the guest houses. That's all they rented. I am allowing them to use the grounds, briefly, for a ceremony and reception. Use of the grounds does not include my usual parking place, my usual walking routes, the pastures, the animals, the trees, shrubs, or gardens, all of which belong to me and have not been rented to anyone."

"Oh, gracious, I'm not sure she understood that. . . ."

"I'm quite sure she didn't. She will simply have to bear the misunderstanding."

Allison climbed out of the car, laden with Shirley's purchases. "I'm going to take these back to your room. You want me to hang them up?"

"Would you, Alli? Thanks. While you're back there,

lock the back door and be sure my curtains are drawn. I'm going to find my coconspirators."

She found J.Q. keeping an eye on the front from the kitchen. Xanthy, he said, was observing the fracas from the cover of the library.

"They weren't going to let me park!" she complained.

"I know. I guess when we told them their guests could park in that little pasture, they thought we would, too. They have a very proprietary air. I closed the gate to the lower pastures and put a padlock on it. I found a bunch of kids down there chasing the sheep."

"Kids?"

"Three of them, about eleven or twelve. They belong to various members of the wedding. I told them we don't chase sheep, and if I caught them down there again, I'd have them arrested for trespassing. They were evidently interesting enough to take pictures of: I also chased away a photographer who was wandering around down there laden with equipment."

"Besides all those video cameras?"

"Besides, yes. This one had dark glasses and a strange hat. Rather like the Gollux. Oh, also, the bride's mama has tinted the pool water green."

"She's *what*?" Shirley dropped into a chair, dumbfounded.

"She says it goes better with her color scheme. I told her I didn't know she was Irish. She says no, the groom's family are from Mexico, so the color scheme is red, white, and green. There are over two hundred chairs set up back there."

"Lord. Never again."

"I hope you mean it this time. You'll have to practice in the mirror saying no, even if people grovel."

Shirley poured herself a Scotch. "You want me to take over this post?"

"If you'll watch from here, I can go back down to the barn. Those kids are more or less at loose ends until things start, and I wouldn't put it past them to try and sneak back down there. Jenny's gone for the day, so there's no one down the hill to keep an eye on things."

Allison had come in during this, and now she offered, "Would you like me to call Ulti? He'd be glad to help."

"Not a bad idea," Shirley opined. "Ask him if he'd mind earning a day's pay to dress up a little and mingle with the guests. He can be our security force."

"Me, too. They've never laid eyes on me."

"Sure, you, too, if you like."

As Allison departed Xanthy wandered into the kitchen to refill her wineglass.

"I'm having a nice time back there," she observed. "Sitting and sipping and eating cheese and fruit while I stare out the window. They've built a kind of balloon arch for the bride to be married under. I wonder if they missed the symbolism of being married while surrounded by hot air. And they've tied tulle bows to the trees. Silly looking."

"When's the ceremony?"

"Three-thirty."

Shirley glanced at her watch. "Another hour."

"It's quite a production," said Xanthy, in a wondering voice. "Like something in India or Taiwan. I must get back into place." She departed, taking the wine bottle with her.

Shirley fixed herself a drink and sat at the table, where she could watch the comings and goings without being observed. In about thirty minutes Ulti arrived, met Allison in the front patio, and the two of them strolled arm in arm among the assembling guests. Shirley took a deep breath. Ulti looked entirely too handsome in suit and tie, and as for Allison . . . Well, the dress became her, put it that way. That child was growing up gorgeous, more's the pity.

The gathering grew larger, people began to break away in clusters, moving here, moving there. Gradually, the movement increased toward the terrace area, where the chairs were set up. When the drive was almost completely empty, Shirley joined Xanthy in the library. The chairs on the terrace were empty. The people were all standing, chatting, moving about like bubbles in a pot.

Shirley glanced at her watch again. It was almost four. "They're late."

"I know. All the people came back and sat down, people took pictures, still and video, and then they all got up again. Wait. There's someone with a guitar."

The guitarist sat on a chair up front and began to play.

"He's good," Shirley commented.

"He needs a microphone," said Xanthy. "We could hear him if everyone shut up."

"What's that man doing over by the fence?"

"I think he has bladder trouble. Or he's camera shy. He's retreated to that fence to pretend interest in the view about four times already."

Quiet came. The guitarist played. And played. And played, now and then glancing over his shoulder at the arch through which the bride was supposed to approach. The people on the chairs became restive. It was four-thirty.

"There's a man with a carpet," exclaimed Xanthy.

"White carpet. How nice. I wondered how she was going to keep her satin slippers unstained by grass."

The carpet layers, accompanied by photographer, unrolled a good many yards of white carpet. The guitarist heaved an audible sigh and started over on his repertoire.

Twenty minutes later the flower girls appeared, then the eight bridesmaids, then the maid/matron of honor, then the bride, on her father's arm, all in white with a voluminous veil.

"I understand they've been living together for the past four years," said Shirley. "You'd think she could have saved something on the veil."

Xanthy pursed her lips. "I spent part of the morning eavesdropping on gossip. This wedding is, I have learned, the result of a feud between the bride's and groom's mothers. The groom's mother did not recognize the bride as her son's intended, since there had been no formal betrothal. The bride's mother, on the other hand, resented this lack of recognition. This ceremony, which is being taped from start to finish and is also the subject of a photo essay for some magazine, legitimatizes the entire affair. Hence the bridal gown and veil. For all intents and purposes, she is a virgin bride and this is the joining of two noble houses."

"Chicken's blood on the bedsheet tonight, you think? To satisfy the groom's mama?"

"I doubt they'll go that far."

The ceremony began. The sun sank in the west. The audience began to hold their hands up to their eyes in order to see through the glare. The official shifted, casting his own shadow on the page he was reading from.

An hour later the ceremony and ancillary rituals were

over. Everyone rose and streamed away, toward the caterer's tent and the music. Xanthy and Shirley went back to the observation post in the kitchen.

"How late will that go on?" Xanthy asked, gazing from the kitchen window.

"All our other weddings have had the good taste and the good sense to stop anything audible by nine. I have a feeling this one won't."

This one didn't. There were mariachis. There was a dance band. There was a recurrent clatter of firecrackers plus a few skyrockets. It was still going on at midnight, though much diminished, when Shirley bade Ultimo farewell and Allison good night.

"Ulti was really great, Shirley," Allison crowed. "He stopped two fights. He helped a drunk lady over to one of the houses so she could recover. He found another lady's shoes. . . ."

Shirley was so tired she was only half listening. "Were you also making yourself useful?"

"Me? I stopped a kid from pulling up a rosebush and some other kids from breaking the trees out by the pool and another kid from stealing a rabbit."

"They must have been on the bride's side," Shirley commented, yawning. "The groom's side were far too well mannered."

"One of the kids' mothers got kind of snippy. I told her I worked for the owner, juvenile security, because that's what Ulti was telling people. She got this look like she was really confused. . . ."

"No more than I." Shirley sighed.

"You're tired. You're sad, too."

"I confess it. I am."

Allison threw her arms around Shirley and hugged her. "You got your hopes up. I'm sorry."

"Me, too, love." She returned the hug. "Enough of all this. We all need sleep, and I refuse to consider the wreckage until morning."

5

SHIRLEY DID WHAT she could to guarantee sleep: a hot shower and shampoo; an application of herbal lotion—Allison's gift; a freshly washed nightgown; sheets tightened and smoothed and pillows likewise. The noise outside had dwindled away. No more fireworks, no more guitars, no more slamming car doors. Darkness, not quite absolute, softened the edges of reality, and she courted sleep by counting—as her mother had often urged her to do—her blessings.

Blessing one: the wedding was over and by Monday all evidence of it would be gone. Blessing two: never again never. Blessing three: Allison had an acceptable boyfriend who was really something of a sweetheart. Don't focus much on that one; sweethearts can mean problems. Blessing four: her favorite season was coming on, with winy air and golden trees. Blessing five: Littlepage wasn't Littlepage, so despite her pain, she could be thankful that she had discovered so soon the falsity of his lures and enticements. . . .

The phone rang.

She opened one eye. It was one A.M. The phone was across the room on her desk. Let it ring. Which it did, switching to the message service on the fourth jangle. Good. She returned to her blessings, feeling drowsiness come.

Five minutes later it rang again. This time she opened both eyes. Someone was determined to talk with somebody else. Suppose it was someone trying to contact one of the guests? They were supposed to use the private phones in their own houses. They were given the numbers in advance, but often they didn't remember or just didn't bother. Suppose someone was dead. Dying.

The phone stopped ringing. She sank back onto the pillow, wide-awake. In a moment she'd call the message service, just to be sure it wasn't an emergency.

The phone rang. She stumbled out of bed, tripped over the dangling end of a sheet, almost falling on her face before managing to pick up on the third jangle.

"Shirley? This is Janice Beardsley! Damn it, what have you done with David Littlepage?"

She sounded both drunk and angry.

"Janice, do you know what time it is?" Shirley asked, not alert enough to be anything but plaintive.

"I don't care what time it is! What have you done with him?"

Wakefulness came, bringing ire along in the van. "I haven't done anything with him, Janice. I've only seen or talked to him once."

"He was supposed to get back to us yesterday. He said no later than Saturday."

Now she was fully aroused, and fury simmered.

"No later than Saturday, what?"

"He called here again on Wednesday. He was very strange. He seemed confused about what he'd told us when he called the other time. Maybe he had jet lag or something. I apologized for you. I told him you weren't yourself because you'd had this tragedy, these newlyweds who'd been killed. I told him that's why you hadn't believed him when he visited you, because you were upset, that I'd talk to you about it. I'd already left lots of messages on his machine, and I'd already sent him all the material from when Glenn and Marty disappeared, the newspaper accounts, everything! He said he'd be in touch with us by Saturday!"

Shirley took a deep breath and tried to rearrange facts to deal with this new onslaught. This was not the time to get into the truth or falsity of David Littlepage. It was too late; she was too tired.

She temporized. "I haven't seen the man or talked to him since Tuesday. At that time I told him to let me know if he came up with anything."

"You accused him of being a con man!"

"I did nothing of the kind!" So much for calm. She could feel steam rising from the top of her head and condensing into a little black cloud with lightning flashing in it. This was all she needed at one-ten in the morning! "I told you to consider that he might be, that's all. I never said a word to *him* about being a con man."

"You didn't agree to pay him!"

"That's true," she snarled. "But *you* did. Maybe his informant was delayed. Whatever happened, I didn't do it."

Janice began sobbing. "I had such hopes! I was sure

162

this was the clue we needed. I was sure Glenn would come back to us. . . ."

Shirley gritted her teeth until her jaw hurt. "Janice, you're tired out. Please, get some sleep and then call me when you're rested. We'll talk about it then."

More sobbing at the other end, plus muttering to someone else, probably her husband, plus the phone hang-up. Shirley stood there, bemused, hearing another click on the line without hearing it until she herself hung up and stalked back to her bed, where she lay, simmering, now remembering: *click, click. Click, click.*

Click. As of someone hanging up. Which could have been someone on an extension at Janice's end, but could equally have been someone here. Who of her own household would still be up? And why?

She cursed and muttered and got herself out of bed, into her slippers and robe, down the long hall through the cavernous living room, through the dining room to the kitchen, making a good deal of noise about it and turning on lights all the way.

The kitchen was dark. When she clicked on the desk light, it disclosed a litter of papers on desk and floor. The file drawer was open. When she'd left the kitchen, the desk had been clear, but it was now scattered with the contents of the "Departed Guests" file, particularly, she saw as she looked through the records, those who had stayed during August. And someone had turned the large wall calendar back to August instead of September. What in hell?

A sound at the door brought her upright. J.Q.

"I thought I heard someone over here," he remarked sleepily. "What are you doing?"

"I just arrived," she snapped. "Whoever was actually 'doing' made quite a mess of it."

He came over to stare owl-eyed at the confusion, muttering to himself, reading half aloud, looking at the calendar, then back at the papers. Finally, he picked up a sheet and read the name. Postern. He looked up at the calendar and checked off the name Postern. Next name, next name checked off.

"Here," Shirley said, puzzled. "Let me read the names." She shook the sheets into a pile, all facing the same way, and began to read the names. "Williamson."

"Check."

"McCandless."

"Check."

"Nussbaum."

"Check."

When they had finished, there were only two names on the calendar that were not checked off. Hoffmier and Jones.

"Hoffmier's in the 'Unpaid Bills' file," J.Q. mused. "I haven't paid the travel-agency commission yet."

Shirley nodded thoughtfully. "Jones's sheet is still back in the library. I made a copy of it for Lieutenant Ohlman, and I guess I left it there. Do you think this searcher was looking for a specific name?"

"Possibly. Or something that would tie an alias to a known individual. Like an address, or a phone number."

"It could have been anybody!"

"How did he get in?"

"Everybody got in, J.Q. People were coming and going like ants. Anybody and his cousin could have come in. People at a wedding don't know all the other people who are there."

"Did Ulti and Alli see him, maybe?"

"We'll ask them tomorrow. I'm more concerned about how anyone got into this room."

J.Q. actually flushed. "I'm afraid I left the kitchen door unlocked. I intended to come back over and make a cup of bedtime cocoa, but I fell asleep."

"Well, if he, she, or it was looking for something to tie Jones or Hoffmier to a specific address . . ." Her eyes fell on the sheet in front of her. "Wait a minute. Here's the Posterns. This sheet was on top. Their address is also Los Angeles, and they were here at the same time Jones and Buscovitch were. They overlapped by three days."

J.Q. leaned over her shoulder, putting his finger on the entry *Number of Guests*. "Two of them?"

Shirley said, "They were a couple. I remember them. Middle-aged. Very pleasant. The woman was a cancer researcher and he was some kind of professor."

"On this sheet, they're just a couple who live in Los Angeles," mused J.Q. "Maybe our snoop thinks they're the ones he's looking for."

"You're assuming he's looking for Jones?"

"Salome told you someone was looking for Jones. Or Buscovitch." He stared at her thoughtfully, as though he'd just noticed her gown and robe. "What brought you over here?"

She yawned gapingly. "I was just falling asleep when Janice Beardsley called. She bawled me out for getting rid of David Littlepage. I told her I didn't do any such thing. Then when she hung up, I heard a click on the line. As though someone else had hung up the phone. It could have been at her end, of course, but it got me all nudgy, so I came over here."

"You think our snoop picked up the phone?"

"Yes, I do," she said defensively. "I have absolutely no reason to think so, but I do."

He thought about it for a moment, coming up with nothing relevant. "Cocoa?" he offered. "Better late than never? We're doing no good standing about in the middle of the wee hours."

"Lord, J.Q., if that phone rings again, I shall jerk it out by the roots. Yes, by all means, cocoa. Or sleeping pills!"

"Cocoa has fewer side effects." He fetched the ingredients, heated the milk, then combined everything with a whisk and set the hot cup before her. "A natural sleeping draft."

"If Salome sent the stuff she promised on Friday, it'll be here Monday," Shirley murmured.

"You think it'll have something relevant in it?"

"Oh, hell, J.Q. I don't know. The only way I can make sense out of all this is to assume that Jones made off with some great wad of money, and his daddy, from whom he stole it, is trying to get it back without involving law enforcement. This could be because the source of the money isn't legal, or it could be because Daddy doesn't want his son labeled a thief. Something led Daddy's agents to Salome's place. Telephone records, maybe. That's where I'd start if I were tracing a child of mine. If Sonny called the girl from home—or from school, for that matter—Daddy could have learned who the girl was that his son was besotted with. Then other phone calls might have led Daddy to the rooming house."

"What led them here?"

"Haven't a clue. Something they found in the room? However they found out, something led them here, then for some reason, the agents killed Jones and Buscovitch."

"Would Daddy have wanted them to do that?"

"It could have happened accidentally. Or maybe things got out of hand. Or maybe Daddy was fed up with his son—wait a minute. We're not at all sure it is his own son. Could be a stepson? Or foster son, or adopted son? Maybe whoever the boss is, he told his guys to get rid of Jones. I don't know. There was a time I'd have considered knocking off any young person unlikely, but according to the television news, kids are killing off parents and parents are killing off kids at a great rate. We should expect it to happen, actually. It happens with animals, too, when the population stresses build up."

"And why are these people still hanging around here?"

"Because they didn't find the money? Because we had it, or rather the police had it and that fact hasn't appeared on the news."

"Hell, Shirley, that won't wash! The murderer didn't even take what was in the kid's wallet!"

"I know," she said fretfully. "It doesn't make much sense, does it?" She stood up, stretching. "I'm going to finish this back in my bedroom. And I'm taking the phone off the hook."

"Just unplug it. Anybody calling at this time of the morning can leave a message."

She turned and went back the way she had come, turning off the lights, hearing J.Q.'s mutter and the snick of the lock on the kitchen door. Locking the barn door after the horse was stolen. Oh, well, like cocoa, better late than never. At least their visitor couldn't get back in.

Shirley slept in on Sunday morning, and thus missed the Sabbath frenzy that began early with the large contingents of guests milling about in the driveway before leaving for church and large contingents of local friends

167

of the bride or groom milling about everywhere as they arrived to tear down and cart away the ritual infrastructure. Shirley was awakened at eight-fifty by one worker calling to another worker as the folding chairs were loaded into a trailer.

She got up, dressed, washed her face, combed her hair, and stomped down the corridor to the kitchen. J.Q. had beat her to it, and the smell of coffee wafted her the last few feet.

"What's happening out there?" she asked.

"Two trucks are ferrying the wedding presents away from here to some undisclosed location."

"Ferrying?" she asked, eyebrows up. "Back and forth?"

"This is their third trip. According to one of the guests who is staying here, the Big House living room is stacked with gifts, floor to ceiling."

"They're stowing folding chairs, out back."

"The balloon arch has been removed. Great quantities of caterer's cookware have been packed. Assorted persons have come in here three times already, asking if we found this or that."

"What kind of this or that?"

He referred to a list on the desk. "Allison started the list, then she went off riding with Ulti. I told him to take your horse because it needs the exercise. So far we have three lost earrings, one singleton and one pair, with great sentimental value. One pair shoes, with great sentimental value. One large coffee urn, with intrinsic value in the several-hundred-dollar range. Assorted cutlery and stemware, unsentimentally rented. If they don't take it all back, minus five percent for breakage, they lose their deposit." He turned the list over. "Two pairs of eyeglasses, one bifocal, one reading. A pearl necklace, with great sentimental value, worn by a young lady who partook of conviviality to the point she lost all contact with reality and had to sleep it off in the Garden House. She thinks someone must have removed her pearls while she was sleeping."

"Is that all?"

"No." He peered at the list. "The bride's mother, wouldn't you know, lost a small plastic folder with some business cards in it."

"My heart aches for her."

"Well, the name and number for the photographer who was doing the photo-essay type thing on the wedding was in it, and she wants to reach him but can't remember his name, so she's fit to be tied."

"And that's it."

"More or less."

"I trust there was no loss of life."

"Not that I'm aware. Of course, I haven't dragged the swimming pool yet."

"Or searched the barn."

"Right. Another cup and I'll be up to searching the barn."

"Have another cup."

"Thank you. I will."

They sat, staring silently out the window at the antlike activity outside. It had the same fascination as watching surf: the ebb, the flow, the constantly alternating shush and tumult.

Shirley remarked, "The rental company won't pick up those heaters and the dance floor until tomorrow. They don't work on Sundays."

J.Q. nodded. "I hope someone is removing the tulle bows from the trees."

"I hope someone is cleaning up cigarette and cigar butts. While they waited for the ceremony I noticed them flinging butts away like mad. People throw all sorts of unlikely things in the most unlikely places. We may find the missing earrings in a magpie's nest."

"I have no intention of looking in magpies' nests," he said. "From the talk I overheard, as soon as the cleanup is done, everyone is going off to see the sights and do the town. Then we can expect a return of peace and quiet."

"Devoutly to be wished." She drank deeply, sighing. "Do we have a gap on the calendar? I need a gap."

He looked at the calendar. "We have a gap. Everyone will have left by noon tomorrow, the eighth, and we have no guests arriving until the Pattersons from Denver show up on Wednesday the tenth. As I recall it's Mom and Dad and five kids. So, we have a gap of a day and a half, at least."

"Let's take the horses and pack and go up in the Jemez or the Sangres and camp out, just overnight. I haven't done that in years."

"Aaah," he said, casting a wary eye. "Sleep on the ground, you mean."

She considered, absently stroking her steel knee, rotating a slightly achy shoulder. "Well, maybe not. It has been sort of rainy. Better try that close to home, just to see if I can. Even on a mattress, it twinges on me. We could take the horses and go riding in the Jemez, anyhow. Spending the night isn't necessary."

"I'm willing," he said, rising to rinse out his cup. "It's past time to feed the critters. Hold the fort."

He went out. She refilled her cup and stood outside the door, watching the scurrying multitudes. Two empty pickup trucks arrived in front of the Big House and were promptly filled with packages, some in brown paper, some in gay wrappings. Fifteen minutes later the trucks departed. Five minutes later someone ran across the parking lot carrying half a dozen wineglasses, shouting, "I found them." Later yet, someone else brought out a fabric that Shirley recognized as the bedspread in the Little House, and shook it, hard. Magenta glitter spun away in all directions.

"Oh, great," Shirley grumbled to herself. "They couldn't use rice. The peafowl would have eaten rice, but this bunch had to use glitter." She gloomed at the wall. Glitter was impossible. It stuck to stuff. It wouldn't vacuum. It wouldn't sweep. All it would do was lie there, glimmering at you. Such a nice, ecological addition to the neatly raked gravel drive! Jenny would have a cat fit.

J.Q. came stealthily in the back gate, almost on tiptoe, his face shadowed by his hat brim. As he came nearer she saw that his face was strangely pallid, his expression unfocused, as though he'd been profoundly shocked. All she could think of was that some of the stock might be ill, or dead.

She went to him quickly. "What is it, J.Q.? What's the matter?"

He put down the bucket he was carrying and put a hand on her shoulder, leaning on her momentarily. "I told you I hadn't searched the barn," he said huskily. "Didn't need to, really. Right there in the loft, in plain sight."

"What?" she urged. "What?"

"We've got a body," he said. "In the hayloft. A man."

"A body? One of the wedding guests? Killed?"

"Shot, probably. Blood on his chest. I don't think he was one of the wedding guests. I didn't touch the body

171

and I'm not sure, Shirley, but I think ... I think he's David Littlepage."

"You mean the one who isn't David Littlepage?"

"I mean the one in the picture. In the *Smithsonian* magazine. David Littlepage."

The thought that kept coming into her mind, whatever else was going on over the next few hours, was an old Thurber cartoon in which an irate woman stands in the open door of an office, asking the seallike critter inside, "What have you done with Dr. Millmoss?" One might go down to the barn and ask the sheep, "What have you done with David Littlepage?"

What had they done with David Littlepage? What had anyone done with him?

Which was also what Ohlman and Griego wanted to know. Shirley had called the state police directly, inasmuch as this murder might be a part of the other murder they were already investigating. They had arrived promptly and had started by asking for a list of all persons present the night before. Shirley suggested that the bride or groom might have such a list, or maybe there was a guest book they could see.

"Also, there were people taping everything," Shirley told them across the kitchen table. "I've never seen so many video cameras. You can probably see the face of everyone present."

Ohlman reiterated the same question Shirley had been asking herself: what had she done with David Littlepage? To which she could only answer, nothing at all.

"So what's the connection?" demanded Ohlman.

Shirley had been struggling for almost an hour to come up with an abbreviated outline of the story that would

172

leave her family out, finally admitting to herself that there was no way to abbreviate herself and Marty out of it. It had to start with Marty.

"Sixteen years ago," she said, "my son, Marty, a recent graduate in anthropology, disappeared in Brazil. He has never been seen or heard from since. Last week, a man calling himself David Littlepage—not the corpse— showed up here with Marty's Social Security card, saying he might be able to find out where my son is, or was. The man identified himself as a writer, and he said that he'd recently visited Brazil.

"Subsequently, J.Q. dug up a three-year-old article about Brazil in *Smithsonian* magazine, written by David Littlepage and with a picture of David Littlepage. The picture was not of the man who had come here claiming to be David Littlepage." She got up, went to the desk, and pawed through a stack of miscellany, coming up with the magazine. She opened it and placed it on the table, pointing.

"The corpse is this guy in the picture?" Ohlman snapped at J.Q. "Right?"

J.Q. nodded noncommittally. "I told Shirley the corpse *appears* to be the man in the picture. I can't swear that he is."

"How the hell does this tie to Jones and what's-her-name?"

Shirley said, "People have been looking for Jones and Buscovitch. The landlady of the rooming house where they stayed in California says that people have come to her place twice looking for them. We had a prowler last night, here in this house, who may have been searching for Jones and Buscovitch, or searching for something they left behind, possibly the money we turned over to you. Since the man who called himself Littlepage wasn't really Littlepage, one has to ask what the hell he was up to. All I can come up with is that he could have been simply another spy, trying to learn something about two of our guests."

"But he's not the corpse?" asked Griego.

"No, he's not the corpse." She considered mentioning Janice Beardsley and discarded the idea. "The only reason I can think of why the real Littlepage came here is that he learned he was being impersonated."

"The guy down in your barn was shot. But you didn't hear a shot anytime last night?" This was Ohlman, determined he was going to make her responsible, somehow.

J.Q. snorted. "The wedding party had mariachis playing part of the time, plus a dance band the rest of the time, and they played until roughly midnight. Roughly two hundred people were chatting and laughing. They also set off fireworks every now and then. He could have been mowed down by a fully automatic weapon and we'd have thought it was firecrackers."

Shirley added, "There's one more thing. My foster daughter and a young friend of ours moved around among the wedding guests last night, just being sure everyone's behavior was appropriate, and it's possible they may have seen something helpful."

"They might have seen this guy?" Griego asked.

"I have no idea. You can ask Ulti. He and Allison went off for an early-morning ride, but they'll get hungry and be back soon."

"He a local?"

"Yes. Ultimo Gonsalves. A neighbor of ours."

Ohlman snorted, a little like a bull, Shirley thought, one that was considering knocking down a gate or jumping a fence or goring some unwilling cow into submission. She wasn't being sufficiently cowlike, which irritated him, you could tell.

"You have any theories?" Griego asked in a soothing voice, with a sidewise glance at his boss.

"J.Q. and I have tried to figure that out. The only thing we could come up with was this: The kid, Jones, stole a lot of money from his father. His father doesn't want that money mentioned to the police, so he or someone working for him tries to find the kid. He traces him to Los Angeles, then loses him for a while, then traces him here—"

"How?" demanded Ohlman.

"I don't know exactly how. When I figure that out, I'll tell you. Anyhow, the two kids get married and come here, bringing the money with them. They go on a buying spree in town. They go on a trail ride. Somehow, Daddy's guys catch up to them, and the whole thing goes wrong. The two kids get killed. However, people are still searching the place they stayed, so Daddy must still want his money—"

"Or," J.Q. interjected, "since they didn't take the money in Jones's wallet, we have to consider they were looking for something else."

"Yes," Shirley agreed. "It may be something other than money."

"And this Littlepage guy?"

Shirley shrugged. "The phony Littlepage could be Daddy himself, or someone working for Daddy. Somehow, he finds out the name of this place. He does a little research digging into public business and financial records, which tells him I'm the owner; then he looks me up and finds out I had a missing son sixteen years ago. That seems like a good way to get at me, so he looks for a name he can use, somebody, anybody, with a legitimate connection to Brazil. He comes up with Littlepage. He then lays on a few phony props and comes here pretending to be Littlepage. He could just as well have pretended to be a diplomat or an anthropologist or a biologist or whatever so long as it was a story that would get him close to me."

"When he came here, did you think he was phony?"

"Not necessarily, no. I thought it might be some kind of scam. He was very eager to take pictures of the place and to wander about. He referred to honeymooners at least twice, and he specifically asked to take pictures inside the guest houses."

"But you have no idea about the dead guy?"

She wavered. She might have to tell them eventually, why not now? "Not really, unless . . ."

"Unless what?" Griego urged.

"There was another young man with my son when he disappeared. Glenn Beardsley. The Beardsleys live in Alexandria, Virginia. The so-called Littlepage called them before he came here to me. I think he did that purely for verisimilitude—"

"For what?" Ohlman demanded, scowling.

Shirley took a deep breath. "A real journalist would have contacted them, so he did it to make his journalist act look better. Anyhow, I talked to Janice after the so-called Littlepage had talked with her. She believed him, totally, and of course she fed him all kinds of details that were never in the papers, details he could use to get to me. As a matter of fact, Janice called me last night saying she'd been leaving messages for Littlepage and she'd sent him all the newspaper articles and information about the disappearance sixteen years ago.

"Littlepage didn't give me his address, which I now consider rather odd. If he'd really been after my support, he would have let me know where to find him. I didn't ask Janice where she sent all the stuff, but since Janice believed him totally, she probably looked him up by calling the magazines he said he worked for. If she did that, she got the address and phone number for the real Littlepage. Once Janice started sending him stuff and leaving messages, the real Littlepage would have become very much aware that somebody was pretending to be him."

Ohlman muttered, "I don't get why he'd call this woman at all."

J.Q. remarked dryly, "Maybe to get information about Shirley that he could use when he talked to her. Maybe to find out more about the disappearance."

"Kinda backfired on him," the lieutenant said.

J.Q. nodded. "The phony Littlepage may have learned that the real guy was away for a while, on a job somewhere, giving him, the phony, time to pull off his job and be gone before the real Littlepage came back. Personally, I think he planned to finish his investigation the day he came here. What he really wanted was to find out if Jones and Buscovitch were here. He knew they'd run off together because he fished for information about honeymooners. He didn't get anywhere. He tried to take pictures in the houses, but Shirley put him off. He very much wanted to find out which house the kids were in and get into it."

"Why would he want to?"

"I said why," Shirley grated. "If he didn't kill the kids,

177

if he doesn't know they're dead, then he's looking for them. If he killed them, or knows they're dead, he's looking for something the kids had. The money or something else."

"You had a prowler in your house last night. That could have been the real Littlepage."

"Could be," Shirley admitted. "Depending on the time of death. If he was still alive at one-fifteen—which is when I knew someone was in the house—it could have been him. If we're right about this scenario, however, the person who came into our kitchen and went through our records was still trying to find out which house Jones and Buscovitch stayed in, though he didn't know those names. The real Littlepage had no connection to Jones and Buscovitch, which tells me it wasn't him who prowled our kitchen.

"The prowler found a reservation sheet for a couple who'd come from Los Angeles, a couple who were here the same time Jones was, and if I were the phony Littlepage, at that point I'd go back to L.A. and see if they were the right ones.

"I don't guess Daddy or his minions knew what names they were using. Or about the disguises."

"Disguise?" Ohlman erupted. "What do you mean, disguise?"

"She wasn't really a blonde; his hair wasn't really black. He was probably a redhead, she was definitely dark."

"How in the hell did you find that out?" Ohlman was red in the face, obviously annoyed.

Shirley had no intention of telling him. "It was obvious from their skin coloring. She was dark, he was pale, with pale sandy lashes and freckles."

Ohlman rose to his feet, hitched up his belt, and went out to the car. They saw him through the window, shouting into his phone.

"How did you really get onto the fact they'd dyed their hair?" Griego asked, keeping an eye on his boss through the window.

Shirley smiled grimly and told him about the observant saleswoman. "Also, the landlady in Los Angeles said Alan had a matching car. Matching to what? Even though I'd seen his body, I didn't connect the word *matching* to anything then. It hit me later what she meant. The kid had freckles, light lashes, and very pale skin, so he could have been a redhead, the same coppery red as the car. The two young people changed their appearances to go with their new names, their new official ages, their new home address—when they got one."

"What were they going to do?" asked Griego. "Settle down somewhere around Santa Fe?"

"I have no idea what their plans were. They couldn't have lived here long on sixty-odd thousand, not with her expensive tastes," said Shirley. "Of course, they may have had no idea how far that much money would go, or possibly they stole a great deal more money than we've found."

"They had travel expenses, they bought clothes," Griego said, tallying the points on his fingers. "They bought a car—if they were running away and changing their appearance, they wouldn't use a car people could identify. The car alone was at least thirty thou. Even after that, they had sixty-five thousand left. They must have taken at least what? A hundred fifty? You don't think that much is enough to make somebody come looking?"

"It could be." Shirley nodded. "But is it enough to

justify what we've seen here? At least three guys asking questions in California? Three murders? Plus assorted prowlings and snoopings."

"Assuming Jones did take something additional to the money, where would he have put it?"

J.Q. snorted. "Anywhere between here and California. Any locker or storage facility or safe-deposit box. Any abandoned mine shaft, I suppose, nutty as they were."

"Getting back to this latest killing," Griego said, keeping his eyes on Ohlman, who was still on the phone, brandishing a fist at nothing. "How does he fit in?"

Shirley shook her head. "No idea. Unless he confronted the fake Littlepage and maybe threatened to expose him or something."

"But you didn't see the fake Littlepage among the guests."

"No." She thought about it. "Even though we did watch the crowd, we weren't looking for anyone we knew. Ultimo and Allison were out there mixing, but they wouldn't have known him if they'd seen him. They were in school when the phony visited here, and besides, he wasn't memorable in appearance. Average height and weight, going bald, lines around the eyes, as though he'd worked in the sun a lot."

Griego rose to his feet and picked up his hat. "If you don't mind, let's just keep this conversation between us. H.R. has some kind of burr under his tail. He isn't handling things as well as he should. I figure we should be talking to people in California, telling the media how old these kids really were, providing retouched photographs so we can get IDs. We're not going to get anywhere until we know who they are, but H.R. wants to do it his way, by himself."

"Why?" Shirley said. "He's handicapping himself."

Griego flushed slightly. "He's trying to prove something to the world, particularly to the new captain. And he's taken a real dislike to you, ma'am. He doesn't like the way you find stuff out."

Shirley, annoyed, spoke without thinking. "Well, he doesn't like any woman really, does he? Your sister-in-law is evidence of that."

He flushed more deeply, turned his hat in his hands, then murmured, "You caught that, did you? Since you did, maybe you could give me some advice. The way he's treating Rena, it's got me between a rock and a hard place. She says she fell on those stairs, and I think maybe she did, but maybe she got shoved a little. I say anything and my tail's in a crack. I don't say anything and it's like I'm aiding and abetting."

"What does Rena think?" Shirley asked gently.

"She's scared to death of him. She left him once before, went to her mother's place in Texas, but he found her. She thinks he'll kill her if she tries it again. She doesn't want me doing anything, for fear he'll take it out on me, or on Lupe."

"There's a shelter in town, one that can protect her."

"That's what I told Lupe. She's been trying with Rena, but Rena says that's the first place H.R. would look. Being a cop, he knows where it is, of course. We all do, and the way he's been lately, I don't think a locked door would stop him."

"You have a point. She needs a real hideout, then. Are there children?"

"No. And that's part of the trouble. It isn't her. It's him, but he won't hear that. Something has to give, soon." He grimaced, as though at himself, let himself out, and joined Ohlman in the driveway.

J.Q. said flatly, "I wonder what he'd do if she were his sister instead of his sister-in-law."

"He isn't irresolute, J.Q. He just doesn't know what to do. His wife is urging him to do nothing. Her sister wants him to do nothing. You know the pattern."

He made an unpleasant face.

A moment later Griego knocked lightly on the door, sticking his head in to say, "The lieutenant says he's not going to release the body for transport until your daughter and her friend get back. He wants them to look at him, see if they recognize him as somebody that was walking around with the guests last night."

Shirley frowned. "Could we bring them to the morgue or wherever?"

He half nodded. "You could, but that's clear down in Albuquerque. Medical investigation is done at the university med school. Actually, I suggested to H.R. that he wait because it would save you the trip."

J.Q. rose and went out, saying, "I know where they were riding. I'll go see if I can hurry them up."

Griego went out and spoke briefly with his boss, who climbed into the car in which both men had arrived and sped off, throwing gravel. Dog, hit by flying stones, yelped briefly from the driveway then appeared whining at the door, Griego close behind her.

Shirley set about soothing her pet, who was agitatedly licking her flank.

"Wounded?" Griego asked.

"Bruised. No blood showing. She'll have a sore spot for a while."

"Damn!" he said feelingly. "He's an explosion waiting to go off."

"What's he in such a boil about today?" Shirley asked.

"It's not just today. He's never what you'd call cheerful, but this started about six months ago when they brought in another guy for the captain's job. H.R. figured he'd earned the promotion. Then there's Rena. He figures it's her fault they don't have children, no matter what the doctor says. So he boils over at a few civilians and uses too much muscle on a suspect or two, and the new captain calls him on using undue force. H.R. figures that's somebody else's fault, too. It's like he's building up to self-destruct. I'm afraid he may take somebody with him when he does."

She looked at his brooding face, then out at the vacant drive. "How about some coffee, Raul? Let's sit out in the patio. I've been avoiding it the last few days, but the place seems to have emptied out. Did you get everyone identified?"

"We've got the names of all the people staying here— they're all family of the bride or groom, all from out of state, none of them likely suspects, and they won't even be much help identifying other people at the wedding, except each other. We also located the guest book. We've borrowed that to make copies, and we're running copies of all the videotape we've located so far."

She led the way to the patio table, adjusted the large umbrella, and sat down. From the pastures below, she heard horses talking. "J.Q.'s back," she said. "Or maybe he never left. I hear more than one horse."

They waited silently. In a few moments J.Q. came through the gate, closely followed by Ulti and Allison, both unusually sober. Griego rose, took off his hat, and offered his hand. Allison shook it gravely.

"Hi," Allison said to Griego. "I'm Allison, and this is Ultimo. J.Q. says you want us to . . . look at a person. . . ."

"His face wasn't injured," Griego assured her. "We merely want to know if you recognize him as being someone who moved around among the guests yesterday. I understand you were keeping an eye on things."

Allison heaved a deep breath. "We were mostly out around the pool, being sure people didn't break glasses there. Actually, one person did, but Ulti fished the pieces out of the water. It was at the shallow end, and we could see it all right."

Ulti offered, "And we walked out in the driveway, back to the terrace, and around the houses. It was crowded, but most everyone seemed to know people. There weren't any loners that I saw."

"There was the man who said he was looking for a bathroom," said Alli.

Ulti frowned. "Right. I forgot him. Well, they had one house for the men to use and one for the women to use for bathrooms, you know. And this guy was jiggling the door of the Garden House. I asked him if he'd lost his key and he sort of stuttered something about needing to go, so I showed him where the men's bathroom was and he went off in that direction."

"Could you describe him to a sketch artist?"

Ulti shook his head. "I saw more of his backside than I did his face. When he spoke, he took out a handkerchief and sort of blew his nose, and he was still blowing when he went off. I don't think I can help you."

"How tall? How heavy? What color hair?"

"Shorter than me, taller than Allison. Maybe five-eight? Not skinny, not fat, just sort of ordinary looking. Brown flat hair. He wore dark glasses, so I don't know about the eyes."

"What was he wearing?"

"Slacks and a sports coat. They were brown, too."

Griego nodded. "Well, it was worth a try. Could mean something, or he could just have been a befuddled guest. Are you up to coming out to the ambulance and taking a look?"

Allison looked over at Shirley, who nodded. She took another deep breath and said, "Sure. Let's get it over with."

J.Q. moved off with them. Shirley, after a moment's hesitation, followed. The gurney was waiting at the back of the ambulance, the driver and his assistant standing by.

Griego unzipped the bag. Allison looked. Ulti looked. J.Q. and Shirley looked. Shirley saw that he did, indeed, resemble the David Littlepage in the photograph. She had never seen him before in the flesh, not that she remembered. Allison shook her head. Ulti shook his.

"That's not the man who was trying the door," he said. "This guy has curly, blond hair. I don't remember seeing him, and I think I'd remember that hair."

"Again," Griego said, "worth a try. Thank you."

He nodded to the ambulance crew, who promptly loaded the body.

"I'm catching a ride into town with them," Griego said, offering Shirley his hand. "Thank you."

"That other matter," Shirley said in a low voice. "I may be able to help. Ask your wife to call me."

He gave her a slightly puzzled look, then nodded.

They watched the ambulance depart, then dropped into the chairs around the table.

Shirley looked at the circle of morose faces and remarked, "Now that our Sunday is irreparably ruined, our calendar gap obviously taken up with another murder, how shall we spend our day?"

"I've never been near a murder before," Ultimo said. "Not even close."

"Shirley has," Allison remarked. "She attracts them, like flies."

J.Q. objected, "It's not an attraction. It's a statistical anomaly, and that's all."

Shirley laughed without humor. "Can anything else go wrong?"

J.Q. nodded. "Sure it can. When the bride's mother is interviewed by the police because you and I found a corpse, when her videotape and everyone else's videotape is confiscated, I should imagine we're in for another tantrum. I sincerely hope the bride and groom are away on honeymoon."

"In Rangoon," murmured Shirley. "Or Outer Mongolia. Where they cannot be reached, by anyone. As I devoutly wish we all were."

"Good morning!" Xanthy called in a cheerful voice, emerging from the house. "Last night's revelry did go on and on, didn't it? Once I got to sleep, I didn't want to wake up! What a lovely, peaceful Sunday."

She looked quite confused when Shirley put her head on the table and pounded it weakly with both fists.

Shirley called Roger's office first thing Monday morning, leaving a lengthy message. The package from Salome McCreary arrived around noon, by which time the last of

186

the wedding guests had gone, leaving only peace and quiet behind. Shirley paid the collect shipping charges and set the carton on the patio table, then went inside to get a knife. J.Q., deep in *The Wall Street Journal* western edition, looked up as she found the weapon of choice.

"Anybody I know?" he asked, staring at the blade.

"Package by UPS," she murmured. "From the lady in Los Angeles. You want to see?"

He heaved himself upright and followed her out into the sunlight. The day was warm, not hot. Clouds hung low in the west, promising the chance of thunderstorms in the afternoon. Autumn anemones made a pale blotch of color in the front garden, set off by the last of the phlox and the first of the chrysanthemums. Xanthy came out of the house and joined them as Shirley slit the taped joints.

Regarding the open carton with interest, she asked, "And this is?"

"What the victims left in their Los Angeles room." Shirley opened the carton on a clutter of papers, odds and ends. "One pair of shoes." She set them on the table. Loafers, about size six or seven.

J.Q. picked them up and turned them over, running his fingers along the insole and around the heel. "Worn," he said. "These were Buscovitch's."

The carton held several unmatched socks and pieces of underwear: one bra, two pairs of panties, one pair of male bikini briefs. "Probably left in the bed linens," Shirley remarked, remembering the diary.

An envelope, addressed to *Helen Beskovitz*. Inside, a letter beginning *Nitsy, you nut*, and signed *Beegee*. No return on the envelope. Postmarked . . . New Mexico.

Albuquerque. Which meant nothing. The letter could have originated anywhere in the state. Wordlessly, Shirley passed it to Xanthy.

" 'Nitsy, you nut,' " she read. " 'I thought you were kidding! You really did it. You crazy thing. I've really missed you since we moved here, and I'm so glad you're coming. Call me when you get to town. I want to hear all about it. I want to meet HIM! Beegee.' "

"Someone here in New Mexico knows her," said J.Q.

"Knows ... knew her well," Shirley affirmed, digging more deeply into the box and pulling out several thick, slick magazines. "Here's the *New Mexico Tourist Guide*. And another one from Arizona. Another one from Nevada. She mentioned those in the diary, didn't she."

"Let me see New Mexico," J.Q. directed. He put it on the table and leafed through it. "Here. Our ad. And wouldn't you know. A big red check mark and a note, 'sending broshoor.' " He handed the book to Xanthy.

She leafed through it, looking for other check marks or notes. "They checked several places, all of them in or near Santa Fe."

Shirley said, "Which is probably how they were traced here. The men who looked through the room saw this lying there, then they leafed through and found the check marks."

J.Q. remarked, "Santa Fe could also be the town Beegee referred to."

"I wish Beegee had told us her last name," Shirley muttered.

J.Q. took out his pipe, loaded it, lit it, and sent a puff of smoke across the opened carton. "Is Griego looking for missing teenagers?"

"He says he is. The lieutenant is."

"Is he looking locally?"

Shirley sat down with a thump. "Probably not. Why would he? He assumed they were from California. As I did."

Xanthy mused, "Are they necessarily from out of state at all? I don't think we've paid enough attention to the diary. Let me get the copies we made." She went inside, returning in a moment with a notebook, a pencil, and several loose sheets of copy paper, which she referred to as she jotted.

"Now. In the first place, we learn that she is in school. She says the rooming house is better than school insofar as sharing bathrooms is concerned. He is also in school. She says he wants to finish school. Surely she doesn't mean that particular school. She means he wishes to finish his education. Weekend after next, she says, is vacation and his father will be gone, and they'll rent a place. Then, she says, they drove all around Hollywood, which he knew pretty well because his folks used to live near there."

She set the pages aside and asked rhetorically, "What does this tell us?"

"It tells us the end of June is pretty late to end a school term," grouched J.Q.

"In public or the usual private school, yes," Shirley mused. "A remedial one, perhaps? A boarding school for problem kids? Or maybe just kids whose parents have no time for them?"

"The mention of sharing the bathroom establishes that she was definitely in a boarding school," Xanthy said. "He may well have been. And you're right. One of the things private schools sometimes do is extend their year to ten or even eleven months, with short midsummer and midwinter holidays. Sometimes, regrettably, they are as much custodial as educational, if not more so. The fact that his father will be gone during his son's short vacation could be indicative."

Shirley said, "Helen says they drove around Hollywood. Not drove to, but drove around. Does that imply that Hollywood was close to where their schools are?"

"I think that's a possible assumption," Xanthy said. "But the schools are not necessarily close to where their parents live."

"No," Shirley said excitedly. "Not close to where Alan's family is, but maybe close to where Helen's family is. He can only get there occasionally during vacation. She can get there oftener. She lives nearby. He doesn't."

"Where do you get that?" asked J.Q.

"From what Salome McCreary said. That she seldom saw him, and that Helen wasn't always there. Helen was at school during the week, and so was Alan, but maybe Alan was farther away."

"What about the other magazines she spoke of?" Xanthy went on. "Are they in the box?"

Shirley handed Xanthy the Arizona one, keeping the Nevada one for herself. Flipping through it, she found no check marks or notes, as there had been in the New Mexico book. She looked in the box again.

"No Hawaii," she said. "But she did mention Hawaii."

"She talks about leaving a false trail," Xanthy commented. "All that bit about surfing. Hawaii was supposed to be a red herring, so they wouldn't have left the magazine in a room their folks weren't supposed to know about. They'd have left it in their rooms at home or in their rooms at school."

"His or hers?" Shirley asked.

"Certainly his, maybe both," said J.Q.

"I find this enigmatic," said Xanthy, reading from the sheet in her hand. " '. . . Nevada is all gambling. We should stay away from there. Besides, we need a place Alan's dad won't look for us. Like in that Mystery movie.' Mystery is capitalized, which may mean absolutely nothing."

"What's the date on that?" Shirley asked.

"June twenty-fourth."

Shirley said, "*Mystery!*, capitalized, is a PBS show. They do Poirot and Miss Marple and Sherlock Holmes and all the old British standbys. Alleyn. Who's the P. D. James sleuth? Dalgleish."

"Dalziel and somebody," offered J.Q.

Xanthy mused, "If Helen was in or around Los Angeles, it should be possible to find out what episodes of *Mystery!* were broadcast there at around that time."

"If it was the regular program, it's network, isn't it?" J.Q. asked. "The same all across the country?"

"Maybe we don't need to find out," Shirley said thoughtfully. "Helen says, 'We need a place Alan's dad won't look for us.' What well-known mysteries deal with hiding things where people won't look?"

"The classic one is, of course, 'The Purloined Letter,' " said Xanthy. "Was that dramatized on television? Somehow I have difficulty imagining the Helen I know from her writing and your descriptions as a person who watched that kind of thing."

"Alan might have," Shirley said.

J.Q. remarked, " 'The Purloined Letter' theme was to hide something in plain sight. How does that apply?"

"The thing that strikes me," Shirley mused, "is the dismissal of Nevada. She says it's gambling, they should stay away from there, besides, they want a place Alan's father wouldn't look for them. The proximity of ideas says to me that Alan's father might for some reason look in Nevada."

Xanthy asked, "Because, perhaps, he lives in Nevada?"

"Well, he could, couldn't he?" Shirley said. "I keep coming back to that money. Gambling would certainly explain it!"

"So where are we?" grumped J.Q.

Shirley took a deep breath. "To reprise: Alan's father may live or work in Nevada, and he once lived in or near Hollywood. Alan himself goes to boarding school in or around Los Angeles. Alan's father has access to lots of money in large bills. Helen also goes to boarding school in or around Los Angeles. Is there any possibility it's the same school?"

"Not if your argument about her living nearer makes any sense," J.Q. said.

"She might go to the same school as a weekday boarder," said Xanthy. "Monday through Friday, home on weekends. He might be a full boarder. In which case, her movements on weekends aren't the school's business, but his are."

"So it could be the same school. Or it could be two different ones, a boys' school and a girls' school—"

"Which might have joint social affairs, allowing the two young people to meet," said Xanthy.

"Possibly! Anyhow, Alan and Helen fall in love, discuss marriage, are discouraged by at least one parent, Alan's father—"

"We don't know that," Xanthy said. "We only know Helen thinks so."

"Right. They wait until their lives aren't under examination, until school is on vacation and Alan's father is away from home—does this say to you that Alan has no mother?—then they drive around Hollywood and rent a room in a boardinghouse. Even though his school is on vacation, Helen is still in school—"

"Different schools," said Xanthy firmly. "Or her school is out, and she's supposed to be home."

"Right," Shirley acknowledged. "She is still in school or at home, but can still get to the rooming house more frequently than Alan."

"Which means he's under supervision somewhere else," said J.Q. "Either at home or in a camp or something."

Shirley nodded again. "The kids use the boarding-house as a mailing address from which to build false older identities for themselves."

"Also as a trysting place," offered Xanthy, glancing through the more erotic passages in the diary.

Shirley agreed. "Right. They are greatly influenced by television. They get a lot of their ideas from television, including how to hide money and how to get false papers and perhaps, if we're right about Poe, where to hide themselves.

"When they have their documents and are ready to run off together, Alan steals a large amount of money from his father, plus, perhaps, something else of value—"

"Why something else?" asked Xanthy.

"Because of the murder. It could be about more than money. Alan leaves clues at home to indicate he has gone to Hawaii. Both of them change their appearance, and leave for New Mexico, where they have made reservations to stay with us for a while. Alan buys a car somewhere, in California or here or on the road, and once he's in New Mexico, he confuses the trail by putting a license plate on it that belongs to another car, perhaps a junkyard car. Their idea, according to the diary, is to find a place to live permanently.

"Typically, they do not bother to clean up the room they are leaving. It never occurs to them that someone may trace them to that room. Alan's father does find out about the boardinghouse—possibly by examining phone records—and sends people or goes himself to find out where Alan has gone. They find a New Mexico tourist guide with our facility, among others, checked in red, and that brings them to our door."

"Okay so far," said J.Q. "Not necessarily true, but eminently logical."

Shirley went on: "Meantime, the young people have been killed, but since the lieutenant will not give their correct ages and descriptions to the press, no one yet knows they are dead except thee and me and the killer or killers, a category which may include Alan's daddy."

"Well stated," said Xanthy. "A very nice summation."

"Which may be totally and absolutely wrong," Shirley muttered.

"Of course. But it will do to get on with. I'm about to fix myself some lunch. Does anyone else care for something?"

Shirley joined her in the kitchen, where they made sandwiches and iced tea, carrying them out onto the patio.

"This morning I got a call from Julie," Xanthy said as she settled herself. "She got the bonsai this morning, FedEx. She loves it. She was amazed I got one of that quality here. I had to tell her all about poor Mr. Akagami."

"*Poor* Mr. Akagami?" asked J.Q.

Shirley told him about the internment, the loss of prop-

194

erty, still able to get exercised about it though it had happened almost fifty years before. "He couldn't have been more than a teenager at the time," she said. "But of course his parents lost everything."

"That wasn't the worst," Xanthippe remarked. "It was *how* they lost everything. Mr. Akagami told me their property, their farm, had been coveted for some time by a neighboring mogul. Not films, I think, something else. Banking, or oil. The elder Akagami wouldn't sell it. It was to go to his oldest son—"

"Our Mr. Akagami's older brother?"

"Nosura Akagami's older brother. His name is something like Oshibo. I didn't like to ask Nosura Akagami to spell it. Anyhow, when they had to leave the farm, there was a conservatorship set up, and this rich neighbor subverted it somehow, through Washington channels, and got the property for almost nothing. It had been worth quite a bit, but after the war, the Akagami family received only a pittance."

"The property couldn't be reclaimed?" Shirley asked.

"Evidently not."

"Akagami certainly told you a lot!"

"Well, I asked for it, I guess. I saw the elderly gentleman glaring at you, and I called our host's attention to it. He told me the story, and part of it was that his brother was engaged to marry a girl from Hawaii, and when the war was over, her parents wouldn't let her marry him, penniless as he was. He's still terribly bitter, after all these years."

"At the whole country, I should imagine," J.Q. remarked.

"No. Actually not, according to his brother. Not mad at the country, but furious with wealthy people who use their money to cheat the law and abuse others. Evidently there have been all too many examples right up to the present time, not excluding O.J."

"So why was he glaring at me?"

"His general bitterness has been sort of endemic lately. Nosura Akagami told me his brother's health is failing. He had a heart attack early in the summer."

"He looks a lot older than his younger brother."

"About twelve years older, which would make him seventy-something. Actually, Nosura Akagami says he couldn't have started his business here without his oldest brother. It was he who had all the experience and talent. The whole family has tried to make it up to him, but he never married, never let it go."

"Sad," Shirley commented. "Damn. That is sad. I wonder if it's too late to do anything?"

"Reparations were made years ago, weren't they?" J.Q. asked.

"Government ones, yes, such as they were. But what about a civil suit against the evildoer?"

"Long dead, I'm afraid," said Xanthy, stacking their plates. "Did we look at everything in the box?"

"Not quite." Shirley had set it on a nearby bench, and now she retrieved it, lifting out the top layer that they'd already looked at. At the bottom was a scatter of paper, some torn from newspapers and magazines, others lined yellow pages torn from a legal pad, some bearing phone numbers and cryptic messages. Among the clutter was a Fotomat envelope of developed snapshots.

Shirley dealt out the pictures. Dark-haired Helen on the beach, in several suggestive poses. Helen in bed, with a lot of skin showing. Helen in the shower, with all her skin showing. Definitely brunette.

"My, my," said J.Q. "Very nubile."

One picture of Helen and Alan together, Alan's flaming coppery hair glinting in the slanting rays of a sunset that had turned the sky behind them to apricot and rose. Then six pictures taken against a blue wall: three of Alan, with dark hair, three of Helen, now blond.

"They'd have needed photographs for fake driver's licenses," said Shirley. "These must be the ones they took after they dyed their hair."

The rest of the shots included one of a dog, one of a red-haired woman playing with the dog, two of the same woman and an elderly man standing on a tiled portico and involved in passionately angry argument.

"His mother, no doubt," said Xanthy. "You're wrong about his not having one. I wonder if the man could be his father?"

"Maybe they're divorced," Shirley suggested, staring at the angry faces. "He's a lot older than she is. He must be seventy or more."

"Let me see the negatives. Maybe it's the end of the roll," J.Q. offered. He looked at the negatives in the envelope, nodding. "Right, the ones of the dog, woman, and man were at the end of the roll."

"He wanted a picture of his parents, to remember them by?" Xanthy offered.

"He didn't want it enough to take it with him when he left," Shirley commented. "I think he was just shooting pictures, the way we do when we've got something we want to get developed but there are a few shots remaining on the roll. He actually wanted the pictures for ID. The others were just fluff."

"How many pictures are there of dog, woman, and man?" J.Q. asked.

"Four," Xanthy replied.

"There are six on the negatives," J.Q. said. "One of dog, one of woman and dog, four of the couple arguing . . . fighting. In the last one, he socked her!"

Shirley took the negative from his hand and stared through it, making out the forms with some difficulty. Tiny. Reversed. But J.Q. was right. He was hitting her a good one.

"Are you giving this to Griego?" J.Q. asked.

"I'm thinking of it. He could always say he asked me to get the stuff." She looked from the photo of Alan, with dark hair and a dark wispy mustache, to the one of the elderly man. "That must be his dad," she said, handing them over. "They look exactly alike."

Xanthy peered, adjusted her glasses, and peered some more. "Not so ruthless," she opined. "The boy is actually rather soft looking."

"The girl did boss him around," J.Q. said.

"She certainly did," Shirley remarked, remembering the boot salesman's story.

"His expression isn't ruthless, true," Xanthy said. "But you're right that the features are almost identical. There's a great family resemblance."

6

"I T COULD BE family," Roger said on Tuesday morning. His call had wakened Shirley and brought her across the room still half-asleep. She stood by the bedroom window in her nightgown, narrowed eyes staring out at the barely cracked day, trying to make sense of it.

"What family, Rog?"

"You called yesterday." He waited, patiently giving her time to catch up. There was a two-hour difference in time zones. People on the East Coast got used to being patient with Westerners, as though they were slightly retarded—and not only in a chronological sense. What time was it? Six-something.

She pulled herself together. "Yes. I said David Littlepage had been killed here. It was the same Littlepage as the Littlepage who wrote for *Smithsonian* magazine, but it wasn't the same Littlepage as the guy who came here claiming to be Littlepage."

"Right. Well, I have no idea who your pretender was, but the real David Littlepage was Carlo Luccio's son."

Luccio. Luccio? "The godfather-type Luccios?"

"You've heard of him?"

"I don't particularly remember any Carlo, but I've heard of the Luccios. Was Carlo one of the big fish? Wait a minute while I find a pencil."

"Don't bother to take notes, I'll fax you the whole thing. Let me just give you the outline now.

"Carlo Luccio was born in 1903, a younger son of a younger brother of the very large Luccio family. His cousins were the big fish, but Carlo was definitely one of the tribe. He married Lucrezia Bonafacio in 1925, and two years later they had a son, Filippo. A few years later they moved to California from the East Coast. Evidently Lucrezia had some chronic health problem. She never had another child, she was ill for years, and she died in 1943. Six years later, when Filippo was twenty-two, Carlo married a second wife, Lillian Littlepage, a Connecticut girl attending UCLA. She was two years younger than Carlo's son, Filippo. Lillian and Carlo had a son, David, in '52."

"David Littlepage? Not David Luccio?"

"Be patient. Evidently Lillian became disenchanted with the Luccio family. When David was about eight, she took him and returned to the East Coast, resuming her family name. She went back to college, became quite a well-known photographer, a writer of travel pieces in some of the better magazines, and she has half a dozen travel books to her credit."

Shirley thought about this for a while. "Did David keep in touch with his father? I'm surprised what's-his-name, Carlo, let her take the boy. I thought those families were rather possessive about their kids."

"David stayed in touch, yes. He still does, according to my sources. I don't know how or why Carlo let Lillian leave him. Maybe she had something on him. Anyhow, Carlo died in '74. David was twenty-two at the time."

"What about his older half brother, what did you say his name was?"

"Filippo. He's a full generation older than David. Twenty-four, twenty-five years."

Shirley smoothed her hair with one hand. Her head itched, but the irritation seemed to be inside her skull. "It's all very interesting, Roger, but what did you mean when you said it could be family?"

"Well, your fake Littlepage could have been a family member, or at least someone who knew the family. He finds out who you are, he sees the business about Brazil, whoopy-do, who does he know who's been to Brazil? Though the real David grew up with his mama, he has always visited back and forth. They all know him, at least they know enough about him to phony up a brief visit. Or, considering who the family is, maybe they had some reason for killing him. Maybe Lillian Littlepage did have something on them, and it threatened to come out."

"During a wedding? In New Mexico? Does the Luccio family have anything to do with New Mexico?" She heard her voice rising stridently and choked it down.

Roger waited until she subsided. "As a matter of fact, yes. Filippo has a second home near Albuquerque, quite a showplace from all accounts, and he is reputed—put that in quotes—to be recently much involved with the Indian casinos."

She was abruptly sobered, remembering all those thousand-dollar bills. "Is that his thing? Gambling?"

"In an ancillary way. He did a short stretch in a federal prison for laundering drug money through a Las Vegas casino. I think it was '75 through '79, something like that. He had a minor interest in a Las Vegas club, but the gaming commission took it away from him when he was convicted. He has never had any direct connection with the drug trade, not that we know of, either buying or selling, but he's intimately involved with the money end of the family business."

"How about his own family? Does he have one?"

She heard the rustle of paper at the other end. "Filippo seemingly wasn't much interested in women during his younger years. According to people who knew him, he had a lot of female friends, but the relationships were ephemeral. The year he got out of jail, he married a showgirl from the same Las Vegas club he'd had a share in. Maybe absence made his hormones fonder. Let's see. Her name is Arlena Delgado. She was twenty-six at the time they were married. They're still married, so far as my information goes—"

She interrupted him. "Are you going to send this information to the state police here in New Mexico, Roger?"

"If you want me to, yes."

"Please give them something to chew on. But don't let them know where it came from. Ask one of your friends at the FBI to do it."

"Speaking of my friends at the FBI, the Social Security card was a fake. Chemically, the ink didn't match. It appears to be a rather hasty job, according to the same technicians."

She'd expected it, but still, her stomach felt as though it had dropped away from her. "Thank you, Roger."

"I'm sorry, dear."

"Yeah. Well." She gritted her teeth to keep them from chattering. She took a deep breath. "I'm sorry, too, but I'm glad to know. I would have hated to go kiting after some con man, spending my time building up hope and then tearing it down again. It wasn't the card that had me going, actually. How in hell did an impostor come up with that marmoset-skin bag?"

"It no doubt belonged to the real David Littlepage. As I said, the family knew him well. He visited back and forth all the time, he no doubt had his own room or the use of a guest room at Filippo's house. He could have left belongings there."

Staring blindly out the window, she nodded, then, aware he couldn't see the nod, said, "Yes, Rog. That's probably true."

"Do you want me to get hold of the Beardsleys?"

"If you can have someone do that, still keeping me out of it, yes. If I tell them, they'll think it's my fault that he wasn't real."

"Illogical, dear. But true. Killing the messenger, I think it's called. You can get the details from the stuff I'm faxing you, and I'll talk to you again soon."

She dressed and headed down the corridor to the kitchen, hearing the fax machine in full whine as she passed the library door. Much of the time it lived in a closed cupboard, disconnected. She never admitted to the guests that she had one. If they knew, she'd spend half her time running back and forth with faxes. This one's real-estate deal, and that one's edited copy for the ad campaign, and this one's article for the medical journal,

203

and that one's something else. If they needed a fax that bad, let them bring their own or go stay at the Hilton.

J.Q. looked up as she entered. "I heard the phone."

"Roger," she told him. "With news." She poured coffee while giving him a brief recap. "He's faxing me all the stuff. I heard the machine screeching at me when I came past."

He handed her the milk and poured coffee for himself. "If some member or minion of the Luccio family was pretending to be David Littlepage, what were they looking for?"

She shrugged. "What we've always assumed they were looking for: money or something even more valuable. Alan's father must be associated with Filippo Luccio in some capacity, working for him or for the casino. If he's responsible for the money, and if his son took a good chunk of it, that would leave him in a very bad position. If he has access to records, and Alan took incriminating records . . . Well, if that's so, Alan's father may be quite desperate to get them back."

J.Q. fetched his paper from the counter. "From reading that diary, I don't get the picture of Alan as the son of a casino employee." He unfolded the paper on the table, ready for the morning-ritual read while Shirley did the crossword in the Santa Fe paper.

"I'm not talking about a croupier, J.Q. I'm talking about someone at least at the managerial level." She stared into her cup. "Remember that Alan went to private school, which has to have been expensive. He had an expensive car even before he stole the money. Salome was shown a picture of it. I don't understand the bit about money laundering, which is what Filippo went to jail for. How do you launder money at a casino?"

204

He glanced up from the headlines. "If you made a deal with the management, you could give the casino stacks of money under the table. Then you could win that money back, right out in public. When the IRS came looking you'd say. 'Hey, this money? I won this at the casino.' "

She thought about it. "The dealers would have to be in on it, of course, and if there was a lot of money, you'd have to have a sizable team of gamblers, a lot of different winners, and they'd have to pay taxes on the winnings."

"It would be pretty cumbersome for large amounts," J.Q. admitted. "Another way, needing fewer players, would be to cook the books at the casino to show business on the books that never happened. Show people losing more than they actually did."

"You mean, bank the drug money a little at a time, as though it were casino income."

"Something like that. I suppose casino wins are accounted for, probably table by table, but so much actual cash flows through that an extra ten or twenty percent could go unnoticed. Particularly if you set it up slowly and kept the cash flow constant so there were no huge, suspicious deposits. You'd need to do a nice clean job of fudging the internal records."

"And I suppose the casino employees would get a share, for their trouble."

"Whoever was directly involved. The bookkeepers, at least."

"So if it's happening here in New Mexico, then the Indian pueblos that own the casinos are corrupt?"

"Not necessarily. I doubt very much that any of the Indian-owned casinos are actually managed by the tribes. The casinos are only a year or so old, not long enough for any of the tribespeople to have gained any real experience.

They'd have hired managers. And the managers hire auditors. And the auditors either don't see what's going on, or they do and get paid off."

"So Alan's daddy could be a manager. And Alan might have had access to some very important records."

He shook his head at her. "Anything is possible, but beware of imagination running riot. We found nothing of the kind."

"It could be in a safe-deposit box somewhere. It could be hidden here at the ranch."

"In the hayloft, no doubt. Which explains what the real David Littlepage was doing there. He whacked his nephew—for some reason yet to be determined—but before he killed Helen, he choked the location out of her, and she said she'd hidden it in the hayloft? Then when he got to the hayloft, he got shot for some reason unknown by someone we've never heard of."

She swallowed coffee. "No. That makes no sense."

"It really doesn't," he said. "None of it makes any sense at all."

She bridled. "One thing does! We've said all along those thousand-dollar bills meant Daddy was involved in something not quite licit. We've talked drugs and gambling. That part ties in."

"In. But not up. I'm afraid we can't tie it up.'

"Clarity will no doubt emerge."

"Don't count on it," said Xanthy, coming in from the patio. "Clarity often refuses to emerge. Along with sympathy, generosity, and good sense."

"You sound snappish," Shirley observed. "Like me."

"I did not sleep well. I took the magazine with David Littlepage's article in it back to my room last night, and I read the article. It was insightful and extremely well

206

written. He was a man I would like to have known. The thought of his being murdered here in our midst was very depressing."

Shirley regarded her closely. Her white hair, which inclined to wispiness, was slicked back into a schoolmarm bun, very tightly twisted. Her collar was buttoned. Her glasses, which sometimes tended to drift down her nose, were firmly in place. All unmistakable signs of irritation.

"You're annoyed," Shirley said. "Is it at our lack of progress? If it is, I have some new information."

Xanthy made a cup of tea and sat down expectantly while J.Q. ostentatiously ignored them and Shirley once again recounted Roger's story of the Luccio family.

"Well," Xanthy remarked when the tale was done. "That explains Helen's strange remarks about staying away from Nevada and needing a place Alan's father wouldn't look. Since they laid a false trail to Hawaii, they felt he would not look for them in his own backyard."

"Meaning New Mexico."

"Probably. Also, it may explain why the boy was in boarding school. I have a niece whose husband works in Las Vegas. He's a software genius, much in demand. He and my niece live in California. He goes to Las Vegas on Monday morning, and he comes back home on Friday afternoon. She tells me a lot of professional people with children live in California even though they work in Las Vegas and Reno and even Lake Tahoe. They don't like what the gambling culture does to young people. Maybe Alan's father doesn't want him exposed to that culture. Or maybe Alan had already started that school before his father followed Mr. Luccio to Albuquerque."

Shirley mused, "You know, in that diary, there was no mention of Alan's mother, or of Helen's mother or father. Just Alan's father. As though he were the only one of any importance. I wonder why Luccio moved from California to New Mexico?"

"Who says he moved?" J.Q. demanded. "Just because Luccio has a residence in this state doesn't mean he spends much time here. New Mexico has a lot of absentee landowners. Luccio could still be living in California, and Alan's father could be there with him. The boarding school could be for convenience, not conviction."

Shirley put down her cup, muttering, "We're not going to get any further with this until we know who Alan really was, and I, for one, am not going to postpone breakfast until I find out."

She did, however, call Raul Griego while her toast was making, to ask him if the corpse had been definitely identified as David Littlepage.

"That's who he is," said Raul. "His mother flew out here from Baltimore and identified him. She was listed in his wallet as the person to notify in case of accident."

"That'd be Lillian," said Shirley.

"How did you know?"

"I have some friends on the East Coast who know of the family," she said weakly.

"Well, she says she's coming out to see you. I told her about the guy pretending to be her son. I thought she had a right to know. Don't mention it to H.R. He's still refusing to tell anybody anything."

"How is he getting away with that?"

"The captain's been at a conference in Denver, and H.R.'s getting worse by the minute. I think Rena's being in the wheelchair gets to him. And I think she's staying in the wheelchair because she feels safer there."

"He won't hit a cripple?"

"Something like that. I'm not sure that's true, by the way. Or maybe not true for long. He may work up to it."

"I'm not sure either, Raul. And unless she plans on being crippled for life, it's no solution."

"That's what Lupe says."

"Did you ask her to call me?"

"I told her, but she says it's family. You know. Private."

"Death can also be family, but it's seldom private. Tell Lupe I have the number and address of a family in Colorado who would offer Rena a refuge. The woman grew up in an abusive home. She now has a little extra time and money and a couple of small guest houses, so she takes in women who are in the same position. Tell Lupe I would be happy to drive her there myself."

"That's no solution, either!"

She turned to see smoke pouring from the toaster. "Raul, think about it. My kitchen's on fire. Talk to you later."

J.Q. looked up from his paper, jumped up, and unplugged the toaster. Xanthy opened the window and turned on the exhaust fan over the stove. Allison came in and remarked, "Well, I'm glad to see we're all started on another peaceful day."

J.Q. operated on the toaster with a fork, pulling out the charred bread, which had somehow stuck below the slot and refused to be ejected. Shirley got out a frying pan and made her toast on the stove.

Xanthy said, "You were talking to Sergeant Griego about his sister-in-law?"

"I was. He says the local shelter for battered women is no good because the lieutenant knows where it is. He's right. When the police are the aggressors, it's damned hard to find a safe place to hide."

"Were you referring to Consuelo Farmer's place in Manitou Springs?"

"I was. I think it might be at least a temporary solution for Rena." She sat down with her toast and coffee. "Not that she'll take advantage of it. I think she's frozen into that wheelchair. It's her security blanket."

She turned to the crossword and plucked a pencil from the desk. Xanthy made herself a cup of tea and took a section of the morning paper. Allison joined them, bringing a banana to slice over her cereal. J.Q. jabbed his thumb, muttered an imprecation, and threw the toaster into the trash basket.

Shirley glanced in his direction and remarked, "I never liked it anyhow. It wouldn't do bagels."

The phone rang. Still muttering, J.Q. picked it up and growled, "Rancho del Valle!"

Long silence.

"Mrs. Caravel, we haven't found any earrings. We haven't found any shoes. We haven't found your business-card folder. We haven't found the coffee urn. We have found about a ton of cigarette butts. The people who put down your dance floor didn't put runners under it, and there's a large plot of burned grass. Someone pushed the screen out of the screen door in the Ditch House. The fireplace in the Frog House was full of broken glass. Two of your relatives who were staying here complained that their bathing suits were ruined by the green dye you put in the pool. We'll be charging you for draining and refilling the pool. . . ."

Long silence.

"No idea. Your daughter did not confide her honeymoon plans to us."

"Rangoon," whispered Shirley.

"Certainly," said J.Q. "We try to oblige."

He hung up with some force. "Silly woman had some guy doing a photo essay of the wedding for some magazine called *Bride*? I don't believe there is such a magazine."

"There is," said Xanthy disapprovingly.

J.Q. shook his head in disbelief. "She's frantic to get her business-card folder back because she's lost his address and can't remember his name."

"If she doesn't go away, I'm going to forget mine," Shirley growled.

Outside the door, Dog gave the annunciatory bark that meant someone was coming. They heard wheels on gravel, then the sound of a car pulling up outside the patio wall. J.Q. opened the kitchen door, waiting as a thin, graying woman came through the gate.

"I'm Lillian Littlepage," she said, "I'd like to speak to Ms. McClintock."

Shirley was right behind him. She took Lillian's hand with murmurings of sympathy and drew her into the kitchen. Allison slipped away, leaving a vacant chair at the table. Lillian sat. She accepted a cup of black coffee. Xanthy expressed her sympathy, saying she had read an article by David, so well done.

"He was talented," Lillian said, reaching into her jacket pocket for a handkerchief. "And he was a good person. And I've been afraid for him since he was a baby."

"Why?" Xanthy asked. "Was he exceptionally adventurous?"

"Not for anything *he* was," she said. "For what they were. Are."

"The family," Shirley said. "You mean Filippo Luccio."

211

"You knew?" Lillian looked at her in amazement. "How did you know?"

"A friend in Washington dug up the history for me. Sergeant Griego said he told you about the impostor."

"Yes. I couldn't imagine why . . ."

"It may have been pure coincidence. Someone was trying to gain my confidence and get access to this place. My son disappeared in Brazil, years ago. Your son had been in Brazil. Someone put those two facts together to make a story I would want to believe, just to get next to me."

"Why did anyone want to get next to you? That's the part I don't understand."

Xanthy said, "Let me tell her."

"By all means," Shirley remarked. "I'm weary of it, believe me."

While Xanthy spoke Shirley carried the dishes to the sink, put on a fresh pot of coffee, and stepped quietly out the door to say good-bye to Allison as she left for school. When she came in, she passed J.Q., who excused himself with a muttered word and went out to feed the animals. Crisply, concisely, Xanthy made her way through the tale and wound it up just as the coffeemaker hissed its final hiss.

"This boy," Lillian asked. "This boy who was murdered. He had red hair?"

"Naturally red," Shirley confirmed, bringing the pot to the table to refill their cups. "Though he'd dyed it black."

"And he was how old?"

"Sixteen, seventeen."

"I wish you had a picture," she said with a haunted expression, eyes wide and disbelieving.

"I do," Shirley commented. The box Salome had sent

212

was stashed in the pantry. She retrieved the photos and put them on the table, dealing them out like cards, one by one.

Lillian did not react to the posed pictures of Helen. When the one of Alan and Helen in the sunset was dealt, however, she cried out.

"Jaime. That's Jaime Luccio."

Shirley dropped into her chair, mouth agape. "Who?"

"Filippo's son. James." Her eyes filled and spilled over. "His mother called him Jaime. And he's dead, too. God, that family is lethal!"

Xanthy soothed. Shirley fetched water and a box of tissues. Lillian wept.

"Tell us," Shirley begged. "Please. Tell us all about it."

"You have to know about Carlo. . . ."

"Tell us about everything."

She got the words out slowly, chokingly. "God, it was such a long time ago. When I met Carlo Luccio I was only nineteen. I was working part-time in a restaurant. He ate there two or three times a week. He said I was a honey of a waitress. I said I wasn't a waitress. I was an artist in the making. He got a kick out of that. He said I made him laugh." She choked on her words, sipped at the water, and wiped her eyes before continuing.

"He . . . Carlo was so handsome. Like a god. That Mediterranean style of looks, the dark hair and eyes, the lips like something Michelangelo carved. He asked me to marry him. He introduced me to his son, Filippo. His son was a younger edition of Carlo but older than I was. Carlo was in his forties, a widower. He had money. He had a courtly charm. I didn't know he could turn it off like a water tap, and I knew nothing about his family."

"You married him," said Xanthy sympathetically.

213

"I married him. He wanted me to have a baby. I guess I wanted it, too. I don't know. I'd quit the university. I'd quit having a life of my own, even though our marriage wasn't what I'd thought it was going to be. He could talk passionately; he could stir me up, but he only made love to me . . . once in a while. Sometimes he tried, but couldn't. I was naive, a virgin when we were married, some of us still were, back then. I assumed it was because of his age. A year went by, two years, I didn't get pregnant. He'd bought this big place in Los Angeles and he was busy building a gorgeous house. He let me help with that. Actually, I did most of it. I have good taste. I bought furniture and saw to the fabrics and the carpets. I also went out a lot, I traveled, I had a lot of gorgeous clothes, I went to the best restaurants. If Carlo didn't want to go, he'd send someone with me. Sometimes one of the family wives, or a couple, or just one of his men as chauffeur. I was like . . . like the house. Something he enjoyed when he felt like it.

"We'd been married three years when he went to Italy with some of the family, a visit to the old country. Filippo and I were alone in the house. . . ." She paused, wiping her face.

Shirley nodded thoughtfully. "And he was young."

"He was young. One night we got to talking, in front of the fire, over a bottle of wine. I confided too much. I cried. He was sympathetic. He said more than he meant to. He told me his father was actually gay. He didn't call it that. People didn't, not then. What he said was, his dad was only turned on by boys, and Filippo had learned that from some old friend of the family. Carlo had had a disease. It was cured, but he was probably sterile. Filippo

214

hugged me, told me he was sorry. We had another bottle, we ended up in bed together. I got pregnant."

"What did you do?"

"It was 1952. What could I do? My period was only a few days late when Carlo came home. I got him a little high that night and seduced him into making love. It wasn't that he couldn't ever, just not often. Three weeks later I told him I was late, maybe I was pregnant. Time went by. I had David."

"Did Filippo know he was the father?"

"He probably guessed. He never said. I never said. Maybe even Carlo guessed, but he never said a word. I found out more and more about what he was into and how dangerous it was, more and more about why he did the things he did, more and more about how cruel he could be. Not to me. He never was to me.

"Carlo gave me money, an allowance. I saved most of it. When David was four, I hired someone to get proof Carlo was homosexual. When I had it, I told Carlo I wanted a separation, that I knew he didn't love me in that way and I couldn't go on living a lie. I told him I wouldn't ask for a divorce, we wouldn't have any scandal. I told him I would keep my mouth shut about his being homosexual if he let me go, let me raise David myself. In that family, in that culture, being homosexual was taboo. It wasn't just sinful, it was dishonorable, antifamily."

"He let you go."

"Yes. He was even rather kind about it. He actually told me that he'd married me to put all the rumors to rest, and since David had inherited my coloring, my hair and features, and didn't look like a Luccio, he'd just as soon the boy grew up somewhere else. I got the implication of that. He didn't suspect Filippo, but he did suspect someone. I never thought of Carlo as an evil man. He was bad, but not evil. He didn't hurt people just to hurt them. He wasn't a torturer. He was nice about our separation and he gave me quite generous child support. I went back to school, I started a career. When Carlo died, Filippo kept up the payments. Filippo helped support David until he was through college, right up until David told him we didn't need it anymore."

"Did David know Carlo?"

"Of course. He visited Carlo every now and then, usually in the summer. That was part of the deal. I didn't mind that, so long as Carlo kept him away from the business. After Carlo died, David visited Filippo. When David was just a little kid, I told him about the family, what they did for a living. It was our secret. I told him he could be fond of his father and brother and enjoy being with his father and brother, but he must never get involved in their business. I told him to disappear whenever men came to the house or whenever the family discussed anything private so he couldn't be drawn into it. I believe he kept that promise, which is what makes this all so . . . maddening."

Xanthy said, "His death may have nothing to do with the family. How did he become a travel writer?"

"David inherited some of the same talents I had. I taught him photography. He taught himself writing. I encouraged him, partly because it wasn't a talent the family could make any use of. If he'd gone into law or accounting, they'd have co-opted him. Actually, he did better at the travel stuff than I did. He traveled in places I'd have been afraid to go."

"What about James?" Xanthy asked.

Lillian leaned back in her chair, folding the tissue between her fingers. "Filippo got to be thirty, then forty, and he stayed single. I wondered sometimes if he was homosexual, too, or maybe bisexual. David said no, Filippo had lots of girlfriends, he just wasn't ready to settle down. In the mid-1970s, Filippo was convicted of laundering drug money. He went to prison. When he got out, I guess he decided he'd better have a family if he was ever going to. He'd have been fiftyish then. He picked a showgirl from the Las Vegas club, the one he'd had a share in. Arlena Delgado. Gorgeous. In her twenties. Very fiery—"

"You know her?" Shirley asked, surprised.

"No. Once I left the family, I never went back. I never talked to Filippo. I never visited Carlo. I was afraid of them, not for what they'd do to me or David, but for what they might drag us into. I know about Arlena because David took photos of her and he told me about her."

"What is she like?" Xanthy asked.

"David says she's beautiful, a bit shrewish, very passionate about things. Well, frankly, I wouldn't have thought she'd be Filippo's type, but she evidently was. David became an uncle, and James was definitely Filippo's son. Whenever David visited the family, he took photos, then he'd send marvelous portraits as gifts. Lots of photos of Arlena, lots of James. David really liked James and the two of them became buddies. No, it was more elder-brother-type stuff, or even fatherly-type stuff. Filippo was really too old when the boy came along. James used to write letters to David, and when the Web came in, he and David talked through the Web. They looked nothing alike. James had Arlena's red hair, but other than that, he grew up to look exactly like Filippo,

217

exactly like Carlo. Same eyes, nose, jawline, lips. Same ears. They could have been clones."

"Where do they live?" Shirley asked.

"After Carlo died, Filippo continued living in the house I'd helped decorate. It would have been surprising if he hadn't. It's a gorgeous house, palatial, set on fifty acres. Parts of it have been refurnished by the showgirl, not in very good taste according to David, but the landscaping is still marvelous. I could show you pictures. . . . I took hundreds of pictures of the way the landscaping developed, turning fields into lawns and gardens, looking out over the avocado groves. . . ." Her eyes were unfocused, remembering.

"What happened to Arlena?"

Lillian picked up one of the snapshots. "This is her, in the photo, fighting with Filippo. She's still married to him. David told me they fight like cats and dogs, but they've stayed married."

"James was in a boarding school?"

"According to David, Arlena insisted on it. She didn't want him around his father's associates until he was old enough to know what was going on. She didn't want him to be aware of what his father did, at least not the details. Actually, I think David may have suggested she send Jaime to private school."

"Would Filippo have large amounts of money around, in large bills?"

Lillian Littlepage's mouth twisted into a mocking smile. "As Filippo himself often asked, 'Is the pope Catholic?' "

"So it was his father's money that James stole."

"I don't know who actually *owns* the money that goes through Filippo's hands. I never wanted to know. I'm sure James stole it from his father's keeping, whoever it belonged to. It was the morals he inherited from his father that let him do it. And the scheming mind he inherited from his father that led him into this . . . whatever he was up to."

"I think it was just an elopement," said Xanthy. "Foolish, but not criminal. Not morally wrong."

"Was it also his father who killed him?" Shirley asked.

Lillian gasped. "Never. Not his father, not anyone working for his father. Filippo would *never* have hurt Jaime. James was like a prize possession. Filippo spoiled him rotten. He gave James a Mercedes convertible on his sixteenth birthday. James had charge accounts at every men's clothier on Rodeo Drive. Filippo didn't devote much time to the boy, any more than he would a painting he paid a million for or a diamond he kept in the safe-deposit box for Arlena to wear, but that was beside the point. James was *his* son. He wouldn't let anyone hurt James."

"Do the New Mexico State Police know about James?" Shirley asked.

"Not from me. They never mentioned him. They didn't tell me about him."

"Who did you talk to?"

"A lieutenant. Olson?"

"Ohlman. He didn't tell you much of anything, did he?"

"No. He just said David had been killed here. And the other officer said someone had been impersonating David."

"Could the impostor have been one of Filippo's men?"

Lillian made a helpless gesture. "I suppose, but I don't see the sense of it. I know how Filippo thinks. He would say, 'If my son took money, so let him take money. Boys will be boys. Eventually, he'll turn up, and then he and I will work it out.' "

"What if he took something more than money?"

"Like what?"

"Like records of drug money laundered for the family."

Lillian drew an astonished breath. "That would be a very dangerous thing to do."

"You mean, it would involve other . . . factions?"

"I mean Carlo and Filippo had always been minor players. Rich men, yes, but not . . . not really top echelon. When I was married to Carlo, I met some of the important men. That's what Carlo called them, important men. If Jaime took something that was incriminating to the important men, then . . . yes, someone might kill him."

"And if your son, David, got in the way?"

"Filippo wouldn't hurt David. But someone else might."

"You don't have any idea who the impostor might be? Fortyish? Thinning hair?"

Lillian shook her head. "David might have known, but I have no idea at all. As I said, I've stayed away from the family since 1956. That was over forty years ago. The person you describe probably wasn't born yet when I left."

"So you think Filippo may not even have looked for James?"

"If James took only money, I doubt very much that Filippo would have become very concerned. Filippo could replace money, and he'd feel James would show up, eventually. If James took something dangerous, however, Filippo would have tried to find him first, before someone else did. To protect him."

"There were two separate inquiries at the boardinghouse in Los Angeles. The landlady says the first ones who came included a very dignified-looking man, like a banker."

"That could have been Filippo. He could have been with any one of several men he works with. He has this entourage of accountants and lawyers. They're all totally respectable looking."

"I don't suppose you'd have a clue as to the girl's name?"

Lillian shook her head sadly. "Sorry. No. But I'm sure someone at James's school probably does. His parents might know. I'm sure David would have known. James told him everything."

Shirley moved restlessly in her chair, frustrated. "The second inquiry was the Friday before Labor Day. I called Salome—the landlady—on Monday, after we found the bodies, and she said the inquiry had been a day or two before I called. Salome said that person paid more attention to the writing on the wall by the phone than he did to the room. My guess is that the person was noting down the number of that phone so he could get records of calls. That phone was probably the one used by Helen— whatever her real name is—to make a reservation here. Would Filippo have sent that person?"

Lillian shook her head. "All I know is, Filippo would not have hurt Jaime, no matter what. He would not have hurt David, even if David discovered some imposture."

"Let's say the impostor was here, and that David confronted him."

"If the impostor worked for Filippo, David would have said, 'Filippo Luccio is my brother.' David knew what the score was with Filippo. He was on good terms with Filippo."

"Would Filippo have suggested to someone that he use David's name to get into my confidence?"

"I don't know. I suppose it's possible."

"Would anyone else have known about David's connection to the Luccio family?"

Lillian laughed. "Everyone in the family knew. In that family, you don't divorce ever and you don't separate often. Once family, always family. They're Catholics, and they regard the church as a kind of magical power plant that helps them do whatever they want. They think God is like them. He doesn't care if they kill people or steal or sell dope, just so long as they're respectful. So, they respect the Church. They obey some of its more convenient rules, like going to mass occasionally. Like no divorce. No abortion. Back in the fifties, no contraception. They're too busy to be much involved, so they depend on their women to observe all the church rituals. Having a good, pious wife is part of the observance, and they themselves make big cash contributions to church needs. The families have always dealt in what they call 'protection.' That's when a little merchant pays you money, respect, every week so your thugs won't wreck his store. In the mind of the family, paying money to the Church is exactly like buying protection. You pay your dues. You show respect. Then God overlooks your little failings. He doesn't bother you."

Shirley sighed. "I'm sorry to keep at you like this. I can't make sense out of the death of those two children, and it bothers me a good deal. Could you talk to Filippo?"

"To Filippo?"

"Yes. Will you? Will you ask him whether he used David's name and persona to get into my confidence? Will you ask him who he sent after Jaime, if anyone?"

The woman leaned on the table, face hanging over it, eyes dripping tears. "There's no reason not to talk to him. There's no more David to protect."

Xanthy said, "Shirley. You're forgetting. He doesn't even know. . . ."

Lillian stared across the table at her, gradually coming to awareness. "Of course," she said at last. "I was forgetting, too. Filippo doesn't know his son is dead. That either of his sons is dead."

Though they talked about it a big longer, Lillian said she was the best person to inform Filippo Luccio about both David and James. David had given her the phone numbers of both Filippo's houses, and she would call him from her hotel, when she'd had a little time to get herself together.

J.Q., who had been silent during their conversation, asked if she'd like him to drive her to her hotel.

"No. I like to drive. It relaxes me."

"Be careful," he urged her.

"If I can drive in Mexico, I can drive here," she said with a wan smile. "Mexican men drive like they're bullfighting. You get points for how close you can miss the other guy."

She turned to Shirley and Xanthy. "When I've talked to Filippo, I'll let you know what he says. I can tell you right now that Arlena is going to fall apart. She is . . . was devoted to James. He was the center of her life."

Shirley, looking at her visitor's haunted eyes, believed Lillian had also lost the center of her life. She hadn't mentioned that David was married or had children. She would have, if they'd existed. David was probably all she had.

223

J.Q. escorted Lillian to her car. She shook hands with him before driving away, and when he came in, Shirley was on the phone in the library. She needed to let Roger know what had happened.

At the end of her story, Roger said, "Don't get involved, Shirley."

"I'm already involved."

"You know what I mean. Do not get involved in trying to find out anything at all about the Luccio family. If someone in that family killed David Littlepage and this boy, James, you may be assured that person will pay for it. If someone outside the family did it, the Luccios will find out. I want you to back off this thing. Don't talk to anyone about it."

"Lillian said she'd let me know what Filippo had to say."

"Listen, but don't ask. I'm serious. When you interfere in a family matter, you could get hurt."

"The boy wasn't killed by the family," she said, unaware until she said it that she'd already thought it out.

"How can you say—"

"He wasn't, Rog! Bet you anything you like. People were looking for those kids the day after they disappeared. Twice, people called here asking for Jaime Yukio, which is what Allison and I both heard. We thought it was Japanese. Whoever it was was asking for Jaime Luccio, and she told them no such person was here. Nobody came here looking for them. If anyone went looking for them, they went to Hawaii. We got the calls because some lodging places in and around Sante Fe were checked in red in the tourist guide the kids left in the boardinghouse room.

"But nobody came here looking for them before they

died. The kids were killed on Sunday. The preceding Friday, late in the afternoon, somebody went to the rooming house in Los Angeles and looked at the phone in the hall to get its number. That was, I believe, so the calls on that phone could be accessed. Luccio no doubt has a contact at the phone company."

"Where are you going with this, Shirley?"

"My point is, it was Friday afternoon, before Labor Day weekend. The kids were killed on Sunday. There wasn't any time! The phone-company offices would have been closed on the weekend."

He made a tsking sound. "Doesn't hold water, Shirley. All telephone information is on computer. I'm sure the Luccios have a pet hacker somewhere who can get that kind of information or any kind of information, day or night, weekend or no weekend, holiday or no holiday. If they're into gambling, they need ready access to people's financial history, their personal history. That's probably how they got to you!"

"All right, Rog, but look at what happened. The kids get killed on Sunday, but people are still looking for them! The fake Littlepage was looking for them, or what they had—"

"Maybe he killed them before they could tell where they hid whatever they had."

"And why would he do that? If his job is to find X and bring it back, he doesn't slam a shovel into the head of the only person who knows where X is. My point is, Roger, that the phony Littlepage wasn't sure this is where James/Alan was staying. He wanted to get into the houses so he could see where they were staying."

"How could he tell?"

"Well, he probably had certain things to look for, but

225

also any space occupied by those two for more than five minutes would be unmistakable! Who would know that better than the kid's family! Even if all Filippo's minions were looking for the kid, at the time of the killing none of them knew for sure where the kid was. Moreover, up until I told Lillian, none of the people trying to find him knew he was dead."

"You want me to identify the kid for the police?"

"Thank you, but no. If Lillian doesn't, I will. The bastard lieutenant can't accuse me of intruding on police business when I learned about it. I was commiserating with a mother who lost her son."

She put in a call to the state police. Griego called her back within moments, and she told him the young couple had been identified, at least the young man had. Knowing who he was, probably they could find out who she was.

"James Luccio," he mused. "Next of kin is this Filippo Luccio guy?"

"His father, and he has a place in Albuquerque. Lillian Littlepage is already letting him know. She was at one time Filippo's stepmother. David was his half brother. James was his son."

"Ohlman is going to think this is some kind of mob war, with us in the middle."

"Well, he's paranoid."

"You're probably right. Listen, Shirley, about this place in Colorado? I talked to Rena again."

"You want me to make arrangements?"

"I think Rena's going to call you."

"I trust not from home with her husband there."

"No. No, I think she has better sense than that. Not much better, but some. She'll call from a pay phone, when she goes grocery shopping."

"I'll be glad to help when she does."

He muttered something, then asked, "You think he'll come here? Luccio?"

Shirley thought about it, but only briefly. "I can't see why. The bodies are in Albuquerque. I would assume he'll bother the state police down there."

An assumption in which she was very much mistaken.

7

Janice Beardsley called about one o'clock that afternoon. She had heard from someone who had told her the score about David Littlepage. She was newly contrite, though still weeping.

"You must think I'm a fool," she confessed, sniveling.

"No," Shirley admitted. "I wanted to believe it, too."

"But you didn't believe it."

"Let's say I delayed belief."

"The man who called me from Washington said the writer is dead."

"The real David Littlepage? Yes. They found his body here. Sunday. Two days ago."

"If I hadn't looked him up, if I hadn't called him, if I hadn't sent him all that stuff, he wouldn't have gotten involved."

This was quite true. Shirley thought about lying,

soothing, temporizing. She did none of them. "He might not have."

"He wouldn't have been shot," she howled, determined upon guilt.

"You don't know that, Janice. You're leaping to conclusions, again. We don't know why he was shot."

"He was shot because he ran into the man pretending to be him!"

"Why would the man shoot him? Pretending to be someone else isn't against the law. A little pretense is hardly worth a murder. If it were, there'd soon be no media people left."

Janice gulped, a swallowed, half-hysterical giggle. "Will you let me know when they find out? I feel so guilty."

"You know, Janice, at our age, we need to quit feeling so responsible for everything else that goes on. Let the younger people be responsible. We've earned a little irresponsibility."

Another drowned giggle. "You will, though, won't you?"

"Sure, Janice. I'll let you know."

J.Q. brought in the mail. "There's a car parked in the field where all the wedding guests were parked!"

"A leftover car? How come we didn't see it yesterday after everyone left?"

"You didn't go out all day, and I only went to the mailbox. We'd have seen it if we'd driven out. It's a green car, parked behind a cottonwood. I wouldn't have seen it today, except the sun sparkled off the windshield. I suppose somebody could have put it there this morning."

She considered cars left in foreign fields. "Littlepage

had to get here somehow. Nobody's asked how he got out here on Saturday. Or Sunday. Whichever."

"I didn't go close enough to look at it."

"Let's do," she said urgently. "It's not a crime scene. He wasn't killed there."

His expression was doubtful, but he didn't protest. They got into the Jeep and went down the drive to its intersection with the paved road, then down that road to the field in which the wedding guests had parked. The field was small, only a couple of acres, outlined by fence on three sides, and on the fourth side by cottonwoods along the acequia that separated the little field from the rest of the property. The only use Shirley and J.Q. had made of the area was to let Beauregard and the other horses graze there from time to time and for overflow parking.

The car wasn't particularly obvious until the wind ruffled a branch and the sun poked through to glint from the windshield. Shirley got out and opened the gate. J.Q. drove through. She left the gate open and got back into the Jeep. They bumped along over the rocky ground.

"You know," she said, "we didn't look out here for things like earrings and business-card folders."

"I'll suggest it to Mrs. Caravel next time she calls." He pulled up next to the other car. They got out and walked around the boxy vehicle, careful not to touch it.

Shirley fished out a handkerchief and used it to try the doors. Locked. Inside on the backseat lay various camera cases and boxes of film, several file folders, and a short stack of books. The front seat held two pairs of sunglasses and several hats of various types, both narrow-and wide-brimmed. A set of bright stickers on the back

230

bumper said, OMAHA, PARIS, PONAPE, DZIBILCHALTÚN, BETELGEUSE.

"Funny man," she observed. "This is definitely David's car."

"He was here early on Saturday, then. Before the wedding. The first cars that came parked straight across, and by two-thirty or three, that row would have been blocked in."

Shirley sighed. "We know he found out about the impersonation through Janice Beardsley. He called her last Wednesday, after which he probably decided to come out here and find out what was going on. Do you think he realized his family was part of the situation?"

"No idea."

"This car has New Mexico plates, and with all those stickers, it's obviously not a rental. It may be David's car, which he keeps at Filippo's place. David may have known his family was involved in this. I mentioned dead newlyweds to Janice, and she mentioned dead newlyweds to David. He may have had a hunch they were involved, but he wanted to find out first, before he upset anyone down in Albuquerque."

"If he knew James and his girlfriend were married."

"According to Lillian, David would have known if anyone knew. Why don't you call Ohlman and tell him about this car. Ohlman isn't mad at you."

"Why is he mad at you?"

"In case you hadn't noticed, he doesn't like women. Raul says it's because I find stuff out. The lieutenant would regard that as trespassing on his territory."

"Are you going to get Rena to safety?"

"I told Raul I'd help. If Rena calls me. She has to want to. I'm not into kidnapping."

"I can drive her to Consuelo's," he said, almost unwillingly.

Shirley shook her head. "So far as that goes, we can put her on the bus, J.Q. Consuelo would be glad to pick her up at the bus station."

"In a wheelchair?"

"Rena can walk. She's just not going to."

"I can't understand that mind-set. She knows he's dangerous. She knows he's going to hurt her again. But she's just frozen."

"When abuse goes on long enough, that's how people get. The sensible time to act is the first time it happens, but if people behaved sensibly, what would the soap operas do for plots? Ninety percent of what passes for plot in melodrama and movies and opera comes about because someone doesn't act. Doesn't tell anybody. Doesn't admit anything. Doesn't go anywhere. If the characters acted decisively and sensibly, the plot would be over in half an hour."

"Well, Griego did say Ohlman had found her once before when she tried to get away."

"She went to the most obvious place she could! Her mother's. Good Lord, if I had to hide, I'd figure out someplace nobody would ever, ever look for me."

"Like where?"

"Ponape. Dzilbilchaltún. Betelgeuse."

"Where on earth is Dzilbilchaltún?"

"In the Yucatán," she said shortly. "One of the lesser-known archaeological sites. I've been there."

He kept a straight face. "And Betelgeuse?"

"Haven't been there yet."

He laughed and climbed back into the car. She waved him off.

"Let me look around out here awhile, J.Q. Maybe I'll find a clue."

She began to cover the ground as he drove away, setting a track parallel to the ditch, about ten feet from it. The pasture had been mowed to accommodate the parking, so there were no large clumps of grass or herbage to hide anything. Within the first few crossings she'd found a bracelet, a pair of glasses, and a new, unopened package of condoms. Perhaps intended as a joke gift for the groom.

No earrings. No shoes. She stopped momentarily to admire two horses playing in a neighboring field, challenging one another, then running away with their tails high. Lovely animals. She went back to her search of the ground. Another pair of glasses, this one smashed to fragments. And then, almost at the gate, a small shiny leather wallet with the word *Caravel* in gilt lettering. Mrs. Caravel's business-card folder. How did it get out here?

She picked it up, then looked up as a long, black car came easing along the road and drew up at the open gate. People wanting directions, perhaps. She dropped the folder in the same pocket as the other found objects and went toward the car. The passenger window opened and a vulpine face stared out at her. "Can I help you?" she asked.

"You McClintock?" asked the man in the front seat.

"Yes," she said warily. "I'm Shirley McClintock."

The back car door nearest her opened. A tall, bulky man unfolded from the backseat. She turned toward him politely.

"Get in," he said.

She backed up. He stepped forward, so quickly it

233

seemed almost superhuman, and fastened a hand on her upper arm.

"Get in," he repeated, pushing her toward the car.

"What is this?" she cried. "Who are you looking for?"

"Mr. Luccio wants to see you," the fox-faced one said. "Get in."

She got in, thrust from behind, to find herself confronting Lillian Littlepage, who was squeezed into the far corner of the backseat, red-eyed, pallid-faced.

"Lillian," Shirley said. "What is this?"

"It's Filippo," she responded in a husky murmur. "I told him, over the phone. He said he was coming, but instead he sent these people! He couldn't understand what I was telling him."

"Nobody's going to get hurt," said the big man, crushing into the backseat next to them. "Mr. Luccio just wants to talk to you."

"He could have called," Shirley snapped. "I'd have been happy to talk to him."

"Mr. Luccio, he don't like the phone," said the man in the front seat.

Fox, Shirley thought. The man in the front seat was a fox, the one in the back was a bear. Plus the driver, who looked a little like a weasel. All predators, that was for sure. She eased herself away from the heavy thigh against hers, moving toward Lillian. As the car pulled away she got a glimpse of J.Q.'s astonished face. He was standing at the mailbox. He had probably seen the whole thing. Silently, Shirley urged him to get the license number and call Roger. Not Ohlman. Roger.

The car eased down the side road, not spinning wheels, not making a spectacle of itself. It turned toward the highway, reached it, and came abruptly up to the speed limit. Just to the speed limit, Shirley noted. As usual, half the traffic was going at least ten miles an hour above.

"I tried to explain to him that you didn't know anything about it," Lillian murmured from beside her. "He was all right when I told him about David. I mean, he was sorry, he cried, but he was all right. Then . . . I told him about James. . . ."

"What did he say?"

Lillian almost whispered. "He didn't. His voice got . . . strange. Then he told me to stay there, at the hotel, that he was coming to see me. But it wasn't him. It was these three men. They asked about you, I told them who you are, where you live. I didn't realize what they were planning—"

"Nobody's going to get hurt," the big man said again, in a slightly offended voice. "You don't need to get all bent out of shape. The boss just wants to find out what happened to his boy."

They were speeding toward Santa Fe. There was no way to go around it.

"You're taking us to Albuquerque?" Shirley asked.

"To Mr. Luccio's place," the big man confirmed. He was more bearlike with every moment. His very voice was furry. "It's outside the city a way."

"You realize my manager saw you pick me up? He got the license number of the car. He's probably reporting a kidnapping right now."

The big man moved uncomfortably. "Mr. Luccio says bring you. We're going to bring you, that's all. That's no kidnap! Nobody said nothing about ransom or hurting nobody." He sounded quite outraged, as though his honor had been questioned.

Shirley sat back, took a deep breath, and settled herself.

If she was in for a trip lasting at least an hour and a half, no point in driving herself crazy during it. "You know my name," she said. "How about introducing yourselves."

"That's Juice," said the big man, pointing to the driver.

"Giuseppe," said the driver. "Call me Joe." He indicated the man beside him. "He's Ben."

"And you?" Shirley asked her seatmate, who was unaccountably scowling at the driver's back.

"I'm Joe. He's Giuseppe. That's why we call him Juice, so we don't get us mixed up."

"And all three of you work for Mr. Luccio? Here in New Mexico?"

"Juice and me, we live on the place," said the fox. "We take care of the cars and the grounds and see the pool people do their job and the house people do theirs, and if there's guests or Mrs. Luccio is there, we see they get chauffeured around. Joe, he moves around with Mr. Luccio."

"Did you by chance go to a boardinghouse in Los Angeles, looking for Mr. Luccio's son?"

The fox regarded her blankly. "I din' look for him. Mr. Luccio, he looked for him. Kid left him a note sayin' he's gone to Hawaii."

The man beside her spoke again. "The kid left his dad a note about Hawaii, so the old man hires some guy that specializes in finding people? You know? Like guys that skip on bail?"

"A skip tracer," Shirley offered.

"Right. So this skip tracer starts lookin' at phone bills. And he finds all these calls back and forth, back and forth from the kid's school to this place in L.A., so they go lookin' for the place."

"The boardinghouse."

"That's what I hear between him and her."

"Between Mr. and Mrs. Luccio?"

"Right. They fight a lot, so I hear a lot. Hell, everybody hears a lot."

"You got a mouth on you," muttered the driver. "Oughta keep it shut."

Joe said calmly, "Listen, Luccio just wants to know what happened to his kid! The more the . . . the lady knows, the better she can tell him."

He turned to Shirley once more. "Anyhow, Mr. Luccio, he goes with this skip-tracer guy, they find a lot of stuff in the place, only it's the girl's place, and it looks like he's run off with this girl and Hawaii's prob'ly not the right place. There's stuff in the room makes them think maybe the kid and the girl are in New Mexico."

"Did someone phone my place to ask about them?" Shirley demanded.

"That'd be the lawyer. Browne hyphen Murch," said Ben.

"Bastard," murmured Big Joe.

"You don't like him," Shirley observed.

"Son-of-a-bitch," opined Big Joe.

"Anyhow, he don't get anyplace," Ben continued. "Because you said the kid wasn't there."

"What we said was, there was nobody there named Jaime Yukio," Shirley said angrily.

"Yukio!" Ben sniggered. "Like he's a what's-it. Can't call 'em what we used to call 'em. Now they're Asian."

Shirley said stubbornly, "Yukio is the way we heard it. The boy who was killed called himself Alan Jones. His driver's license said he was Jones."

"Told you you shouldn't'ta talked in fronta that kid,"

Big Joe said to Ben. "Told you not to go shooting your mouth."

"Telling him what?" asked Lillian, fascinated despite herself.

"Where to get fake IDs, driver's licenses, all that stuff," said Big Joe. "With Jaime sittin' there swallowin' it all down. I told Ben the kid's mom would nooter him. Cut him right off. She didn't want Jaime knowing any of that stuff."

"Didn't want him hangin' around us," said the driver. "She made that real clear."

"Is that what you called him?" Shirley asked. "Jaime?"

"It's what his ma called him," the fox agreed. "Mr. Luccio, he calls him James."

"So none of you ever searched the boardinghouse?" Shirley persisted.

"Just Mr. Luccio and the skip guy and Browne hyphen Murch," said Big Joe.

"You all know Browne-Murch?" Shirley asked.

"If the boss is someplace, the hyphen is there, too," said Ben. "I think they both sleep with the missus. Or maybe all three of 'em, includin' the accountant."

"Don't say that where anybody can hear you," Giuseppe offered. "Unless you want to end up dead."

"It was the lawyer who went to the boardinghouse a week ago last Friday or Saturday?" Shirley demanded.

"That was him." Big Joe nodded ponderously at her. "I drove him. The skip-tracer guy was out here in Santa Fe, and he called the boss and told him to get the phone number where the girl called from."

"The pay phone."

"That's the only one there. I'da got her a cellular, if it was me."

"Alan ... James didn't have the money to do that," Shirley mused. "Not when they moved the girl into the boardinghouse."

She fell silent, thinking it over. So far it was pretty much as she'd thought, and thus of little or no help. Luccio was going to want to know who killed his son, and she hadn't a clue. It didn't seem that it was any of Luccio's men, certainly not Luccio himself. So who?

"It doesn't make any sense, does it?" Lillian asked plaintively.

"Not to me it doesn't," Shirley agreed.

"That's what the boss says," opined Big Joe. "Him and the missus both."

The rest of the journey was quiet. Big Joe leaned his head back and went to sleep, breathing heavily. Ben took a book from the glove compartment and buried himself in it. Giuseppe drove, humming to himself at intervals.

They did not go into Albuquerque. Well before reaching the city, they turned off toward the Sandias and began climbing. Almost two hours after Shirley's abduction, they turned into a long, paved drive that wound among groves of large trees and stretches of bluegrass lawn that didn't belong in New Mexico. The house was like a jewel in this setting, white stucco with red tile, fronted by a seven-tiered Spanish fountain set in a stone-rimmed lily pond among topiary evergreens.

"Nice," said Lillian, almost humorously. "Almost an exact copy of the east garden I designed for Carlo in Los Angeles, and totally inappropriate for this setting."

The men conferred while Lillian and Shirley stretched their legs.

"He's into vistas, isn't he?" Shirley commented, looking down over the valley toward the city.

"His father was, too. Carlo kept adding ground to the place in Los Angeles. I think he more than doubled the size of it in the forties."

"What's this place, about three acres?"

Lillian looked around. "Looks like he's got three acres landscaped. Knowing the family, he could own a lot more, and there's probably an eight-foot fence around it."

Joe gestured at them, and they followed him through planked double doors fastened with huge ornamental iron *clavos*, down a long tiled hallway, and through an arch into a library. Oak shelves and leather bindings, Oriental carpets, furniture upholstered in leather.

The man behind the desk could have been upholstered in leather, for he did not look like a living man. Deep-set eyes, dull as carved wood. Skin of that distinctive yellow brown that betokens illness among olive-skinned people. The color of corruption, Shirley thought, wondering where the thought came from.

Lillian went past her, directly to the desk, to lean upon it. "Filippo, what is this? Why have you done this?"

"Sit down," said a red-haired woman who came forward out of the shadows. "Please, do sit down. I'm sure Filippo meant no disrespect."

The words were polite, but the voice was cold. Looking at the two of them, Shirley's first thought was that it had been Arlena—for this was certainly Arlena—who had dispatched the muscle trio to pick them up. She decided to get out of the line of fire, moving aside to half hide herself in a huge leather wingback chair.

The man at the desk grunted. It seemed to take a great deal of effort for him to form words. "You." He pointed at Shirley. "Tell us what happened."

240

Good Lord. Shirley moistened her mouth, swallowed deeply, and focused on keeping it brief.

"Last June a person called our place and made a reservation for the end of August and early September. She gave us the names Helen Buscovitch and Alan Jones. She sent a money order for the deposit, and it arrived a week later. The address she gave us was in Los Angeles. Later I learned it was a boardinghouse. The phone number Helen gave us was the number at the boardinghouse.

"They arrived at our place in an expensive little red car on Tuesday before Labor Day weekend. They said they were newlyweds. They did some sightseeing. They did some shopping. On the Sunday before Labor Day, they went on a trail ride from Silver Saddle Stables, up into the Pecos Mountains. They wanted to plant a tree while on the trail ride, and they borrowed a spade from me. The spade was a special kind, a birthday present.

"They didn't come back from the trail ride. They left all their things in the house. I called the owner of the stables. He said he thought they'd left, but their car was still at his place. I was worried about them, plus, I wanted my birthday present back. My assistant and I rode up the trail, looking for them. We found my spade halfway down a hill, so we searched the area and found their bodies. We called the state police. So far as any of us knew, their names were Helen Buscovitch and Alan Jones; they were twenty-one and twenty-two years old; she was a blonde and he was dark-haired. That's what their driver's licenses said.

"Later the police found out the driver's licenses were phony and that the young people were only teenagers who had dyed their hair. He was actually a redhead, she was dark."

241

She sat back in the chair. Silence.

Arlena Luccio spoke from behind her. "What was this business about the tree?"

Shirley looked at the man behind the desk. "It was a sentimental thing. They wanted to memorialize their honeymoon. They wanted to come back every year and visit their tree."

" 'Which would grow, as their love would grow,' " said Arlena, obviously quoting. "My son. He wrote poetry. He wrote that and left it for me. All about a girl and a tree."

"They died where they planted this tree?" the man croaked.

"Where they started to plant it, yes," Shirley answered. "I think they were killed before the tree was planted and some animal may have carried it away."

"How did David get mixed up in this?" Lillian demanded.

"My fault," the man muttered. "I thought David was in Japan. I told Mitchell to use his name. David had some stuff from Brazil in his room, his notebooks, some souvenirs. Mitchell took one of David's notebooks and some of the stuff. He called the Beardsley woman from here, saying he was in Washington."

Shirley asked, "Mitchell was the skip tracer you hired to find James?"

He nodded, turning his head to stare out the window. The light showed the glossy channels where tears had dried on his cheeks. "My lawyer works with a computer man, a hacker. He can find out anything about anybody. We wanted to find James quickly. . . ." A spasm racked his neck and face, and he fumbled in his breast pocket for a pill bottle, slipping a tablet into his mouth, reaching

242

for the glass on the desk, swallowing the tablet with difficulty.

"I assume," Shirley said, "that James took something belonging to you. Something you needed to get back without making a . . . big stir about it."

Arlena laughed, a short, barking noise. "Oh, no, we didn't want any stir. If the wrong people found out, James might have been killed."

Abruptly she broke into tears and left the room.

"Who knew my boy was going on this ride?" asked the man behind the desk. "Besides you?"

"I didn't know until ten minutes before they left, when your son asked to borrow the spade. My assistant was with me, and he was with me all day. Your son made the arrangements by phone. The police searched the house they had lived in. I think if there'd been any kind of tap on the phone, they'd have found it."

Actually, she wasn't at all sure of this and reminded herself to look into it when . . . if she got home herself.

"You believe James met his killer by accident?"

The pain in his voice was only partly grief. With sudden perception, Shirley knew that his illness was deadly. The man was dying.

"You believe it was random?" He leaned back, rolling the pill bottle in his palm like a worry stone.

What could she tell him? "Mr. Luccio, I don't believe anything. I don't know anything. The two children were the last people in the world to be killed for any reason. They weren't shot by accident, she wasn't raped, he wasn't robbed. That's three major reasons for violence right out the window. We did find money in the house, after the police had searched it. The money was hidden in a lamp."

243

"How much?"

"He had about sixty-five thousand when he died."

"He took a hundred sixty."

"Well, he bought a car. And they spent quite a bit in Los Angeles and Santa Fe."

"I could have made that much up. Nobody had to know. You think he had a good time." The words came out one by one, milked reluctantly from some reservoir of agony.

It was a statement, not a question, but she agreed. "I'd say so, yes. He was having a good time. A very romantic time."

"That's good. If it's got to happen, better it happens when there's happiness. Not like this, all the happiness gone."

Lillian said, almost in a whisper, "It wasn't your fault, Filippo."

"Ah, Lily, then whose fault was it? David, he was mine, too. You think I didn't know that? He made me proud. He was a good son to you. Even to me, and he didn't know I was his father. Somehow, me being his father, that got him killed. Me using his name, letting that weasel use it. I don't know how *they* found him, but they did."

Shirley asked, "You think *they* killed James and his girlfriend, whatever her real name was—"

"Nita. Nita Morella. I knew all about her. I didn't want him to marry her. The family is no good. The mother is a whore, a gambler, running off and leaving her children. She spends half her time with her sister, and the sister's no good. And he was too young—"

Shirley went on as though there had been no interruption, "And you think *they* also killed David?"

244

"I'll find out," he said, pushing himself erect, using both arms and struggling to get there. "I still have a little time. I'll find out."

He pressed a buzzer on his desk. The door opened and Joe came in.

"Take them home," Luccio said. He dropped into his chair once more, temporary strength spent. "My apologies for bringing you here like that. These days . . . I don't have time to wait for later."

He was still sitting there when they went out, through the hallway and out the huge doors into the sun once more.

"He's dying, isn't he?" Shirley whispered.

"Yeah," said Joe, looking guiltily around himself. "Some kinda cancer. It's all through him. The kid . . . he didn't even know."

"James didn't know?"

"Mr. Luccio, he didn't want him to know."

"Did you know David?"

"Mr. Luccio's brother? Sure."

"Did he know Mr. Luccio was dying?"

"He knew. Mrs. Luccio told him. The people who work for Filippo close, all of us, we knew. Yeah. When we came out last week, and David was here, that was a real surprise. He came to be with his brother awhile."

Lillian spoke. "The Luccios came here from Los Angeles last week? And David was already here?"

"Tuesday, Wednesday a week ago, the skip guy calls Mr. Luccio and says he thinks James is out here around Santa Fe somewhere. Thursday we got to the house here, and here was David. He was supposed to be in Japan for a month, but some VIP got sick and the whole thing got canceled."

"When did David leave here?" Shirley asked.

"The next day. Early Friday. He said he had a story to do in Santa Fe, but he'd be back by Sunday."

Seeking out the false Littlepage, no doubt. And seeking two newlyweds, who might be family. Seeking them where Janice's communications had indicated they might be found, at Shirley's. Probably unaware that Filippo had sent the false Littlepage in the first place.

Joe helped them into the backseat of the black car, then took his place as driver. Though it had taken three to bring them, evidently one man was considered enough to take them home.

Lillian expressed Shirley's feelings exactly when she said, "Lord, what a tangle."

"Where's Mitchell?" Shirley asked suddenly. "The skip tracer."

"Mr. Luccio wants to know that, too," said Joe. "We haven't seen him since Friday, around noon."

Shirley thought silently for some miles. "Joe," she murmured, "were you there Friday, when Mr. Luccio talked to Mitchell?"

"Me? Sure. I'm usually around. I can keep my mouth shut when I need to. Mr. Luccio knows that."

"Did Mr. Luccio talk about what was missing?"

"You mean the money? Sure. He mentioned it."

"What about something besides money?"

"That the kid took, you mean?"

"Right."

Joe ruminated, rumbling in his throat. "You know, I couldn't quite figure that. Mr. Luccio, he says he's not too worried about the money, but he says he has to get to the kid by the twelfth of September because he's got to have the information back by then. I mean, that kind of gives you a hint, doesn't it?"

"A hint that it isn't the money that's important?" Shirley offered.

"Right. The kid took information. That's what? Like a computer disk? Like a book? And what's happening on the twelfth of September?"

"That's just three days from now, Friday. A meeting maybe," suggested Lillian. "When some record might need to be produced?"

He shrugged massively. "You got me, ma'am."

Shirley and Lillian looked at one another, then settled into opposite corners.

"You want to call your place?" Joe offered, catching Shirley's eyes in the rearview mirror.

"You have a cellular?"

"Sure. Maybe your friend didn't call out the cops yet."

Shirley called the ranch. J.Q. answered, then immediately cut her off: "Valley Vet? Yes, I did call. May I talk to the doctor."

Shirley dropped her voice to a whisper. "You okay, J.Q.?"

"Doctor, that ram you were worried about finally did it," he said. "Ruptured his brain, I think, banging his head on posts because he couldn't get to the ewes."

"Right," she said automatically, brain running frantic circles. "What's his condition now?"

"He's very agitated, like he's having fits."

Shirley couldn't think of anything to say.

J.Q. had no such problem. "You can't come until this evening? Fine. Call first, his condition may change."

She clicked off the phone. The ram ... would be Ohlman. He couldn't get to the ewes. Which meant Rena had been taken somewhere by someone. And J.Q. was in no hurry for her to come home. She felt sweat beading along her brow and reached into her pocket for a tissue. She came out with Mrs. Caravel's folder, which dropped onto her knee, open. She stared at it for a long moment, put it back in her pocket, and clicked the phone again. Information.

"The home of Raul Griego, in Nambe." They gave her the number and she called it.

"Lupe? Listen, this is Shirley McClintock. Is your sister all right?"

Long burble, full of excitement.

"When did J.Q. make the arrangements? I see. And you put her on the bus? Right. Would you see if you can reach Raul, please, and if you get him, tell him I think H.R. is at my place, probably blaming me for Rena's being gone and maybe holding Mr. Quentin hostage."

Agitation at the far end.

"I have no idea how he would have found out. Maybe Rena herself said something to him. Maybe she left him a note. I may need help with him."

Another burble.

"I hadn't thought of that. I'll call you back."

Lillian murmured in an exhausted voice, "More trouble?"

"In a manner of speaking. The police lieutenant in charge of investigating the deaths happens to be a Paleolithic type who takes his frustrations out on his wife. I mentioned to her sister that I had a friend in Colorado who would give her sanctuary, and evidently today was the day. She must have called for me, J.Q. took the call and made the arrangements, and her sister put her on the bus. The caveman has since found out she's gone. The sister's husband works with him. She mentions that her husband, brother-in-law of the abusee, may be with his

248

boss at the moment, in which case, he's in no position to intervene."

"Hey," said Joe. "You want somebody to intervene, that's me. Nothin' I like better'n doing some cop."

"You've been very civil," Shirley said. "I wouldn't want to get you in trouble."

"Hey, if this guy is violent, I wouldn't get in no trouble. Make Browne hyphen Murch do a little work for a change." He adjusted the rearview mirror to see her face once more and smiled at her. "Besides, you'd be a witness, right?"

They dropped Lillian off at her hotel in Santa Fe. Shirley told her she would call when things were straightened out at home. Then Shirley, now in the front seat beside Joe, rode the last few miles while frantically trying to come up with a plan.

"How long does Mr. Luccio have, you think?" she asked.

"Not long. Some other guy, he's taking over. Mr. Luccio, he's transferring the business—" He stopped talking.

"When?" Shirley asked.

He stared out the window, answering only reluctantly. "The end of the week. You think that's what's happening September twelfth?"

"James took some records or something like records," said Shirley. "He wanted to marry that girl, and he didn't want his father to stop him. My hunch is, he used the records to blackmail his father into letting them go."

"Didn't he know what'd happen?"

"Didn't he know? Of course he didn't, Joe. He didn't know his father was dying. You said so yourself. He probably thought that once he and the girl were married and the honeymoon was over, he'd bring it back."

"So now Mr. Luccio's so sick, and these VIPs coming to this meeting and it's gonna hit the fan. Anybody smart's gonna be somewhere else."

They swung from the highway into the two-lane county road that led past Rancho del Valle. Shirley took a deep breath.

"Let's go past, Joe. There's a place a little way down the road where I can see the driveway next to the house."

They drove past and parked while Shirley walked down the arroyo bank to a place where the trees gapped, letting her see the parking area. One police car. She got back in the big black car and asked for the phone once more.

"Lupe? It's Shirley. Did you get hold of Raul?"

Long hushed explanation.

"Right," Shirley said dispiritedly, hanging up.

"So what?" Joe asked.

"So, Raul is down there with his boss, and both of them are with my friend J.Q. I think I am the villain in the piece, the one the lieutenant wants to slaughter."

"So? Whadda we do?"

She thought, trying to visualize what was going on. They were probably in the kitchen-cum-office. H.R. was probably holding a gun on the other two, if he hadn't already killed somebody.

"Maybe we can get you into the room with them, behind him. That'd be good, get you behind him. In case they're looking out the window, I'll crouch down in the backseat. You drive up, park, go knock on the door. J.Q. comes to the door—"

"J.Q. the guy standing there when we picked you up?"

250

"Right. The bad guy is almost a skinhead, his hair is so short."

"I ask for a brochure?"

"Right. Then you follow J.Q. over to the desk, and when I show up a minute or two later, you should be behind the bad guy. He will probably be holding a gun."

He seemed to find nothing exceptionable in these instructions, leaving Shirley to wonder momentarily if a strong-arm type might not be a pretty good thing to have around. She opened the back door and held it barely shut as she lay down on the backseat. The car went sedately down the drive and parked in front of the house. Joe got out and went through the gate to the door. She heard his knock and J.Q.'s voice and the retreating voices as they went into the kitchen.

She opened the door and slipped gracelessly out onto the driveway, like a too large package, scrambled into a stooping waddle, and skulked through the gate, keeping as low as possible. The kitchen door had been left slightly open. She could hear J.Q. talking to Joe, telling him about the rates. She pushed the door a bit wider and looked in. Raul was facing her, H.R. was standing beside him but facing Joe and J.Q., his hand along the side of his leg, with a gun in it. Fine! Why couldn't Paleolithic types stick to clubs and rocks?

Joe was in as good a position as he was going to get. She opened the door and called heartily. "Hello there."

H.R. turned away from Joe, toward her, face flaming, his arm coming up. Joe took one step, reached around H.R., and grasped both of the lieutenant's wrists in hands the size of boxing gloves. Raul took in the situation in one quick glance, stepped forward, and wrenched the gun out of the lieutenant's hand.

H.R. was struggling, bellowing, twisting wildly to get out of Joe's grip. Joe remained solidly in place, like a monolith.

"Ya got cuffs?" he asked Raul in a conversational tone.

Bemused, Raul took his cuffs from his belt and cuffed H.R.'s hands behind him.

"Now what?" Joe asked, holding on to the cuffs.

"Interference," H.R. screamed. "I'll have you on interference."

Joe put a large arm across H.R.'s neck and levered up, effectively shutting H.R.'s mouth.

"Shut up, H.R.," Raul said wearily. "I'll be the first one to testify that you threatened a civilian with a gun, that you said you were going to shoot another civilian on sight, that the reason for it was you been beating on my sister-in-law for over a year, that it was you pushed her down the stairs and damn near broke her back."

"To which I will add a few words," said J.Q. "Concerning invading a private house and threatening the occupants with grave bodily harm, and so on and so on."

"Best thing for you to do is keep quiet and settle down," said Raul. "Best thing for you to say is you've been feeling crazy lately. Your mind hasn't been working right. You've been losing sleep. You think people are out to get you. Maybe you do that, the department shrink will recommend discharge and no criminal charges because nobody got hurt except Rena, and she probably won't testify against you if you leave her alone."

Taking the still-struggling prisoner with him, Joe eased past Raul and J.Q., saying to Shirley as he went out, "It's been a pleasure meeting you, ma'am." Raul followed him, and the other two watched from the kitchen as Raul and Joe used another set of handcuffs to shackle H.R. in the backseat of the police car.

Joe departed with a wave of one hand. Raul closed the car doors and headed back for the house. Shirley and J.Q. were both sitting at the kitchen table when Raul came back in.

"You okay?" he asked her.

"No problem."

"J.Q. said you were kidnapped."

"Well, it may have looked like that. Say it was a command performance."

He heaved a deep breath, glancing guiltily out at the police car in the drive. "I need to use your phone. If I'm going to keep this quiet, I'll need to go directly to the captain. He's got a private line, and I don't want this on the radio."

Shirley and J.Q. went out into the patio and left him to it.

"You had an afternoon," said Shirley.

"We both did," he agreed. "I called about Littlepage's car, but neither Ohlman nor Griego were there. I left a message. Rena called. I told her to call me back in fifteen minutes. I got hold of Consuelo and she said she'd meet the bus. Rena called. I told her to have Lupe put her on the bus. With you off God knows where, I wasn't about to drive her there myself.

"Then about an hour ago that nutcase came storming in here, telling me he was going to shoot you and probably me, and where were you. Raul was trying to calm him down, and the lieutenant actually drew on him, took his gun away from him, told him to shut up or he'd kill him and his bitch wife along with half the county.

"I told him you'd been in Albuquerque all day, and

253

you didn't know where his wife was, but he didn't believe that. Evidently the stupid woman left a note telling him who helped her. Shirley, is there any way we could, in future, help only reasonably intelligent people? I honest to God believe that evolution is attempting to improve our species by killing off the stupid ones. Guns. Drugs. Cigarettes. Driving drunk. Gangs. Women allowing themselves to be beaten to a pulp. All of these lethal activities help eliminate the stupid ones. I really think society ought to stop agonizing over this and start cheering the process on."

"You did have a bad day," she commiserated.

"It was an epiphany. A revelation," he insisted.

"Why don't we have a drink? Why don't we go out to dinner? Where, by the way, was Xanthy during all this?"

"I didn't tell her about your being snatched. Didn't want to upset her. About mid-afternoon she said she was going to pick up Allison after school and go to the nursery. She said she wanted to see what trees and shrubs they had with good fall color. When they finished planting, there were still a few square feet unbotanized, and she sees no reason for the New Mexico monochromatic autumn."

"Duochromatic," Shirley mused. "Yellow and green."

They sat silently for what seemed a long time. Raul came from the kitchen and dropped into a chair opposite them.

"I forgot to tell you. When they searched the body, Littlepages's body, they found this." He took a plastic folder from his pocket and passed it across. It contained a letter on lined yellow paper, and a Rancho del Valle envelope addressed to David Littlepage in Washington, D.C.

Shirley read the letter aloud.

" 'Hey, Dave, I'm married. Nita and I, we're married! I took some money from Dad, and I took his book, you know, his *book*! I left him a note telling him we'd gone to Hawaii, and if he came after us I'd burn the book but if he left us alone, I'd bring it back. . . .' "

Shirley lowered the letter and said, "He drafted this letter first. We found some scraps of it in the wastebasket in the Garden House, after your people had searched it."

She returned to the letter: " 'Anyhow, we don't like it here much, so we're going back to L.A., and when you come out next month, you get the book and give it back to Dad. We put it in the barn here at this place, up where the hay is, down along the back wall. Tell Dad I didn't mean it about burning it. Tell him I'm sorry, but he just didn't understand about Nita.' "

She turned over the plastic folder. "The envelope was dated the twenty-eighth of August, the Thursday before Labor Day."

"What book is he talking about?" Raul asked.

J.Q. started to say something, but Shirley froze him with a look.

"Something the murderer took. Obviously, David Littlepage went to look for the book, the murderer followed him, killed him, and took the book."

"Something the Luccio family needed back?"

"I presume so."

"That guy who was here. He's a Luccio man?"

"He's just the chauffeur," Shirley said, straight-faced. "Mr. Luccio wanted to know the details of his son's death, and he's accustomed to getting what he wants, when he wants it. Lillian Littlepage and I were taken to his place near Albuquerque, we told him what we could, he thanked us and sent us home."

255

"No kidnap."

"Not really, no."

"No new, helpful information."

"One item only. The phony Littlepage is missing. I can think of only two reasons for him to be missing. One, he's dead. Two, he took the book Mr. Luccio wants but he doesn't intend to give it back to Mr. Luccio. He could be intending to sell it back, or to sell it to someone else. In either case, it gives him the best motive and opportunity for murdering David."

"But nobody saw him here on Saturday."

"We weren't really looking," Shirley told him. "He is not a memorable person. If he put on different clothes and a pair of glasses, I wouldn't have known who he was."

"Maybe he wasn't here until later," Raul suggested. "Maybe the other guy, David, wasn't here until later."

"David was here Saturday, during the day," Shirley said, taking Mrs. Caravel's folder from her pocket, opening it, and pushing it across the table. "Mrs. Caravel dropped this out in the field where we found David's car. He had to be one of the first ones parked there on Saturday. That card on top is his. According to Mrs. Caravel, she had a man doing a photo essay on the wedding. That would have been a perfect front for David."

"Your kids didn't recognize him."

"It was the hair they didn't recognize. The front seat of his car is full of pairs of glasses and various hats, and it was a sunny day. J.Q. mentioned a photographer, laden with cameras and wearing a funny hat. I'm sure Mrs. Caravel told everyone she had hired him, which means the phony Littlepage no doubt caught onto him and carefully stayed out of camera range."

"Littlepage, the real one, was here to get this book?"

"Two reasons. The book, and someone here had been impersonating him. I honestly don't think he knew the phony Littlepage was working for Filippo Luccio. David came here first on Friday. The place was swarming with wedding preparations, people everywhere. He did what journalists do, he got into conversation, found out what was happening, and sold himself to the bride's mother. That would give him the freedom to move around, into every house, into every corner of the grounds."

"He could have gone into the barn, then," Raul said.

"No, I was—" J.Q. started to say.

"No," Shirley said hastily, giving J.Q. another look. "J.Q. was working down there all day, with the animals, and with the man who maintains our grounds."

"That night, then?"

"No. The housekeeper's place is right across from the barn. It was a dark night. If he had turned on any lights in the barn, he would have been seen. I know he didn't go back to Filippo's place. Either he took a room in town or he camped out overnight."

"But you think he went into the barn the next night, while the party was going on."

"Exactly. And he was followed there by the phony Littlepage, whose name, by the way, is Mitchell. And I'm convinced that when Littlepage found what he was looking for, Mitchell shot him."

"No proof of that," said Raul. "Well, at least it gives us something to go on with."

"What are you going to do with him?" asked J.Q., nodding toward the driveway.

"Captain's sending a car with two guys he can depend on. I'm filing a report saying what happened, direct with the captain. That was the job H.R. thought he'd get. I don't know why he thought so. He's always been a hothead."

He got up, started for the gate, then turned to ask, "You don't have any ideas about the kids, do you?"

Shirley shook her head no.

"This guy, Mitchell, he didn't do it?"

"They were killed on Sunday the thirty-first. He was still looking for them the following Tuesday."

"What made him follow Littlepage?"

"He knew Littlepage and James were buddies. That's the kind of thing skip tracers are interested in. Who's friends with whom. Who visits whom. Who confides in whom. If James had confided in anyone, likely it had been David."

"Gotcha." He looked up, hearing what they all heard, the sound of a car approaching.

Shirley stood up just enough to observe flashing lights. "Take him away," she said wearily. "And by the way, will you please find out from Lupe why Rena left her husband a note. I'm really interested in that woman's mental processes."

He flushed, lifted a hand in farewell, and was gone. Outside in the drive there were scuffling noises, muttered curses, a brief howl of rage, then doors closing and cars pulling away. Until they were completely gone, Shirley and J.Q. did not say a word.

"What were you giving me the evil eye about?" J.Q. demanded when all was quiet.

"I didn't want you telling him you were moving hay on Friday before Labor Day," she said.

He frowned. "What difference . . . oh. I see."

"The kid hid the book in the barn on Thursday. At that time there was only, what? One layer of bales?"

"Two layers against the wall."

"So the kid only had to drop the book a foot or so to put it in the space between the studs. On Friday, you and your helpers put most of a semi load of hay down there, eighteen tons, maybe? And you pretty well filled the loft. The book is probably still there."

"You don't think Mitchell got it?"

"How many bales would he have needed to move?"

"Depends on whether the book is at one end or in the middle. I've got them stacked to the ceiling, about eight deep. If the book is at the bottom in the back corner, he'd have had to move the whole load. And there was no place to put it unless he threw it out onto the driveway."

"Right."

"So why kill Littlepage?"

"Because when he found Littlepage in the barn loft, Mitchell challenged him, asked him, 'Where's the information?' Littlepage would have said, hey, Luccio's my brother, the book's under all this hay, let's explain this to the people here and do this together. Mitchell says no, he wants the book. Littlepage says, don't be an ass, and he starts to leave. So, Mitchell shoots him. He doesn't want a partner, he doesn't want Littlepage telling Luccio he knows where the book is, he just wants to get the book himself and sell it to the highest bidder."

"You're guessing."

"It fits what happened."

"But Mitchell didn't get the book."

"He couldn't get it. We had wedding guests and people moving around and this and that. Besides, I doubt Mitchell reasoned it out before he killed David. If you've never moved hay, you don't realize what it means to shuffle eighteen tons of it."

"In which case, he'll be back?"

"I should imagine. Probably with help. If he's going to sell it to Luccio, he's got a deadline, the twelfth of September. No. Wait . . ."

She stared at her feet, aware of the abyss that had just opened there. "He doesn't have a firm deadline. Not anymore. Luccio wanted it by the twelfth to save his son. His son is dead, and Luccio himself is dying. There's nothing to save."

"His widow?"

"She had nothing to do with it."

"But according to you, Mitchell doesn't know yet that the kids are dead. And we still don't know who killed them."

She rose abruptly, hearing the approach of another car. "It's Xanthy. And about time. I'm starving."

"So are the animals," said J.Q., head cocked, listening to the chorus of baas and brays and poultry cackle from down the hill. "I hear complaining."

"You go feed them. I'll figure out what we're going to feed us." She headed for the kitchen, waving to Xanthy and Allison over the wall. They joined her shortly, full of exclamations about this shrub and that tree and this plant, all of them bright red or purple or orange at this time of year.

Xanthy ran down abruptly. "What's the matter? You're looking all washed out."

"I will tell this story only once," said Shirley. "If there are no interruptions."

The other two stopped moving, folded their hands before them, and adopted dramatically attentive expressions. Shirley swallowed the grin that threatened and told her story as baldly, dryly, and briefly as possible.

"Good heavens," said Xanthy, when she had finished. "And you think this book is still there."

"I think it's still there."

"What are you going to do about it?"

"I'm going to have some supper," Shirley snarled. "As are we all. Then, maybe, we can figure out what to do about it."

They settled on hamburgers, salad, and leftover pasta salad. By the time J.Q. returned from his evening zoo rounds, the meal was on the table.

"You should have used some of the mushrooms with the hamburgers," Allison remarked. "They're still all over the place."

Shirley looked up. The dried fungi were still spread on the windowsills and in the lower of the double ovens. The place did smell earthy. She'd gotten so used to it in the last week, she hadn't realized. "We seem to have a year's supply," she said.

"But no matsutake," Xanthy said. "I do wonder if Mr. Akagami's brother found his matsutake this year."

"Mr. Akagami's brother?" Shirley looked up. "The old man?"

"Yes. When we were at the bonsai shop, Mr. Akagami told me that each fall his brother goes to his secret valley and collects enough for several families."

"Like the man at the restaurant," said J.Q. "Remember. He said an acqaintance of his—"

"Hush," said Shirley. "Be still." She bent across her plate, aware of a chasm off to her left, ahead of her, well . . . somewhere. Matsutake. A palatial estate. Pottery shards. Alas . . . They could have been clones.

"I know who killed them," she said.

8

No GUESTS WERE due at Rancho del Valle until the Pattersons, he and she and five offspring, arrived from Denver Wednesday afternoon. The three muscular workmen who showed up early on that morning went about their business without interruption. Shirley went off in the car. By noon the men had finished, received their pay, and gone away. By five after twelve, Shirley had returned. She accepted a sandwich that Xanthy offered, then moved into the living room to plump the pillows and check for spiderwebs.

Shortly after one, the few specially invited guests arrived. Shirley escorted them into the living room: Filippo Luccio, impeccably dressed, tottering between Joe and Ben; Arlena all in black, tear-streaked and savage, her narrow mouth a crimson slash across her ashen face; Lillian Littlepage, dressed in soft trousers and a sweater, her gray-blond hair making an aureole around her head.

Xanthy was present, and J.Q. When all of them were seated, Shirley took her place in the large wing chair by the fireplace.

"You all want to know how David and James died. I know how, and why. Some I can prove, some I can't. The police know some of this, some they don't, and I'm not going to tell them what they don't know. If I am wrong about any of these details, please feel free to correct me."

She turned to Arlena. "Your son attended a private school in Los Angeles, one with long terms, allowing him the least possible time with the family. I understand the reasons for this. You felt you were protecting him.

"Your son met and fell in love with a girl about his own age, also attending a boarding school in Los Angeles. Her name was Nita. Nita was a weekly boarder, spending weekends with her sister or with friends. Your son was a full boarder. They were both children in every emotional sense of the word, impractical, dreamy, romantic, foolish. James talked to his father about marrying Nita, and you, Mr. Luccio, told him no, in no uncertain terms. You disapproved for many reasons.

"James, however, was determined. He was, perhaps, a little spoiled and used to getting his own way. He and Nita devised a complicated, romantic plan. They would rent a place in Los Angeles in order to give them a street address and a phone number. They would obtain false identification that would identify them as being quite a bit older than they really were. They would steal enough money from you to last them awhile, and then they would run away together after leaving false clues indicating they had gone to Hawaii."

She stopped and sipped from the glass of water on the table beside her. No one offered comment.

"They got these ideas either from listening to your men, Mr. Luccio, or from television. When James stole the money from you, he happened upon a book and he took the book also. James knew the book was important, but he did not know the particular circumstances that made it more than merely important at this particular time. He did not appreciate that its loss could prove a great embarrassment; indeed, under certain circumstances, it would be a death warrant. He was totally unaware of the dangerous implications of what he was doing. He knew you wouldn't hurt him. It didn't cross his mind that someone else might.

"He left you a letter saying he had run away to Hawaii with Nita and that if you let him alone, he would give the book back. Then he and Nita packed up and left the boardinghouse."

Luccio started to say something. She held up her hand.

"You immediately hired people to look for your son. One person went to Hawaii. Another person looked up phone records and located the boardinghouse. You and a skip tracer named Mitchell went to the boardinghouse. You saw a New Mexico tourist guide, with our ad checked in red."

"Among others," croaked Luccio.

"I understand. Among others. Someone called here asking for Jaime Luccio. We didn't get the name right, but it would have made no difference. When James and Nita made their reservations, they did so as Alan Jones and Helen Buscovitch. When they arrived on the Tuesday before Labor Day, they arrived under those names.

"Why did they come here? I believe it was because Nita had a friend here, someone she had known in California, a

265

girl known as Beegee. They probably visited with Beegee, or took her shopping with them. Nita was an inveterate shopper. She liked expensive things. She liked having her own way as much as your son did. Your son was quite besotted with her. At one place they shopped, Nita saw some boots she wanted. They weren't for sale. As they were departing she was overheard to tell Alan, 'Next time, just drop some money on the counter and take what you want.'

"On Sunday morning, the young couple decided to go on a trail ride. They wanted to plant a tree, a romantic notion that they'd picked up somewhere without any idea about the realities of the situation. I told them it would have to be a small tree, to carry on horseback. I said, take water and a spade, meaning them to take a worthless old spade I didn't care about. They borrowed my good spade, which annoyed me. They drove off in their little red car. They went to a couple of the places they had checked and listed, and they found they weren't open that early on Sunday morning. Evidently they then stopped at a public phone and looked up some other nurseries. I called the sergeant who's investigating both cases and asked him if there was any kind of note or listing in the car, and he told me there was a page torn from a phone book.

"On that page was a listing for a little shop that sells bonsai. It's a private house as much as it is a business, which explains why James and Nita found it open on Sunday morning. They went in, but there was no one there. The person who should have been watching the store, the granddaughter of the family, was back in the kitchen, talking to a friend on the phone. I learned this when I talked with her this morning. Alan and Helen wandered around and found a tree they liked. It was one

266

of a matched pair, the more valuable one of the pair, it was on a shelf marked 'not for sale.' They did as Nita had previously suggested. They looked at the other prices, then dropped two thousand-dollar bills on the counter and took what they wanted. The granddaughter finished her call, returned to her post, found the money, saw the tree gone, and went into a funk. She hid the money. She was still quaking when I talked with her, expecting a punishment for her neglect of duty, a punishment that never came."

"A bonsai?" cried Lillian. "For heaven's sake—"

"I'm sure James and Nita had no idea what a bonsai is," Shirley said. "They were looking for a little tree, and here were whole shelves of little trees.

"They put the tree in a shopping bag. They already had my spade and a gallon jug of water, and they drove to the Silver Saddle Stables. Joe Cisneros, under protest, let them pack the stuff up the hill and remain behind the rest of the group while they planted their tree."

She rose, stretched, took another mouthful of water, then sat back down again.

"Now I have to go back fifty-some-odd years."

Lillian looked up, eyebrows raised.

Shirley went on, speaking directly to Filippo. "I have to go back fifty years to a time when Lillian helped her husband, your father, Carlo Luccio, build and decorate the big house in Los Angeles. The land that house sat on belonged, before the war, to several Japanese families who farmed it. When the Japanese were interned, during the war, Carlo Luccio got his hands on the land. The real owners received scarcely a penny. There was at one point a confrontation between Carlo and one of those former landowners. Carlo, in effect, told him to go to hell. The

Japanese man was in his twenties at the time, his entire family had been ruined by the internment, he was horrified to see the land his family had so lovingly tilled being used as lavish grounds for a family known to be . . . shall we say, suspect in their sources of income.

"That Japanese gentleman moved first to Colorado, then here to New Mexico. With his younger brother he established a landscaping service and a small bonsai shop. In that shop he displayed some bonsai that had been in his family for generations, including a pair of small pines, one fairly young one he was training to match the other, and one he had kept with him all through the war. It was very old; it had been in the family for generations; it had great character. Most important, it meant a great deal to him. That tree was family, farm, land, hope. That tree was his soul."

Arlena muttered, "I don't see what—"

"A moment," Shirley said. "Your son and his wife went on the trail ride. They took their little tree and the spade and the water down the hill. They moved some rocks, finding a place for the tree. On a rock a few feet away, an elderly Japanese man was sitting, cleaning matsutake mushrooms he had just collected. When the young people took the tree from the shopping bag and broke the pot off by slamming it against a rock, the elderly man saw precisely what they had in their hands. It was his tree. The one he had kept all during the war. And it was being manhandled and destroyed by the same man who had taken his parents' farm."

Luccio made a gargling noise.

"What follows is inference," Shirley said. "The old man may have asked the young man what the hell he was doing with his tree. The young man may have said it was

268

his tree, he'd left money for it. The old man may have cried that it wasn't for sale, and possibly the girl said something snippy about everything being for sale. Something like that may have been said, or perhaps there were no words at all. In any case, the old man picked up the spade and swung it with all the strength his fury gave him. And when the girl attacked him, he wound something around her neck and strangled her.

"Then he picked up his little tree and all the pieces of the container that he could find. In scrambling around on that slope several times, I later found several small pieces he had missed.

"The elderly man was no doubt distraught. Perhaps he realized at some point that this was only a boy, that though he looked precisely like the ones who had robbed his family, this particular boy had had nothing to do with it. We don't know what went through his mind as he dragged the bodies down the hill, composed them, and put their belongings beside them. He did not pick up the spade. Perhaps he didn't want to touch it again. He went up the slope and untied the horses, driving them down the trail. He went away with the matsutake he had come to collect, leaving only a few trimmed stems to show he had been there.

"When he returned to his shop, he repotted the tree. The pot is a standard shape and size, so he was able to match the one that had been broken off. He put new moss around its roots. He replaced it on the shelf of items that were not for sale. He put the broken pieces in a sack of shards that are used for drainage pieces in the bottom of containers. When I went there early this morning, they matched exactly the pieces I found on the hillside.

"The granddaughter thought a miracle had occurred.

When I finished talking with her, I asked for Mr. Akagami and begged from him the location of his parents' farm. He told me where it had been. I checked with a friend in Los Angeles. That farm is included in the estate of Filippo Luccio.

"Mr. Luccio, that elderly man was robbed by your father. You were a young man after the war, when he came to complain to you, and you went on robbing him. He was robbed again by your son. As Lillian has said, all three of you look as alike as clones."

"He's a dead . . . dead man," Luccio gargled.

"Yes," Shirley said, almost scornfully. "He is. If he wasn't already dead, I wouldn't be telling you this. When I saw him on Friday he didn't look well. He died two days later. According to his family, he'd had a heart attack in June. He'd been warned not to exert himself, not to climb around in the mountains, but old people can be stubborn."

Luccio fell silent, a light like waning embers in the ashy pits of his eyes.

Lillian said, "What about David?"

"Mitchell had already learned, prior to last week, that James's best friend in the family was David. Last Friday, Mitchell found out two things he hadn't known: he learned there was something other than money missing, and he learned that David was not safely off in Japan but was here, in New Mexico. David, meantime, was aware of three things: first, he learned in a letter from James that James had stolen Filippo's book and hidden it in the barn at this ranch. Second, he learned from one of Mitchell's victims that someone was impersonating him at this ranch, and third, he learned that a pair of newly-weds had been murdered here. David may have sus-

270

pected that they were James and Nita, though the news-paper accounts seemed to say otherwise. He would not have wanted to upset Filippo and Arlena unless he was absolutely sure. So, he came here and scrounged a job as a photographer. He hung around and was spotted by Mitchell. Mitchell had seen pictures of him, of course, for Mitchell had read his article and some of his note-books, had boned up on him, so to speak. I think Mitchell intended offering the missing book to someone besides you, Mr. Luccio. I believe he followed David into the barn and challenged him there."

"Was it Mitchell?" demanded Lillian. "Was it!"

"When Mitchell challenged David, I believe he told David that he was working for you, Mr. Luccio. To David, this meant they were on the same side. So, David told him about the letter Jaime had written, a letter saying Jaime was going to California and David should retrieve the book that was in the barn under the hay."

"You're guessing," Luccio gargled.

"I'm extrapolating. I believe that's what happened because Mitchell didn't search David after he killed him. If he'd thought David had the book, he'd have searched him. If he had searched him, he would have found the letter and removed it. The letter was still in David's back pocket when he died. A friend from the state police office let me read it."

Lillian bent her face into her hands.

Shirley fought down the urge to say something com-forting. Now wasn't the time.

"Mitchell knew David was telling the truth, and he killed David to keep him from telling you, Filippo, where the book was. He would have done that only if he had, or was convinced he had, a very profitable deal for the

271

book. You would know better than I who he might have made a deal with.

"Of course, whether he'd thought of it before or not, Mitchell soon realized he couldn't shift all that hay. So, he deferred that particular problem. Book or no book, he was still looking for James because he still didn't know James was dead! No one here knew the real identity of the murdered newlyweds, not until yesterday when Lillian identified them. Mitchell knew James wasn't here because the place was fully occupied by wedding guests, but there was the possibility we had James's address in the office, so Mitchell snuck up the hill and stopped in this house early on Sunday morning, looking for something about a couple from California. He found a reservation sheet that seemed to meet those criteria."

"Why did he care about Jaime?" Arlena cried. "If he knew where the book was?"

"He didn't want Jaime talking for the same reason he didn't want David talking. Mitchell didn't want Filippo to know the book had been here, in the barn, and that David had known it was there, because this would have told Filippo who killed David and who took the book. Mitchell wanted James to be blamed for that."

"He intended to kill Jaime?" Lillian asked.

Shirley shrugged. "In his place, what would you plan to do? If he couldn't get at the book right away, at least he could dispose of James."

"Where is he?" Luccio gargled. "Mitchell?"

Shirley said, "Probably in Los Angeles, snooping around some people called Postern in the belief they may be James and Nita. Or maybe he's done that already. He's had three days to check out the Posterns. He may be hanging around here. If he was spying on the place this morning, he probably knows the book is no longer for sale."

"He killed . . . David?" Luccio asked. "You sure?"

Shirley looked across the man's head to Joe, standing behind him. She shrugged.

Joe leaned forward, saying softly, "She's as sure as anybody can be, boss. Until we find him and ask him. I'll do it, boss. Don't you worry. I'll . . . take care of it."

"Where's the book?"

Shirley opened a folder on the table beside her, took out the small brown booklet, still speckled with hay. "I haven't looked at it. We hired three men to come shift the hay this morning so we could get at the wall. I didn't want the book to be there if and when the state police got around to looking."

"How much you want for it?" Luccio glared at her.

She smiled grimly. "It isn't mine. It's yours." She handed it to him. "The pair of thousand-dollar bills that James left in the bonsai shop are in it. Akagami's granddaughter gave them back to me without a murmur. Like her great-uncle, I believe some things aren't for sale, Mr. Luccio. My sense of justice is one of them."

Joe shook his head at her, half warning, half grim admiration. Luccio gestured weakly. Joe and Ben heaved their boss to his feet and gently half carried him out to the car.

Arlena came to face Shirley with her blazing eyes. "I always knew the family would end up killing him," she said. "I tried so hard. . . ."

"I know," said Lillian, coming to put her arms around the other woman. "So did I."

Together, leaning on one another, they walked to the door, and after a few moments more they were gone.

Shirley gathered up the folder, her glass, held the door for Xanthy, and they made their way into the kitchen, where J.Q. joined them.

"There's a fresh pot," he said. "I put it on the timer."

"A transfusion," Shirley agreed, leaning wearily on the counter. "I need one. I feel like I've been chewing nails."

"You were very hard on a dying man," mused Xanthy. "I thought for a time you might soften it a little."

"Soften his losing a son? I lost a son, Xanthy. Did that man consider my loss? Did his minion, that Mitchell, consider my feelings? Luccio was quite willing to turn the knife in me, over and over, to get what he wanted. Why should I pity him?"

"No reason, dear. You were quite implacable."

Shirley emptied the folder onto the table. The business-card folder. The glasses. The bracelet. The unused condoms, at which Xanthy stared owlishly.

"They could have been a clue," Shirley said defensively.

"I didn't say anything," J.Q. said.

"You thought it."

"What I thought was, I'm surprised you didn't send that book to Roger."

"I did."

"You said you didn't look at it."

"I didn't. I just copied it and sent the copy to Roger while I was in town this morning. Without looking at it."

Xanthy asked, "Does Nosura Akagami know what happened?"

"No. None of his family know anything about it. There's no reason for them to. All my business was con-

274

ducted with the granddaughter, and I was able to get away with telling her almost nothing.

"I did go to see Mr. Akagami to get the location of the farm his people had had in California. I have a friend who has a friend in the mayor's office who has a flunky in the clerk and recorder's office. As soon as they opened, they looked it up for me."

Xanthy shook her head. "You think James and Nita really came here simply because Nita had a friend here?"

Shirley mused, "I doubt Nita had many friends, but Beegee was one. Nita would have wanted to show off her new husband, and their car, and her clothes."

"Poor children," said Xanthy.

"I grieve more for David," Shirley said. "Much more for David. David had a life he had built, that he and Lillian had built. I can grieve for David. Roger told me not to get too close, not to get involved. He said involvement could mean disaster. For David, it did."

"And Mitchell gets away with killing him," said Xanthy.

Shirley shook her head slowly. "No, Xanthy. You only say that because you aren't acquainted with Joe. Believe me, he won't get away with anything. If I thought for a moment that he would, I'd have to tell the police. But . . . I'm quite sure Joe will . . . make him see the error of his ways."

"And old Luccio is dying," murmured J.Q. "And he has nothing to leave behind him."

"It's important to leave something behind you," said Xanthy.

Outside in the driveway, they heard voices. Allison and Ulti and someone else. Shirley rose and looked out the window. Ulti and his friend had given Allison a ride home. She was standing at the gate, cheeks pink, eyes sparkling, her hair whipping in a light wind, grinning at Ulti and he at her.

"Be thankful," Xanthy said. "She's the best daughter you could have."

"Getting to be just like you," muttered J.Q.

"Come now," Shirley argued. "Allison? Like me?"

"I don't mean in height," he said. "What I meant was—"

What he meant was interrupted by a large van coming down the driveway too fast, roof rack laden with bicycles and duffel bags, every window crammed with faces. Children's faces. Demonic, candy-smeared, sharp-toothed little faces.

"The Pattersons," said J.Q.

"The Pattersons are supposed to have five children," said Shirley. "There's more than five in there."

Outside, Allison turned toward the approaching vehicle, her expression changing to one of apprehension.

The van pulled to a halt and disgorged small persons in legions, like a clown car at a circus. A large, loud woman erupted from the backseat, calling in a hearty voice:

"Hello there, Allison! Remember us? It's Dr. Osinsky, with the boys! Our neighbors the Pattersons had a reservation, so we've come along to stay with them. We're staying a whole week!"

"That dreadful woman!" muttered J.Q. "And her beastly children!"

"And her beastly neighbors look like more of the same," Xanthy added. "Allison told me about the children abusing the animals. Abominable."

276

Allison cast a fleeting glance toward the window, took a deep breath, gained six inches in apparent height, and strode purposefully toward the unwelcome herald, Ulti right behind her.

"Oh, Dr. Osinsky, I'm so sorry!" Allison's voice had taken on the quality of an alarm bell, ringing out the troops, clearly audible to the three listening from the kitchen. "We tried to call the Pattersons, but evidently you and they had already left Denver. Our pump has gone out on our well! There's no water. No toilets! No showers! It'll be several days before we can get it fixed."

A mumble mumble, shocked expressions.

Allison again, still bugling: "We'll return your deposit, of course, but for sanitary reasons, we can't let any of the houses be occupied until we have water."

"We think it was hit by lightning," offered Ulti loudly, firmly, shaking his head. "There was a thunderstorm last night. Sometimes it does that, just burns out the well, and the only thing you can do is put a new pump in there. Pity the well man is so busy right now."

"So disappointing for you," Allison cried. "Would you like me to get your refund check now?"

J.Q. was already at the desk, scribbling madly. When Allison opened the door, looking slightly apprehensive, he handed it to her without a word. She took it, smiled a tremulous little smile, and went back to the fray. A few moments later the clowns repacked themselves in the car and the van went out the drive, away, away, away, while Allison and Ulti stared at one another, afraid of what might happen next.

When she was sure the van was gone, Shirley lunged

out the door and went to throw her arms around Allison and Ulti both, caroling something like "callooh callay."

"Just as I said," J.Q. exulted to Xanthy. "Allison is exactly like her! Exactly."

The Shirley McClintock Mysteries

DEAD IN THE SCRUB

While following a wounded deer, Colorado rancher Shirley McClintock stumbles over a human skeleton half-buried in the autumn leaves. A second murder, accomplished with the same arrow that had injured the deer, convinces Shirley to launch her own investigation.

THE UNEXPECTED CORPSE

Two of Shirley McClintock's relatives die in an accident while on vacation, and their ashes are brought home to Colorado along with the unexpected ashes of an unknown distant relative. When their graves are disturbed and yet another box of ashes turns up, Shirley is determined to find out what is behind it all.

DESERVEDLY DEAD

Shirley McClintock's new neighbor has drained the wetlands, poisoned the scrub, and destroyed the wildlife on his property—no wonder Shirley's about ready to kill him. And when someone *does* kill the ruthless greenhorn easterner, Shirley becomes the prize suspect.

by B. J. OLIPHANT

The Shirley McClintock Mysteries

DEATH AND THE DELINQUENT

While vacationing in New Mexico, Shirley McClintock runs into trouble—her knee is crushed and her daughter's friend April is shot. Soon Shirley discovers that April was, at the very least, a thief. And when a very important baby is kidnapped, Shirley's vacation plans go out the window.

DEATH SERVED UP COLD

Now an innkeeper at Rancho del Valle near Santa Fe, Shirley McClintock is a bit put out when one of her guests dies without leaving any trace of where she's from or why she came to Santa Fe. The remaining guests are unmoved, but Shirley suspects murder.

A CEREMONIAL DEATH

When a beautiful New Age healer known as Shadow Dancer is killed and viciously mutilated, extraterrestrials are rumored to be involved. But Shirley McClintock believes the answer lies in more earthly motives, especially in light of Shadow Dancer's tangled past.

by B. J. OLIPHANT

The Jason Lynx Mysteries

DEATH AND THE DOGWALKER
While out for a morning stroll with his dog in a
Denver park, antiques dealer Jason Lynx comes
across the very naturally posed body of Fred Foret.
Fascinated by this carefully staged death, Jason
begins to put together the pieces of this puzzle, and
the picture that emerges is not pretty.

DEATH FOR OLD TIMES' SAKE
After accidentally witnessing the stabbing death
of an old woman at an anti-abortion demonstra-
tion, Jason Lynx is drawn into the investigation
into her death. Every clue pulls him deeper into
her curious past and the dangerous world of the
Denver mob.

by A. J. ORDE

The Jason Lynx Mysteries

DEAD ON SUNDAY
In a desolate New Mexico chapel, the unpopular Reverend Ernie Quivada is murdered. Chic Santa Fe doesn't care about the sordid crime, but interior designer and private investigator Jason Lynx is fascinated. And his intuition tells him there is more to this murder than meets the eye.

A LONG TIME DEAD
When Ron Willis, the brother of Jason Lynx's longtime girlfriend, is murdered, Jason wants to know why. There's not much to go on: only Ron's address book, his desperate search for cash the night before his death, and an unexpected skeleton found near his body.

A DEATH OF INNOCENTS
Jason Lynx and his wife, Grace, find the remains of a girl beneath the porch of their new house—apparently she was raped and strangled twenty years ago. As Jason and Grace examine old photos and letters, a sinister picture clicks into focus.

by A. J. ORDE

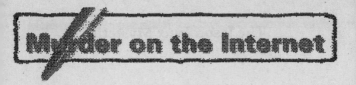

Ballantine mysteries are on the Web!

Read about your favorite Ballantine authors and upcoming books in our monthly electronic newsletter MURDER ON THE INTERNET, at **www.randomhouse.com/BB/MOTI**.

Including:
- 💀What's new in the stores
- 💀Previews of upcoming books for the next three months
- 💀In-depth interviews with mystery authors and publishers
- 💀Calendars of signings and readings for Ballantine mystery authors
- 💀Bibliographies of mystery authors
- 💀Excerpts from new mysteries

To subscribe to MURDER ON THE INTERNET, send an e-mail to **srandol@randomhouse.com** asking to be added to the subscription list. You will receive the next issue as soon as it's available.